The Perfect Combination.

Big Nose Kate Whiskey & *According to Kate:*
The Legendary Life of Big Nose Kate, Love of Doc Holliday

SADDLEBAG DISPATCHES

EST. 2014

Our mission at *Saddlebag Dispatches* is to keep the spirit of the frontier alive by fostering interest, discussion, and writing in the history and legacy of the American West.

SUMMER 2024 • VOLUME 10, ISSUE #1

EDITORIAL

PUBLISHER: Dennis Doty
MANAGING EDITOR: Anthony Wood
COPY EDITOR: Staci Troilo
FEATURES EDITOR: George "Clay" Mitchell
POETRY EDITOR: John McPherson
ENTERTAINMENT EDITOR: Terry Alexander
CONTRIBUTING EDITORS:
Waynetta Ausmus, John T. Biggs, Paul Colt, W. Michael Farmer, J.B. Hogan, Regina McLemore
RESEARCH DIRECTOR: Barbara Clouse
BOOK REVIEWER: Doug Osgood
POET LAUREATE: Marleen Bussma
PHOTOGRAPHER: Patricia Rustin Christen
ART DIRECTOR: Casey W. Cowan
ILLUSTRATOR: Victoria Marble
CONTRIBUTORS:
Reavis Wortham, Sherry Monahan, Paul Colt, Preston Lewis, James A. Tweedie, Alex Slusar, Kimberley Burns, Don Money, Gary Rodgers, D.N. Sample, Doris McGraw, David Cameron, Laura Conner Kester, Kyleigh McCloud, Doris McCraw

BUSINESS

BUSINESS MANAGER: Amy Cowan
ADVERTISING MANAGER: Chris Enss
SOCIAL MEDIA MANAGER: Rachel Patterson

For advertising rates and schedules, contact Advertising Manager Chris Enss
gvcenss@aol.com

For business-related questions, contact Business Manager Amy Cowan
amy@saddlebagdispatches.com

CONTACT INFORMATION

Saddlebag Dispatches, LLC
2401 Beth Lane, Bentonville, AR 72712
479.657.3894

WEBSITE

www.saddlebagdispatches.com

Dedicated to the memory of our late co-founder, Dusty Richards, and our dear departed friends and partners, Velda Brotherton and Bob Giel.

LEADVILLE FEATURES

On our cover: The Prospector by Frank Tenney Johnson. Oil on Canvas, 1914.

CELEBRATING 10 YEARS
SADDLEBAG DISPATCHES
EST. 2014

BEHIND THE CHUTES

Dennis Doty
PUBLISHER

A Tin Star for a Tenth Anniversary

Celebrating a Decade's Worth of Saddlebag Dispatches

Welcome to the Summer issue of *Saddlebag Dispatches* magazine. This issue is themed around Leadville, Colorado, and You'll see some familiar faces among our feature writers.

Before we get too far into exploring the history and characters of the Boomtown Above the Clouds, though, we'd like to pause to celebrate a birthday—ours, to be precise. That's right. The very first issue of *Saddlebag Dispatches* came out ten years ago next month. The brainchild of Dusty Richards, a legendary author who lived and breathed the West, and Casey W. Cowan, an (at the time) admitted Western neophyte whose expertise was in graphic design, started as a small-time e-magazine that few people knew about and even fewer actually read. That being said, it was the start of something new and unique, a magazine combining factual articles on historical Western topics with short-form Western fiction from writers across the genre. Nothing quite like it had ever been published before. In the decade since, it has become one of the premier Western magazines in the country, winning multiple awards and attracting readers of all ages from around the globe.

As part of this celebration, we're pleased to announce that, starting next year, we'll be adding a third issue of *Saddlebag Dispatches* to our schedule. Yep, you heard that right—another entire issue chocked full of your favorite Western content from your favorite Western authors. This new schedule will go into effect next year, with new issues coming in April, August, and December.

Wait, wait, wait... did someone mention awards? Boy, howdy, do we have some of *those* to talk about, as well.

Congratulations are in order for two authors from our Winter 2023 Cochise County issue who have been named finalists for the Will Rogers Medallion Awards in October—W. Michael Farmer for "Finding Farmer" and Michael Norman for "A Death of Crows."

Moreover, "A Death of Crows" was our winner for the inaugural Longhorn Award for Western Short Fiction. Mr. Norman now sports a custom-engraved silver trophy buckle from Montana Silversmiths in addition to taking home the prize money.

Our *Saddlebag Dispatches* Marketing Director, Chris Enss, landed a finalist position at the Will Rogers Medallions for her book *An Open Secret: The Story of Deadwood's Most Notorious Bordellos* (published by Two Dot), and Western Food Columnist Sherry Monahan is a finalist for *Signature Dishes of America: Recipes and Culinary Treasures from Historic Hotels and Restaurants* (released by Globe-Pequot). Hats off to both of these talented ladies. It should be mentioned that Chris Enss is also a finalist for Women Writing the West's 2024 Downing Journalism for her excellent article, "The Attorney Teacher: Sarah Herring Sorin."

Our very own Saddlebag *Dispatches* Research Director, Barbara Clouse, is up for a Medallion of her own in the Children's Illustrated Fiction category for *The Healing Lodge,* the heartwarming story of a young Native American family who seeks help in saving their dying daughter at a special place where people from different tribes came together to help their loved ones feel better.

Last but certainly not least, we're proud enough to bust our buttons over two of our regular contributors whose books are also up for medallions—Paul Colt for his *Lunger: The Doc Holliday Story,* and W. Michael Farmer for *Desperate Warrior: Days of*

War, Days of Peace. These two gentlemen are two of the very finest Western writers in the field today, and deserve every such accolade and more.

While we're on the subject of contests, we're looking forward to digging into the entries for our Second Annual Longhorn Prize for Western Short Fiction. The winner will win a custom-engraved trophy belt buckle from Montana Silversmiths. Oh, and did I mention that the winning story will be published in our next issue in mid-December?

Now, on to *this* issue, which is jam-packed with the kind of stories and histories of the West you love, from some of the very best Western writers around.

First and foremost, we are extremely pleased with the responses and submissions to our annual Western flash fiction competition, The Mustang Award. The winner and runner-up share their winning stories in this issue. Additionally, congratulations are in order for last year's winner, P.A. O'Neil. Her Mustang winning short story, "The Great Burro Revolt," featured in last summer's issue, has been named a finalist for the 2024 Western Fictioneers Peacemaker Award for Short Fiction.

What else is in store for you in this issue? Well, let's see…. We have stories of fortunate miners

Barbara Clouse, (top) author of *The Healing Lodge,* Paul Colt (middle), author of *Lunger: The Doc Holliday Story,* and W. Michael Farmer, author of *Desperate Warrior: Days of War, Days of Peace, Chato's Chircauhua Apache Legacy Volume One* are all finalists in this year's *Will Rogers Medallion Awards* in Fort Worth, Tx.

and not-so-fortunate strike-breakers, rich folks and poor, immigrants, Oscar Wilde, sneaky lawyers, Pinkertons, good men and bad, and some in between,, and a search for a missing man that leads to much more.

Still not enough? Well, don't go away! We've got even more in store for you.

Our features writers take a look at the famous and infamous of Leadville including John "Doc" Holliday, Horace, Augusta, and Baby Doe Tabor, and Marshal Mart Duggan, among others. Also included are the fascinating stories of Laura Bell McDaniel and Chief Ouray of the Ute tribe. Last but certainly not least, we have an exclusive excerpt from Paul Colt's bestselling novel *Lunger: The Doc Holliday Story,* recounting Doc Holliday's time in Leadville—and if you know anything about Doc and his history, you can be sure that time was anything but uneventful.

Apart from Leadville, we also have "Anniversary: Part I," the first installment in a thrilling new crossover serial novella from *New York Times* bestselling author Reavis Z. Wortham, and Features Editor George "Clay" Mitchell's exclusive interviews with both the man behind the *Longmire* phenomenon, the one and only Craig Johnson, and Rob Word, host of the highly-rated web-show on everything Western, *A Word on Westerns.*

We have all these and more, so, as usual, pull up a log, have a seat, pour yourself a cup from the camp pot, then settle in for the best in western reading.

Dennis Doty

WILD WOMEN

Chris Enss
ADVERTISING MANAGER

Laura Bell McDaniel

Courtesan of Colorado City

Madam Laura Bell McDaniel's broken body lay in a ditch beside a snowy thoroughfare conjoined with the twisted rubble of what was once her pristine Mitchell sedan. It was late January 1918 when the notorious soiled dove's car crashed just outside Castle Rock, Colorado. Laura's twenty-seven-year-old niece, Laura Pierson, had been driving the vehicle and was thrown from the sedan when it overturned. A blind family friend, Dusty McCarty, was in the car with the women. He survived the accident but sustained several bruises and cuts.

By the time Laura Bell McDaniel was transferred to Memorial Hospital in Colorado Springs, news of the plight of the woman known as the Queen of the Colorado City Tenderloin had already reached clients and citizens where she lived and worked. Many were saddened by the news, and some believed Laura's car might have been forced off the road by those who wanted the house of ill repute she ran shut down.

Laura was born near Buffalo Lick, Missouri, on November 27, 1861. Her parents, James and Anna Horton, were farmers who made sure their children were well educated. At the age of nineteen, Laura married Samuel Dale from nearby Brunswick, Missouri. The two had become acquainted when Laura's father took the family buckboard to Samuel's father, a wagon maker, to be repaired. The couple left the Midwest shortly after they were married for Colorado, where they settled in a newly established railroad town called Salida. Sam and Laura welcomed a baby girl into their lives in 1884 and named her Eva Pearl Dale. Marriage and fatherhood did not sit well with Samuel, and he left a few months later.

Faced with the challenge of raising a child on her own and with no viable employment opportunities, Laura ventured into the business of prostitution. She purchased a home close to the house where her mother lived. Her mother, Anna, had relocated to Colorado when she and James began having marital problems. Anna opened a boarding house, which she ran with Laura's two younger sisters.

One of Laura's regular callers was John Thomas "Tom" McDaniel. The two spent a considerable amount of time together and traveled to Leadville on occasion in the winter. It was during one of those trips that Laura's home caught fire and burned to the ground. Foul play was immediately suspected, and one of Anna's boarders was accused of setting the blaze. Morgan Dunn was considered to be a man of questionable character by most Salida residents, and he was quite enamored with Laura. He was extreme-

Undated photos from a Cripple Creek brothel. The woman on the left may be Laura Bell McDaniel. *From the Pikes Peak Library District collection*

ly jealous of the relationship she had with Tom.

Laura had insurance to cover the home in case of a fire. While waiting for the insurance check to arrive, she moved to a house near the red-light district of town. She and Tom continued to see a lot of one another and eventually became engaged. They were married on April 7, 1887. Less than a month later, the duo were involved in a scandal that threatened to end their lives together.

On Friday, April 13, 1887, the day before the newlyweds were scheduled to go on their honeymoon, Laura confided in Tom

Tom didn't stay home, however. He returned to have it out with Morgan without his wife's interference. The two got into another battle of words, and Morgan suggested they settle their differences in another way. When Morgan placed his hand on his hip pocket, Tom pulled out a gun and shot him five times. Morgan collapsed at Tom's feet, dead.

The sound of the gun firing drew the attention of the next-door neighbors, and they hurried to the scene. According to the May 20, 1887, edition of the *Salida Semi-Weekly Mail,* they found Tom standing inside the

for a sizable insurance check. The *Salida Semi-Weekly Mail* reported Morgan was unarmed the night he was shot. The article also noted he had been recovering from a broken arm and collarbone, injuries he had sustained in a bar fight.

When Morgan's wife, who was living in New York at the time of his demise, eventually learned about her husband's death, she wrote the judge presiding over Tom's case to ask him specifics about the killing. She learned not only that Morgan had run afoul of the law on occasion, but also that he had been laid to rest in a pauper's grave without a service or friend to see him off.

Tired of the idle gossip surrounding the case, Laura and Tom decided to give an interview to the editor of the *Salida Semi-Weekly Mail* and correct the issues being talked about. Far from clearing up matters, the interview prompted more questions. The McDaniels told the paper Morgan had removed his coat and placed it on the bed prior to the shooting. Actually, the victim was found by police wearing his coat when he died. As for Morgan placing his hand on his hip pocket, Laura's mother claimed that never happened. The McDaniels told the newspaper editor Anna was wrong.

Not long after the trial, Tom and Laura left Salida and somewhere along the way parted company. By 1888, Laura was living in Colorado City alone. She purchased a home where she started her business and began referring to herself as Mrs. Bell McDaniel.

Laura's brothel was one of the most spectacular in town. It featured a ballroom, chandeliers,

> ## THE WEST IS OVERUN WITH BAWDY HOUSES AND SOILED DOVES.
>
> ### GOLD MINER CHARLES BARTLET
> *in a letter home to his family in Virginia, 1872*

that Morgan had tried to kiss her. Tom was furious to hear someone had tried to take advantage of his wife. "Why didn't you kill the son-of-a-bitch?" he shouted at Laura. Tom decided to confront Morgan about his actions, and Laura was unable to reason with him. The pair arrived at Anna's home and charged inside, Tom ready to fight the forward boarder and Laura trying to intercede. Morgan, who was eating dinner when Tom approached him, was initially nonplussed about the incident. When Tom continued to press him on the issue, he became belligerent. A yelling match ensued, and before it became physical, Laura managed to talk her husband into leaving and going home.

front door. His wife and mother-in-law were holding onto him and crying, "Oh, Tom!" The neighbors told police that Anna screamed, "Why did you do that?" Tom was arrested and tried for his actions, but the court found him not guilty. He claimed what he did was done in self-defense.

The residents in and around Salida not only doubted Tom's version of the story but also the motive Laura offered for why he went to see Morgan. Not everyone believed he was driven by jealousy alone. It was suspected that Tom killed Morgan to keep him from ever talking about setting fire to Laura's home. Citizens were convinced Tom and Laura hired Morgan to burn the home in exchange

History...
Adventure...
Natural Beauty...
Colorado...
On Another Level!

At the intersection of historic mountain communities, the highest mountain peaks in the Rockies and a thirst for outdoor adventure, are the mountain towns of Leadville and Twin Lakes.
It's time to experience Colorado on another level!
LeadvilleTwinLakes.com

LEADVILLE
TWIN LAKES

and expensive furniture. She had servants, a bartender, and a cook. Laura entertained powerful, well-known, and wealthy individuals.

Laura and many of the other soiled doves in Colorado City conducted themselves in public with restraint, moderation, and dignity. When the women took walks and shopped, they confined themselves to the red-light district. There was no solicitation, and they were polite to everyone

her to have an education and to choose a different path in life than she had. It is not known if either Laura or Anna visited with Eva while she was away or even where exactly Eva attended school.

Many colorful characters paraded in and out of Laura's life and business. John "Prairie Dog" O'Bryne, a hack driver and brakeman for the Atchison, Topeka, and Santa Fe Railroad; notorious female gambler Minnie Smith;

Tenderloin of Colorado City" did not falter in the early 1900s. Her business did, however, suffer from the usual problems associated with running a bordello—unruly patrons, rivalries with competing houses, and desperate employees who tried to kill themselves. There was also the occasional tussle with law enforcement. According to the April 30, 1903, edition of the *Colorado Springs Weekly Gazette,* Laura and eight other

In Cripple Creek, prostitutes and dance hall girls were required by law to wear aprons over their short dresses, lest anyone possibly be offended at the sight of their ankles. This undated photograph is from a gathering at Crapper Jack's, and may include Laura Bell McDaniel.

they met. Laura was known for being generous with her earnings. She frequently gave money to the homeless, helped them find a place to live, and also gave to charities that provided food and clothing to the needy.

Anna Horton was never too far from her daughter. She moved from Salida to Colorado City in 1890, and mother and daughter visited often with one another. Laura sent her daughter Eva Pearl to a boarding school. She wanted

and mining and real estate magnate Charles Tutt were just a few.

In June 1893, Laura filed for divorce from Tom. The marriage was officially dissolved four months later. By the turn of the century Laura's mother, her sister Birdie, Birdie's husband, and their infant son all lived together in the same home down the street from Laura's house. In 1901, Eva Pearl was also a resident in her grandmother's home.

Laura's reign as "Queen of the

women were arrested for prostitution, and an indictment against her for running a house of ill repute was returned to a grand jury. She gave a bond in the sum of five hundred dollars. "Evidence before the grand jury is to the effect that the houses have been run under the protection of the authorities of Colorado City who have collected monthly fines from each house," the *Colorado Springs Weekly Gazette* article read. "The arrests were entirely unexpected; an unsuccessful attempt to escape was made. Other and sensational developments in regard to the morality of the county, it is rumored, will follow."

After making a court appearance in June 1903, Laura decided to move her business to Cripple Creek. Less than two years later she returned to Colorado City. When her mother died in 1905, she relocated again to Cripple Creek but kept her place in Colorado City. She was now running a bawdy house in both locations.

Historians speculate Laura changed addresses multiple times because laws against prostitution were strictly enforced in the early 1900s. Upstanding citizens did not tolerate women of ill repute, especially those who stayed when warned to vacate their premises. Madams who rebelled against the law were sometimes beaten, and their homes were burned to the ground. Laura suffered through many fires and, regardless of the reasons for those fires, she always rebuilt.

Laura's most famous house of ill fame was called the Mansion. The grand brick bordello cost more than ten thousand dollars to build. Colorado City residents were outraged when Laura dared to have another house constructed. According to the May 7, 1909, edition of the *Colorado City Iris,* her actions were viewed as an attempt to reinvigorate the red-light district, which most people hoped was gone for good.

In February 1911, Laura married Herbert N. Berg, the financial editor of the *Colorado Springs Gazette Telegraph.* Her lifestyle did not change af-

ter she was wed, however. She continued as a madam and even placed an ad in the Gazette announcing she was still open for business. She discreetly referred to herself in the ad as a "keeper of furnished rooms." Local authorities paid several visits to Laura's house and fined her for running a brothel. From 1909 to 1911, she paid more than four hundred dollars in fines for "keeping a disorderly house."

Laura's husband Herbert died in mid-1916, and the following year law enforcement concentrated their efforts on ridding the community of her business. On November 20, 1917, the Colorado City police served Laura with a warrant to search her property. She wasn't sure what they were looking for and was surprised when they produced thirty-four bottles of liquor reportedly stolen from the home of one of Colorado Spring's most wealthy citizens, Charles Baldwin.

Laura was arrested for "receiving stolen liquor." She was taken into custody and charged. Bail was set at $1,500, and her trial was scheduled for January 18, 1918. Laura retained a pair of attorneys with a substantial background in representing soiled doves. James Orr and W. D. Lombard asked the court for additional time to prepare their client's case, and the request was granted. The court date was moved to January 24, 1918.

Witnesses for the prosecution consisted mainly of police officers and detectives. They alleged that on November 12, 1917, Laura Bell purchased several bottles of stolen liquor. Among the items she supposedly bought were Gordon's

gin, champagne, and high-grade whiskey. Charles Baldwin, the so-called victim, did not appear at the trial. He had been called out of town and did not know when he would be returning.

Laura's longtime friend, Dusty McCarty, came forward to testify on her behalf. When he took the stand, he explained to the court that the liquor had been planted at her home. Dusty maintained two men who frequented her business were the real culprits. The case against Laura was dismissed.

The day after Laura's case was closed, she, her niece, and Dusty decided to take a drive to Denver. Laura Pierson was driving when the car jumped off the pavement at forty miles per hour and flipped over. Rumors abounded that the Colorado City police were behind the crash. Laura died from injuries received in the wreck. Some believed she paid the ultimate price for defying the law in court.

After an elaborate funeral, Laura was buried at Fairview Cemetery in Colorado City. Her niece was laid to rest beside her. Laura's daughter was the sole heir of her estate, which amounted to more than fifteen thousand dollars in cash and property.

Laura Bell was fifty-six when she passed away.

Chris Enss *is a* New York Times *bestselling author who has written about women of the Old West for more than thirty years. She's penned more than fifty books on the subject and been honored with nine Will Rogers Medallion Awards, two Elmer Kelton Book Awards, an Oklahoma Center for the Book Award, three* Foreword Review Magazine Book Awards, *and the Laura Downing Journalism Award.*

SHERRY MONAHAN

Sherry Monahan is a multiple Will Rogers Medallion award-winning Culinary Historian with over sixteen books. She's a member of the James Beard Foundation and the Authors Guild. She enjoys sharing the history behind food and drink because tasting history is better than just reading about it.

Victorian Recipes with a Side of Scandal is Sherry's latest book. Monahan creatively weaves Victorian-era recipes with the true, and sometimes scandalous life of an English socialite named Ethel Barry. Discover how this young woman grew up in a proper English home and attended all the right schools but found salvation in a kitchen—a place she wasn't supposed to be. She was expected to find a suitable husband in her class, get married, manage a household staff, and have children. But that's not exactly how her life turned out because she broke Victorian protocol.

Cooking, which she never learned because her parents had staff for that, turned out to be her escape when she was "exiled" in America. She turned to food to sustain them in California as she quickly discovered that her life didn't turn out the way she expected. Learn about Ethel's life through over seventy-five Victorian-era recipes she either made or enjoyed. It's served with a side of scandal, like when she went skinny-dipping and when her divorce appeared in multiple U.S. newspapers with wild accusations.

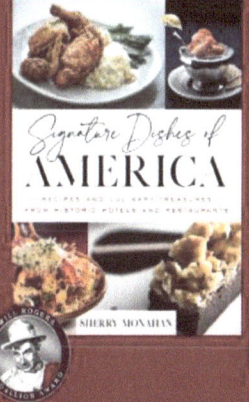

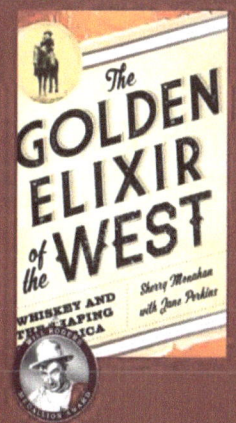
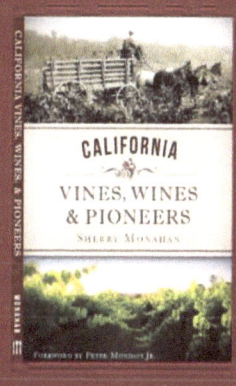

Visit sherrymonahan.com to learn more about Sherry and over sixteen of her books. You can aslo scan this code now.

LIVELY LIBATIONS

Sherry Monahan
CULINARY EDITOR

Please Don't Shoot the Pianist

Mix Him Up a Tom and Jerry, Instead.

Leadville, Colorado's mining boom began in the 1870s when silver and lead were discovered. Between 1878 to 1879, the population hovered around six to eight thousand individuals. Reports filled the newspapers across America when western papers compared each new boomtown to the last. A paper in Deer Lodge, Montana, noted Leadville claimed it was larger than Deadwood. In Leadville, a hardworking miner earned three dollars per day, and he often spent it in a saloon or dance hall. Whiskey cost twenty-five cents per drink and was a lot cheaper than milk.

The whiskey in Leadville was not the best, however, and a Kansas paper noted that it, "is 90 degrees above the high-water mark."

Another shot was taken at Leadville's whiskey by a St. Joseph, Missouri, newspaper. "Leadville whisky assays ninety-eight percent of pure spring water. That kind of beverage will strike with consternation the average stomach of the St. Joseph prospector."

Despite the bad press from some newspapers, Leadville's saloon thrived and many offered a variety of spirited beverages. The Pioneer Billiard Hall served juice apple cocktails, Phil Golding offered imported wines, the Board of Trade offered champagne cocktails, and the Pioneer saloon advertised they served the most "incomparable cocktails" and "mouths water to think of them."

As Oscar Wilde traveled across the West in 1882, he ended up in Leadville. He penned, "From Salt Lake City one travels over the great plains of Colorado and up the Rocky Mountains, on the top of which is Leadville, the richest city in the world. It has also got the reputation of being the roughest, and every man carries a revolver. I was told that if I went there, they would be sure to shoot me or my traveling manager. I wrote and told them that nothing they could do to my traveling manager would intimidate me. They are miners— men working in metals, so I lectured to them on the Ethics of Art. I read them passages from the autobiography of Benevento Cellini and they seemed much delighted. I was reproved by my hearers for not having brought him with me. I explained that he had been dead for some little time which elicited the enquiry 'Who shot him?' They afterwards took me to a dancing saloon where I saw the only rational method of art criticism I have ever come across. Over the piano was printed a notice: *PLEASE DO NOT SHOOT THE PIANIST. HE IS DOING HIS BEST*. The mortality among pianists in that place is marvelous. Then they asked me to supper, and having accepted, I had to descend a mine in a rickety bucket in which it was impossible to be graceful. Having got into the heart of the mountain I had supper, the first course being whisky, the second whisky and the third whisky. I went to the Theatre to lecture and I was informed that just before I went there two men had been seized for committing a murder, and in that theatre, they had been brought on to the stage at eight o'clock in the evening, and then and there tried and executed before a crowded audience. But I found these miners very charming and not at all rough."

The Pioneer saloon took advantage of Oscar Wilde's poems and ran this text in an 1882 ad: *"If a man don't go much on Oscar Wilde's poems he will go strong on the Pioneer Tom and Jerry."* This is the infamous Tom and Jerry cocktail that served all over the frontier, including Leadville.

Sherry Monahan *is an award-winning culinary historian who enjoys researching the genealogy of food and spirits. While there's still plenty to explore about frontier food, she's expanding her culinary repertoire to include places and foods from all over America and beyond. She holds memberships in the James Beard Foundation, the Author's Guild, Single Action Shooting Society, and the Wild West History Association. She is also a professional genealogist, and an honorary Dodge City marshal. One of her latest titles,* The Tombstone Cookbook: Recipes and Lore from the Town Too Tough To Die, *won the 2023 Will Rogers Medallion Award Gold Medal for Best Western Cookbook.*

Tom and Jerry

1 egg, separated
powdered sugar
pinch baking soda
1 jigger rum
hot milk
½ oz. California brandy
nutmeg

Beat the egg yolk in one bowl and the white in another. Once they have been beaten separately, combine them together, then add enough powdered sugar to make a stiff batter. Add the baking soda and rum, stirring gently. Add a little more sugar to stiffen the batter again.

Dissolve one tablespoon of the batter in three tablespoons of hot milk. Place in a hot mug. Add the rum, then fill the mug with hot milk until it reaches one-quarter inch from the top.

Top with brandy and a grating of nutmeg.

THE BOOK WAGON

Doug Osgood
BOOK REVIEWER

Mining for (Literary) Gold

Colorado is rich ground for history as well as fiction.

Women's Work

Gold was discovered near present-day Denver in 1858. From that day forward, fortune-seekers flocked to the Colorado Territory. The story of fantastic successes, horrible failures, and the many who just scratched out a living included many women. Brave, spirited, entrepreneurial women rode the boom and bust cycles along with the men—sometimes alongside a man, other times alone, but always against the odds. And women weren't just mining. Many came to the Colorado Territory knowing where folks gathered, services such as laundering, baking, and cooking—as well as more carnal needs—were in demand. *Women of the Colorado Mines* (Far Country Press, 2024) is the story of these women.

Linda Wommack provides short biographies of twenty-four notable women of Colorado mining history. Some, such as Margaret Brown, better known as the Unsinkable Molly Brown, who made a home for many years while her husband sought their fortune. Others, such as Clara Brown, who endured slavery and the loss of husband and children to the auction block, was set free prior to the Civil War. After migrating to Colorado, Clara's business sense made her a wealthy woman without the help of any man. Every story is well researched and provides concise insight into the lives these women lived.

I found myself initially disappointed that the style was more biographical instead of interlocking stories such as Clavin, Drury, or McCullough. By the end, however, I realized how well each vignette painted portraits of who each of these women were at their core and the strength that drove them forward. I would recommend this book to anyone interested in women's history, the Old West, or mining history.

Rating: 4 Nuggets out of 5.

Where Silver is King

In Leadville, Colorado, silver is king, and that's the issue in Ann Parker's *Silver Lies* (Poisoned Pen Press, 2003). As 1879 draws to a close, assayer Joe Rose is found trampled to death behind Inez Stannert's saloon. Most of the town, including the town marshal, dismiss the death as an unfortunate accident. Joe's widow, Emma, asks Inez to settle Joe's affairs, collect any fees due, pay whatever debts remained, and sell the business. Inez discovers assay irregularities and bogus greenbacks, leading her to wonder if Joe's death was really an accident. Someone in town is uncomfortable with the inquiries and makes multiple attempts to quell them. To make matters worse, Inez's own questionable past comes out, placing her under suspicion.

Ann Parker does a masterful job of keeping the reader guessing. Red herrings leap off the pages, yet the real clues blend into the noise-filled background as the story advances. Parker's prose is tight while vivid descriptions transport the reader to Leadville. The plot is well planned. The pace begins at a trot and slowly picks up to a canter by the halfway point, when Parker touches spurs to the plot, whipping it into a hair-raising gallop along a crumbling, twisty mountain trail. Every chapter seems designed to jerk the reader's thinking in a different direction. When all is said and done, she leads the reader to the obvious and inevitable conclusion they never saw coming.

Silver Lies is a fun and challenging read. With twists reminiscent of a good thriller in an Old West setting. Parker makes Inez Stannert worth rooting for. **Rating:** 4.5 Nuggets out of 5.

Reach for the Sky

Robberies of silver and gold ore shipments, both by stage and train, nearly shut down the Leadville, Colorado mines in Paul L. Thompson's ***Hang Shorty in Leadville, Colorado*** (DS Productions, 2022)**.** The outlaws even seemed in control of the town lawmen. Spies inhabited every cor-

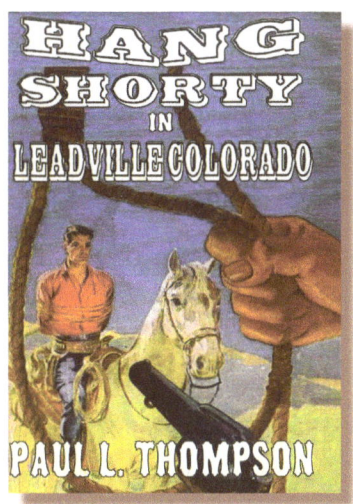

ner, preventing word from reaching state or federal authorities. In desperation, the local newspaper editor, Emmet Darnell, slipped a letter out of town, begging U.S. Marshal Shorty Thompson to come clean up the town. Shorty couldn't say no. He boarded the next train, wondering how a town the size of Leadville could be taken over. On the trip to Leadville, he discovers the gang has set a trap to keep him from reaching his destination. Shorty quickly outwits them, relieving them of their rifles in the process. But he still has to get to Leadville and fig-

ure out who's behind the trouble and why. And try to stay alive in the process.

The plot and characters of *Hang Shorty in Leadville, Colorado,* are straight out of a 1950's b-western. Stilted and cliched dialogue made Thompson's portrayal of Leadville as flat as the cardboard Western towns kids in the '60s played with. The only redeeming quality to the novel was the action. Gunfights, chases, hold-ups, and a little romance drove the plot forward. Unfortunately, even then, predictable outcomes made the scenes much less enjoyable than they otherwise could have been.

The plot of *Hang Shorty in Leadville, Colorado* is as unimaginative as a sober drunkard. At its very best, the novel is a quick read when the grocery ads begin to look interesting. Don't waste your time. This novel isn't worth even picking up for your e-reader. **Rating:** 1 Nugget out of 5.

Doug Osgood

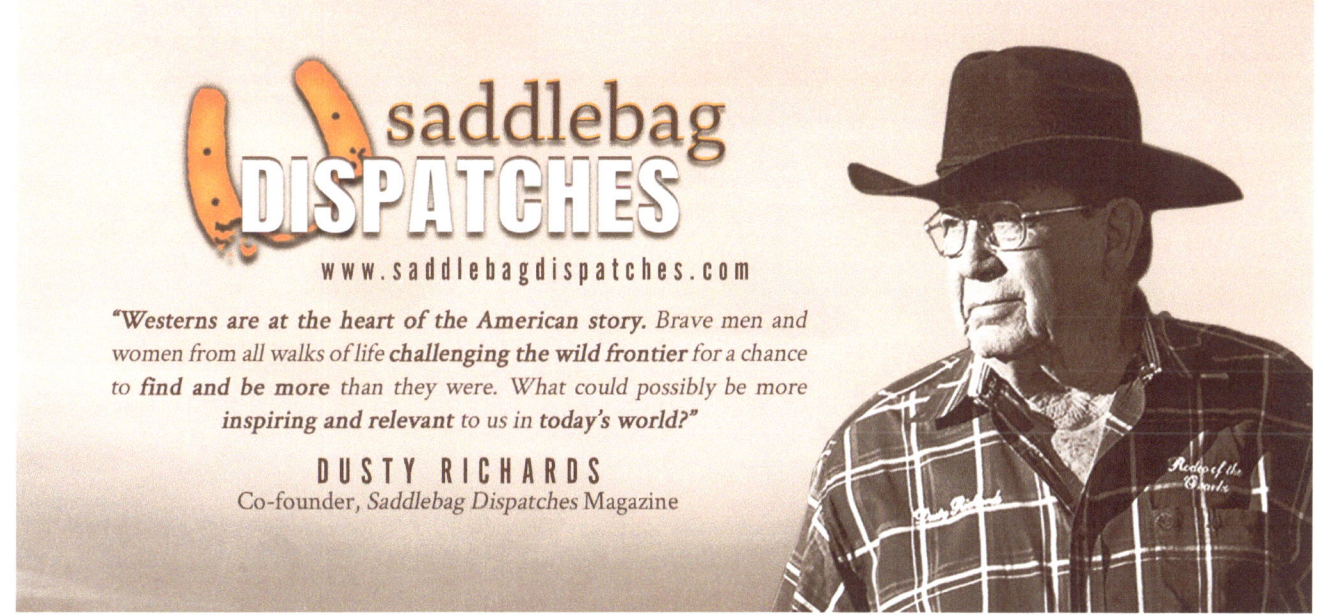

MARLEEN BUSSMA

SADDLEBAG DISPATCHES POET LAUREATE

the LEGEND of LEADVILLE

A round of insults fills the air like water fills a creek.
Loud pistols poke through windows. No one turns the other cheek.
The dueling madams spray their bullets. Life is on the brink.
Guests hide behind Victorian sofas as they spill their drink.

Combative harlots argue over who's more glamorous.
The battle lasts two hours with their fracas and their fuss.
The hoped-for lull appears when firing arms become too tired.
Come daybreak, they may start again unless their will's expired.

Prized metals scratched from local mines line pockets of the rich.
Prospectors flock to this high country with a miner's itch.
Bright gold is fickle as a harlot's heart and fades away.
Black tailings from the gold mines offer up a rich display

that brings back prosperous good times that had left a worn-out trail.
Hotels, an opera house, new schools are built on a grand scale.
The mineral that has reclaimed life in this once dying town
is lead, thus Leadville, soon to be a burg of great renown.

The high times bring low morals as the lawless settle in
like squatters wearing out their welcome with their life of sin.
The city marshal's chased out of town in his first week.
His new replacement, gunned down in a month, leaves their times bleak.

Mart Duggan, who will tame the town, is sworn in by the mayor.
His rep says he's a gunman. Local thugs don't have a prayer.
He escorts crooked deputies and judges out of town.
The incidents of claim-jumpers and armed gangs have gone down.

Mart Duggan hitched his gun belt up and changed the life of crime.
The residents of Leadville, Colorado, can spend time
attending opera—ev'nings at the theater that won't cease.
The thin air near the tree line finally has the sound of peace.

SADDLEBAG DISPATCHES

PROUDLY PRESENTS THE WINNER OF OUR 2024

MUSTANG AWARD

FOR WESTERN FLASH FICTION

LAURA CONNER KESTNER

"A TRAIN TO CATCH"

LAURA CONNER KESTNER

A TRAIN TO CATCH

A SHORT STORY

**Winner of the 2024 *Saddlebag Dispatches* Mustang Award
for Western Flash Fiction**

Clayton kept close watch on the woman as she left the back door of her home and crossed the porch.

In the distance, a locomotive whistle blew. A lonesome sound that drew his thoughts to better days. The days before he'd chased after such a train looking for adventure and riches. He'd found plenty of the first and none of the second. That was when he was younger. Naïve.

Things were different now, and the ache in his heart rivaled the one in his belly.

The woman picked up a long stick as she made her way to an apple tree in a corner of the yard, stopping once to glance in his direction. Had she heard him?

Clayton eased back, into the shadow of the woods just beyond her place.

Was she worried about encountering a stranger? Unfortunately, she should worry. Strangers could rob you blind. That was only one of the lessons he'd learned the hard way.

Go on back inside, Lady.

After several moments, she turned to wave at a young boy in the doorway. "You stay back and out of the way now, hear?"

The boy nodded and she raised the stick, clumsily wielding it to thrash the tree, dodging apples as they fell.

Laughing, she began gathering them in her apron.

Leave one. Please.

Empty pockets and an empty belly had changed Clayton's definition of riches.

Just one.

Pulling his collar up and his hat down against a sudden chill, Clayton wondered when true cold would come calling. Where would he be when it did?

Don't think about it.

Convinced that the woman's attention was fixed on the fallen fruit and her boy, Clayton eased forward again and watched. Smoke curled from a stove pipe of the old frame house. Perhaps she was baking today. Or canning.

Memories rained down on him, as the apples had her. Family gathered around the table, waiting for supper. Pa's words of thankfulness before they all dug in. Ma's smile when the old man mumbled, "Good grub" after the first bite. Love. Kindness. Things Clayton had taken for granted. Things he'd turned his back on, rejected in the name of adventure.

He missed it all with a fierceness that took his breath away at times.

But he couldn't go home now.

Hands in his pockets, Clayton touched the two letters he'd found waiting in Fort Worth—when he'd finally checked. Both sent to him months before, care of general delivery.

The first letter was short.

Pa's sick. Please come home. We need you.

The second one, even shorter.

Pa died.

A punch to the gut he'd remember until his own dying day.

But it wasn't the words on the paper that bounced around in his mind now. It was words left unwritten. *It's too late.* Clayton figured if he showed up at the door now, those exact words would be uttered by his Ma and his younger siblings. Could they ever forgive him?

Throat tight, Clayton shoved the letters and the memories further down, keeping his focus on the woman in the yard. On the apples. No telling how far it was to the next house, and another chance at something to eat.

Apron full, the woman turned, calling out to the boy at the door, "We'll have a feast this evening."

"I wanna help gather them apples."

"You stay right there. Perhaps you can help me cook." She began telling the boy what she'd prepare—including cake and cobbler—as she headed inside.

Help your Ma, boy. Help her however you can. While you can.

After she'd gone, the door shut, Clayton eased forward again. There were still several apples littering the ground. Probably not prime pickings, but he didn't care. Just one. A little something to get him to the next town.

He'd almost reached them when the door reopened. This time the woman had a sack in her hands.

She was coming back for the rest.

Disappointed, defeated, Clayton ducked out of sight again. But she didn't glance his way this time.

She leaned the sack against the tree trunk, then hurried away.

Clayton waited, wary. His gaze swung toward the house. A hand at the window. A wave.

He eased toward the tree and grabbed the sack. His stomach growled as he looked inside. Ham. Bread. *Two* perfect ripe apples.

His spirits lifted as he glanced at the house again. The curtain was closed now.

But someone's mama had cared.

Perhaps his own would, too.

Maybe it's not too late.

If she'd let him, he'd tell her everything. His grief, his sorrow.

But mostly, his regret.

Clutching the precious gift, Clayton turned and walked away.

He had a train to catch. ♘

Laura Conner Kestner *spent 25 years in community journalism before pursuing a career in fiction.*

She is the author of five books–four historical Western fiction, and one contemporary. Her most recent writing endeavor is flash fiction, which she enjoys immensely. She is honored to be a finalist for the 2024 Saddlebag Dispatches Mustang Award.

Laura is grateful for the opportunity to write (it's a childhood dream of hers), and so grateful for those who are willing to read her work. She is a proud four-time Will Rogers Medallion Award finalist, winning the Gold Medallion in 2021 in the inspirational fiction category.

Born in Fort Worth, Texas, Laura is a Christian, wife, mother, grandmother, and seventh-generation Texan.

Find out more about Laura and her writing here: ***https://www.lauraconnerkestner.com/***

 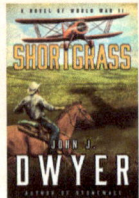 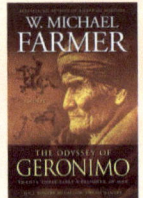 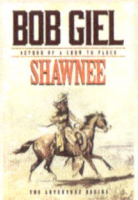 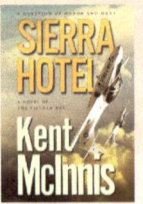 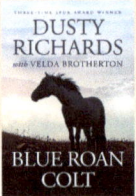 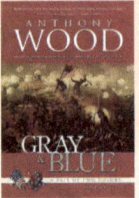

KYLEIGH MCCLOUD

JUSTICE OR EXECUTION

A SHORT STORY

**First Runner-Up in the 2024 *Saddlebag Dispatches* Mustang Award
for Western Flash Fiction**

Sitting with his back against the wall, Colby squinted across the smoke-filled saloon. His bounty: a man with a large scar on his left cheek, playing five-card stud. He dropped his wishful gaze and pulled a folded-up paper from his pocket. The yellowed paper crinkled as he carefully unfolded the tattered poster and studied the description. Did he locate the murderer in Colorado?

A whiskey tumbler thudded, amber-colored liquid sloshing onto the worn table. His twin sister's voice startled him. "Is that him—the man who killed our mother?"

"You'll need to do your part and find out." Colby shrugged. His blurred eyes remained fixated on the wanted poster. He had memorized the name William Mathias Reed long ago. "Remember the signal, if it's him."

Tessie clasped her hand over his and squeezed. "I'll be fine."

Her lacey white hem swished against the floor as Tessie threaded through the crowd, occasionally mingling but undeterred. She approached the target. When her slender fingers brushed along the man's shoulder, acrid bile burned Colby's throat.

A wary eye on his sister, he folded the poster and replaced it in his pocket.

Several minutes passed. Tessie continued her flirtation through touch and a smile with an occasional feigned laugh. With honey-colored hair and vivid-green eyes, few men could resist her.

The suspect drew another card.

Colby fidgeted.

The target revealed his card hand. A relieved sigh came as the man rose and collected his winnings. Tessie deftly snatched a silver certificate off the table. As she pretended to return it, the currency fluttered to the floor. She leaned over and seized her brother's intense gaze.

Colby hoisted his glass and gave a slight nod. Tessie's coquettish wiles seduced William upstairs. He gulped the whiskey, its spicy fire erasing the bitter taste.

Tonight, their father would die.

Heart pounding, Colby set the empty glass on the table. The chair screeched behind him, and he started after his sister five minutes later. He prayed Tessie didn't need her derringer.

The saloon's raucous chatter and laughter faded. Colby hugged the wall as the rustle of men and prostitutes passed in the dim hallway. When he reached Tessie's room, he waited. William's indistinct voice carried and then silenced, followed by a muffled thud. The door creaked open.

"He's out," Tessie said. Colby entered. They forced William's limp body from the floor onto the bed. While Colby secured the murderer's arms to the headboard, Tessie collected the broken glass and mopped up the spill on the floor.

An hour later, Colby shook the splayed man and slapped his face a half-dozen times. When their prisoner didn't stir, he snapped, "How much laudanum did ya give him?"

"He should wake soon." Tessie pursed her lips and stared through narrowed eyes. She placed her hands on her hips with a huff. "I wanted to give him the entire bottle."

"I told ya. You don't want a man's death on your conscience."

"And you do?"

William's head lolled, and he groaned.

Colby slid a hand to his holster. He withdrew his revolver and stood at the foot of the bed, aiming at their no-good, murdering father. His fingers trembled. Shooting a man was different than cans. He swallowed hard and forced his shaky hands to steady.

The prisoner awoke. He stuttered, "Where am I?"

"Your daughter's room," Colby replied in an icy tone.

"I don't have a daughter." William widened his gaze and appeared to search the room for an answer. He blinked. "The last I remember is playin' poker and this young pretty thang …"

"Look at her closer. She should seem familiar."

Tessie approached the bed, her footsteps hesitant. William squinted, and she shuffled alongside the bed. "Eighteen years ago in Dallas you ruined a woman … and soon after she bore twins, she killed herself."

William paled. "Clara?"

"You shamed our mother that she'd rather be dead than raise her children. And now we're here to avenge her murder."

"I-I-I didn't kill her."

Colby cocked the hammer, the noise out of place with the brothel's faint moans and bangs. He clenched his jaw. A gunshot would make people scurry to the room or pursue them. They needed to be ready for a quick getaway.

"Do it," Tessie ordered.

Colby twisted the gun sideways, his finger on the trigger. William flailed against his bonds and pleaded for them to spare his life. He noted the man's slate-gray eyes that resembled his own. "You may as well as."

"What are ya waitin' for? Shoot him."

"If I kill him, that would mean I'm no better." The gun wavered. Colby lowered the revolver and glanced at his sister. He couldn't let her shoot their father because of his cowardice. The headboard banged against the wall as William fought his ties. "I said I'll take care of him."

"You're nothin' like him." Tessie clasped a hand over the revolver's barrel and raised it.

"Please. I'll give ya anything," William begged.

Colby's mouth dried at what he and Tessie had planned. He tried to swallow, but coughed. Was this justice or an execution? Their plan to kill William was harder than he'd thought it would be. "Tessie, leave the room."

"No."

Colby repeated his demand. Tessie scoffed and stomped away, slamming the door behind her. He un-cocked the hammer and holstered his revolver.

"You ain't gonna kill me. You're too much of a coward to be mine." William sneered.

Colby stalked beside the bed and jerked the pillow from beneath his prey's head. He held the pillow over him. His grip tightened as the two men stared. William chuckled and goaded him again. "Do it. I dare ya,"

"I was never your son." Colby pressed the pillow against his victim's face. As William thrashed, he pushed harder until his prisoner slackened. He lifted the pillow. A smirk blossomed on Colby's face while William gasped for air. "I never said I'd make dyin' easy for ya." ♘

North Dakota native **Kyleigh McCloud** *lives in Minnesota with her husband and rescue cat. Writing has always been in her blood. As a result, she attended Minnesota State University Moorhead and graduated with a BS in Mass Communications, emphasis in Print Journalism.*

While Kyleigh loves to read a variety of genres, her favorite is historical romance. She has always felt drawn to the 1800s time period. The Little House on the Prairie series introduced her to this era when she was in fifth grade. Ever since, Kyleigh has admired the people's tenacity to survive back then. She and her husband love traveling the Midwest to visit historical sites.

*Aside from writing westerns, Kyleigh writes contemporary women's fiction and historical fiction. She has multiple short stories published in various anthologies and also has two holiday novellas. To follow Kyleigh's writing journey, check her website www.*__kyleighmccloud.__ __com__*, or follow her at* __www.facebook.com/authorkyleighmccloud.__

THERE'S A LITTLE COWBOY IN ALL OF US!

Discover Cowboy Action Shooting™

The Old West comes alive with a membership in SASS®. Members receive a numbered shooter's badge, alias registration, an annual subscription to The Cowboy Chronicle and much more.

SINGLE ACTION SHOOTING SOCIETY™
Toll Free: 1-877-411-SASS
www.sassnet.com

Legendary Leadville luminary Horace Tabor.

LEGENDS OF LEADVILLE

A legend in its own right, Leadville was inevitably populated by characters as colorful as it's rough-and-ready reputation—people like Horace and Baby Doe Tabor, Sheriff Martin Duggan, and Madame Mollie May.

STORY BY

TERRY ALEXANDER

People knew him as the Bonanza King of Leadville and the Silver King. His good friends called him "Haw." He was destined to be the richest man in Colorado and die in poverty.

Horace Austin Warner Tabor was born to Cornelius Dunham and Sarah Ferrin Tabor in Holland, Vermont in the United States on November 26, 1830. Cornelius owned a farm near the Canadian border, where he raised a variety of grains, vegetables, and fruits in addition to cattle, sheep, hogs, and chickens. During the winter months, his father ran the district school, and Horace and his brothers John and Lyman attended during that time. He also had two sisters Sarah and Emily.

The family lived in a drafty farmhouse without any conveniences. They used primitive tools and oxen in the fields. His mother died in 1846 at the age of forty-nine. In 1850, Cornelius remarried Betsy Welch. She had five children from a previous marriage who she brought into the household. At the age of seventeen, Horace and his brother John worked as granite cutters in Quincy or Boston, Massachusetts. In 1853, William Pierce, a stone contractor from Augusta, Maine, hired Horace to supervise other stonecutters. Here he met Pierce's daughter, Augusta, and fell in love with her.

The pair made plans for marriage. Tabor would travel to the western frontier, get established, and save some money. He would then return to Maine, marry Augusta, and together they would venture to Kansas and fight for the abolition of slavery. In 1855, he and his brother, John, departed for Kansas Territory with the New England Emigrant Aid Company. Their goal was to populate Kansas with anti-slavery settlers. Horace worked at Fort Riley as a stonemason to earn enough money for his plans.

He joined with other abolitionists, including John Brown, who would later lead the raid on Harper's Ferry. Their purpose was to defend Kansas from the pro-slavery faction. They failed to protect Lawrence when Confederate forces sacked and burned it to the ground.

Augusta Tabor had a reputation as an astute businesswoman in her own right and did much to support her husband and family during the decades before they struck it rich in Leadville.

Horace and Augusta were married at her family's home in Maine. After the wedding, the couple moved to Zeandale, Kansas, and farmed along the Deep Creek for two years. They had a son named Nathaniel Maxey Tabor, who went by the name of Maxey. The family moved west in 1859 with other "Fifty-Niners" during the Pikes Peak gold rush. The journey took six weeks in an oxen-driven covered wagon. They settled in California Gulch in Oro City. They began placer mining and operated a small store. By 1861, most people believed the area to be mined out and had moved away.

In 1862, they moved to Laurette in South Park. The town of Laurette would later be renamed Buckskin Joe. They again opened a store, and Tabor was appointed postmaster of the new town. The family prospered, mostly due to Augusta's efforts. She ran the store, operated a boarding house, did the cooking for the boarders, and managed the mail while Horace prospected. By 1863, the family was worth approximately thirteen thousand dollars, a small fortune at the time.

Upon hearing of a rich strike at the Printer Boy Mine in Oro City, the family again relocated and opened another store. This area would become part of Leadville in 1877. Horace was again named postmaster of the new community. The citizens elected him as Leadville's first mayor in January or February 1878. Leadville was a tough, lawless town. One of Tabor's first acts was to hire T. H. Harrison, the town's City Marshal. In 1877, the population of Leadville was between 300 and 350 people, mostly miners. By February of 1858, the population had bulged to nearly 15,000.

Harrison had a fearsome reputation, but the lawless element of Leadville beat him and ran him out of town two days after his appointment. George O'Connor became the next marshal. O'Connor lasted for two weeks before being shot by a former deputy. James M. "Tex" Bloodworth murdered the marshal after O'Connor reprimanded him for spending too much time in the area saloons and brothels. Bloodworth fled after the shooting and vanished, never to be seen in Leadville again.

Tabor's third appointment was Martin Duggan. The man was a tough, hard-nosed Irishman born in County Limerick, Ireland, who'd immigrated to the United States as a child. He was raised in the Irish slums in New York and headed west after the New York Draft riots in 1863. He drifted through the mines of Colorado, working as a muleskinner and a miner. He participated in numerous fights with both Indians and cowboys. In 1876, Duggan began working as a bouncer in the Occidental Dance Hall & Saloon in Georgetown, Colorado.

After his appointment, he had to disarm a drunk who was brandishing a pistol and making threats. Duggan took the pistol from the drunk and beat him with his own weapon. The man threatened to kill Duggan and stated in a stand-up gun battle he would have killed the marshal. Duggan threw the man's pistol into a corner, walked outside, then waited for the drunk to come confront him. When the drunk stepped out, they faced each other about thirty feet apart. The two men went for their pistols, and Duggan got his pistol free of the holster first. He fired three bullets, striking the drunk in the chest and killing him. The man was buried in an unmarked grave, as no one knew his name.

Tabor entered into a grubstake agreement with George T. Hook and August Rische for one-third of their profit from the Little Pittsburg Mine. If the mine failed to make any money, the two miners owed Tabor nothing. His wife disapproved of the arrangement and stated Tabor shouldn't have given the men the supplies. On May 3, 1878, a massive find in the mine kicked off the Colorado silver boom. Tabor sold his one-third interest in the mine for a million dollars then used this money to invest in other mines. He owned part of the Chrysolite and Matchless Mines as well as mines in Cripple Creek, Aspen, and the San Juan Mountains. By 1879, he was one of the richest men in Colorado.

In 1878, the voters elected Tabor as Lieutenant Governor of Colorado. He held this office until January of 1884. During that time, he also served as a U.S. Senator from January 2, 1883 until March 3, 1883, following the resignation of Henry M. Teller, at which point he became United States Secretary of the Interior under President Chester Arthur.

In late May of 1878, Duggan arrested Tabor's friend, August Rische, for being drunk and disorderly. When Rische resisted arrest, Duggan physically lifted him to the curb and escorted him to the county jail. Mayor Tabor came to the jail to protest Rische's arrest. Duggan refused to release the man. Later that same month, Duggan was called to the Pioneer Saloon. Two miners, John Elkins and Charlie Hines, were arguing over the pot in a poker game. A fight ensued and Elkins, a black man, stabbed Hines with a knife. Duggan located Elkins and arrested him without incident. However, when a rumor circulated that Hines was dead, racial hatred began to spread through the town. A lynch mob formed and walked toward the jail, ready to drag Elkins outside and hang him without a trial. Duggan stepped through the door with a cocked pistol in each hand and informed the mob he would kill the next man who took a step toward the jail. The mob dissipated. Hines, who didn't die from his wound, recovered. The judge ruled El-

Martin J. "Mart" Duggan was an Irish-born gunfighter and lawman who finally brought order to the chaos that was early Leadville. While relatively unknown today, Duggan was once one of the most feared men in the West.

Love, scandal, and silver. Horace Tabor's controversial romance with Elizabeth McCourt—better known locally as 'Baby Doe'—shook Leadville to its core.

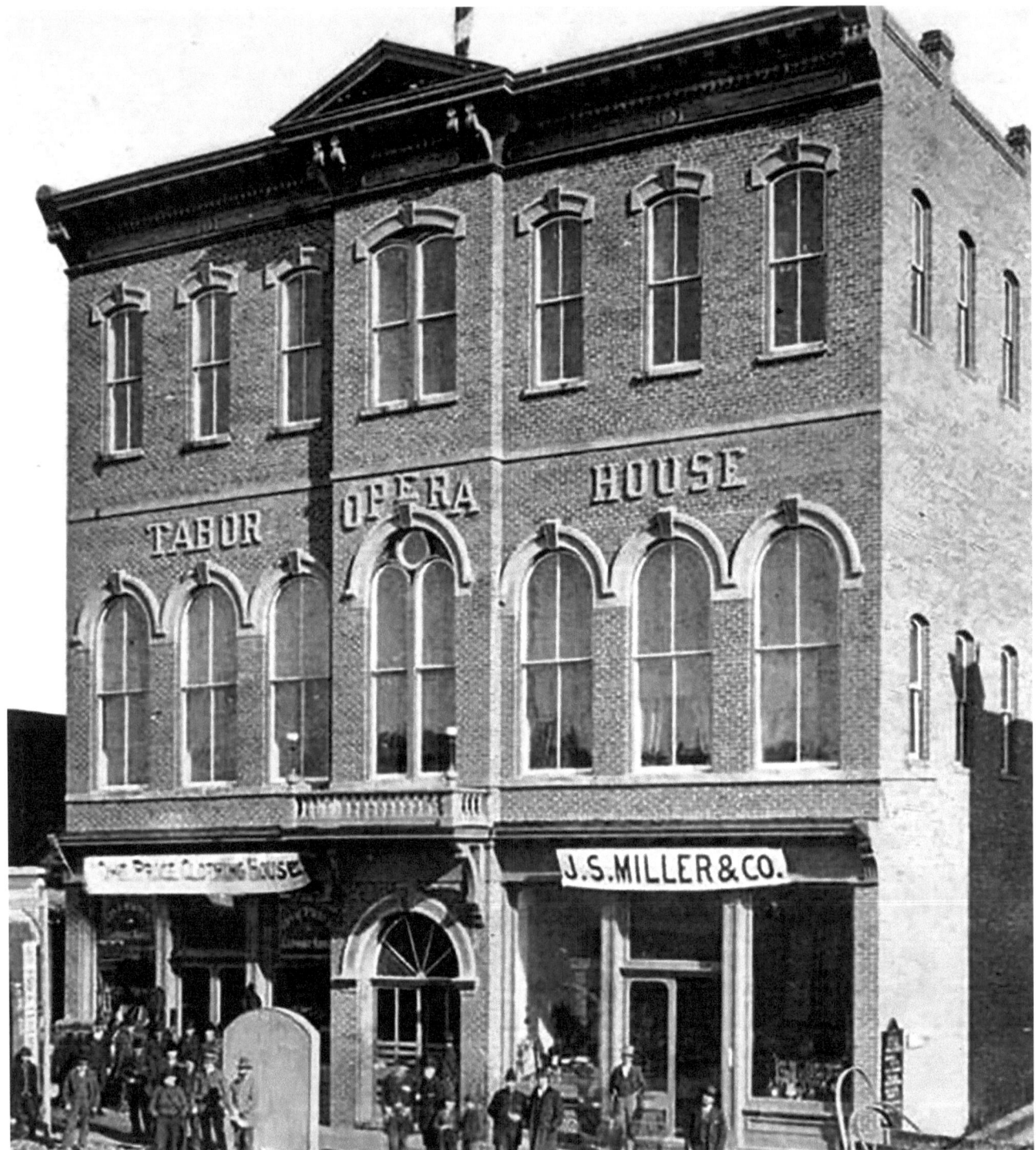

When it opened in 1879, the massive three-story Tabor Opera House was the most costly strucure in the state of Colorado. While Horace Tabor was forced to sell the building in 1893, it still stands today, designated as a National Treasure by the National Trust for Historical Preservation.

kins acted in self-defense. He immediately fled town after his release from jail.

The Tabors moved to Denver in 1879. The relationship between Horace and Augusta began to falter. She wanted to save their money while he continued to be a reckless spender and gamble and speculate on mining properties. The couple moved into separate residences. Augusta lived in their Denver mansion while Horace moved to the Windsor Hotel. Horace had an affair with Elizabeth McCourt, who was nicknamed Baby Doe.

Tabor donated money for the water works, rail lines, schools, and churches in Leadville. At one time he owned 4,600,000 acres of land in Colorado, and

175,000 acres of land in Texas dedicated to copper mining. He established a bank, newspapers, and the Tabor Opera House in Leadville. Augusta required money to support herself and took in boarders. She filed suit against Tabor, seeking financial support.

In March of 1879, Bill and Jim Bush became involved in a dispute with Mortimer Arbuckle over a vacant lot in town. Arbuckle had set up his small shanty business on the lot claimed by the Bush brothers. In a heated argument, Jim Bush pulled a pistol and killed Arbuckle. Arbuckle was unarmed at the time of the shooting. Another mob formed, intent on burning down the hotel owned by Bill Bush and dragging Jim to the hanging tree. Duggan backed down the mob and took Bush to jail. The mob continued to seethe, wanting to punish Jim Bush for Arbuckle's murder. The mob reformed and advanced toward the jail. Duggan took Bush to Denver for safekeeping until the trial. Duggan left the position of City Marshall in April of 1879 when his term expired. He relocated to Flint, Michigan. Pat Kelly was appointed as City Marshall. The lawless element in Leadville again took control of the town. The city council fired Kelly and sent for Duggan once again. The gunman returned in late December of 1879. Duggan fired all of Kelly's deputies left on the payroll and set about arresting anyone he believed to be causing problems in the city. By April of 1880, Leadville was under control, and Duggan stepped away from the marshal's job again.

In May of 1880, Horace Tabor hired Duggan to end a miners' strike over wages. Within a month, the strike had ended. Duggan and miner Louis Lamb had several confrontations during this time. In September of 1880, a witness reported Duggan attempted to run Lamb over with a sleigh while he was intoxicated. On November 22, 1880, reports stated Lamb had committed suicide in front of the Purdy Brothel. Lamb and Duggan had argued earlier, and Lamb walked away. Duggan continued to yell obscenities at Lamb. Lamb walked to the front of the brothel, where he turned and drew his pistol. Duggan drew and shot Lamb in the mouth, killing him instantly. He turned himself in after the shooting and was later cleared on all charges, as the shooting was ruled self-defense. Duggan left town and moved to Douglas City, Colorado.

Louis's widow, Mindy Lamb, swore to get revenge on Duggan. She promised, "I shall wear black and mourn this killing until the very day of your death and then, God damn you, I will dance upon your grave." The quote was widely circulated, and a few days later, local madam Mollie May stopped Mindy on the street. "You don't know me, but I wanted to tell you that what happened to a decent man like your husband was a dirty rotten shame and I'm really sorry for you." The women became friends, often visiting on the street in front of Mollie's brothel. The women remained lifelong friends.

Mollie May sold her house of ill repute to the city in 1881. The community used it as the city hall for many years. Mollie had a new brothel constructed with the aid of her silent partner, Horace Tabor. Mollie was born Milinda May Bryant to German and Irish immigrants in 1850. By 1870, she was working as a prostitute and performed in Jim McDaniel's Theater in Cheyenne, Wyoming. In 1876, she and McDaniel moved to Deadwood, South Dakota. There she met the May brothers, Jim, and Boone. They got into an altercation over Mollie at the Gem Theater. One brother drew his pistol and shot at the other. He missed his brother and struck Mollie instead. The bullet hit a steel rib in her corset, saving her life.

Fannie Garretson bit off part of Mollie's ear in late 1876 or early 1877. Fannie had married Banjo Dick Brown in November of 1876. The three of them were sharing a ride in a closed carriage. Dick let his intentions toward Mollie become public, and Fannie didn't appreciate her husband paying attention to another woman. After the brawl, Mollie left Deadwood for Colorado.

Prior to her marriage to Banjo Dick, Fannie lived with Ed Shaughnessy for three years in Laramie, Wyoming. When things didn't go as planned, she left him behind and moved to Deadwood. She and Brown married later in 1876. Upon hearing the news, Ed left South Dakota and traveled to Deadwood. Shaughnessy roamed the town until learning they were performing at the Bella Union Bar. He began drinking and drank for three days. On the evening of the third day, he went to the Bella Union Bar to catch the show. The following story has been documented on the *Wild West Tech* TV show.

Ed stood in a darkened area close to the wood stove and near the stage. When Fannie appeared, he grabbed the hatchet from the wood box and threw it at her. He then charged the stage. Dick Brown came from the wings and drew his pistol. His first shot hit the stage near the floodlights, the second struck Shaughnessy above the right hip. The fourth bullet struck him above the elbow, and the fourth missed. Shaughnessy fell and struck his head on the hard floor under the piano. A handful of witnesses carried Shaughnessy to the drugstore, where he lingered till five the next morning before dying from his injuries. Mayor Farnum of Deadwood conducted a hearing and ruled the shooting to be in self-defense. It proved the old saying, "Don't bring a hatchet to a gunfight."

She settled in Silver Cliff and Bonanza for a brief time and took up with an outlaw named Bill Tripp. After leaving him, she moved to Pueblo where she became the girl of gambler Sam Mickey and went by the name Jennie Mickey. By 1878, she'd settled in the boomtown of Leadville and brought her old friend Jim McDaniel with her. He shipped over forty thousand pounds of theater scenery, bought a building, then opened McDaniels New Theater. Mollie did very well in Leadville. By 1880, she'd employed ten girls and two men to keep order in the brothel. Her place was one of the most popular in town, and at one time she had the only local working telephone.

Fannie Garretson resurfaced in Leadville in 1880. She did one show at McDaniel's New Theater, and promptly sought employment elsewhere. Mollie and a rival madam named Sallie Purple got into an argument over who had the roughest childhood and who had the finest bordello. The two women cursed and insulted each other then finally they began shooting handguns across the alley at the other's business. The battle ended after two hours without injuries.

In 1881, Mollie became the subject of another scandal when news circulated that she was buying a nine-month-old child, named Ella, from a Mr. and Mrs. Moore. Mollie remained silent until a local newspaper published articles expressing concern over her intentions. Mollie gave the Leadville Herald an exclusive interview, explaining the baby belonged to a decent woman who was unable to care for her, and she was going to care for the child until the mother and father could get on their feet or get assistance from other relatives. Despite Mollie's claim, Ella's family never reclaimed the child and Mollie adopted her. When the child reached school age, she attended Saint Scholastica's Institute in Highland, Illinois. Robert Busk served as her official guardian.

Horace attained a divorce from Augusta without

her knowledge in Durango, Colorado in March of 1882. Augusta filed for divorce in January of 1883, when she discovered she was already divorced from Tabor. She filed a legal case for desertion. They settled the case out of court in late 1883. She was awarded two properties worth $250,000 or a settlement of some $400,000 dollars.

He married Elizabeth McCourt on March 1, 1883, in Washington, D.C., and their union made the Lieutenant Governor a social outcast. The second marriage produced two daughters, Elizabeth Bonduel, nicknamed Lily, and Rosemary Echo, nicknamed Silver Dollar. The Tabors lived a life of luxury and traveled extensively. He ran for Governor during the remainder of the 1880s without success.

Mollie May died on April 11, 1887, from what a local doctor reported as "Neuralgia of the heart." Her funeral was one of the largest processions in Leadville. Mollie's brothel substituted as a church for her funeral. Her good friend Mindy Lewis sat in one of the front row chairs. News of her death circulated throughout the entire state. A three-thousand-dollar hearse transported her coffin to Leadville's Evergreen Cemetery.

Her estate, valued at over $25,000, included some $8,000 in diamonds. Her personal property sold for $1,500, and her house sold to Madam Anna Ferguson for $3,600. The money from the sale went to Ella Moore.

Duggan returned to Leadville in 1888 and accepted a job as a patrolman. The town had progressed beyond the mining camp he had policed eight years earlier. While the town had changed, Duggan's techniques did not. When he roughed up a jewelry peddler and dragged him to jail, a judge fined him twenty-five dollars after he dismissed the case against the peddler. Duggan resigned from the police force and began drinking heavily.

In the early morning hours of April 11th, Duggan engaged in an argument with two gamblers, William Gordon and Bailey Youngston, inside the Texas House. The gunman invited both to come outside to settle their dispute. Fearing Duggan's reputation, each refused. At around four in the morning, Duggan's friends convinced him to go home. He left the Texas House and walked half a block when someone approached him from behind and shot him in the back of the head. Duggan staggered to the Bradford Drug Store before collapsing. His wife ran to the

Leadville, Colorado, circa 1881, looking over the town from the West.

drugstore, and she and many of his friends sat with him till the wee hours of the morning.

He opened his eyes hours later and asked for a drink of water. When asked who had shot him and was it Youngston, he replied "No, and I'll die before I tell you." Duggan took his last breath at 11:00 a.m. on April 9, 1888. No one ever knew why he refused to disclose the name of his attacker. Several people mourned his murder while others lamented the fact that someone else killed him. Bailey Youngston, Tom Dennison, Jim Harrington, and George Evans were arrested for the murder. They were acquitted and released due to lack of evidence.

Many people believed George Evans was hired to kill the former marshal by a group of men with grudges against Duggan. He left Leadville after his release from jail. Mindy Lewis danced in the street where Duggan had been shot down and presented her black widows dress to his widow.

Tabor's fortune vanished when President Grover Cleveland repealed the Sherman Silver Purchase Act. His holdings, including his mansion in Denver, were sold to pay his creditors. He returned to work in the mines for a brief time then called in a political favor and was appointed the Denver Postmaster in 1898. He and his wife then lived at the Windsor Hotel.

He became terminally ill with appendicitis in 1899. His final request to his wife was that she hang onto the claim for the Matchless Mine. Tabor believed the mine would yield another strike. The flags flew at half-mast the day of his funeral. The Aspen Tribune reported ten thousand people attended his final service. His body was interred at Mt. Calvary Cemetery in Denver then was later moved to Mt. Olivet Cemetery in Jefferson County, Colorado.

Elizabeth Tabor moved to Leadville and spent her last days living in a tool shed at the Matchless Mine. After freezing to death in the shed in 1935, she was buried alongside her husband at Mt. Olivet Cemetery.

Augusta Tabor fared far better than her former husband. She made several successful investments, and on her death in 1895 was noted to be among the wealthiest people in Colorado. She left her son a half million dollars and several properties.

Local madam Laura Evans recalled that in 1895, over five hundred sporting girls lived in Leadville. In 1901, the *Leadville Herald* published a story concerning the then-twenty-year-old grown-up daughter Mollie May adopted. Ella Moore, who then went by Lillian, had attempted suicide in Leadville. Quick action by a local doctor saved her life. Upon her recovery, she was last seen on a train headed to Denver, and like so many people in the Old West, she vanished without a trace.

Terry Alexander *and his wife, Phyllis, live on a small farm near Porum, Oklahoma. They have three children, thirteen grandchildren, and four great grandchildren. If you see him at a conference, though, don't let him convince you to take part in one of his trivia games–he'll stump you every time.*

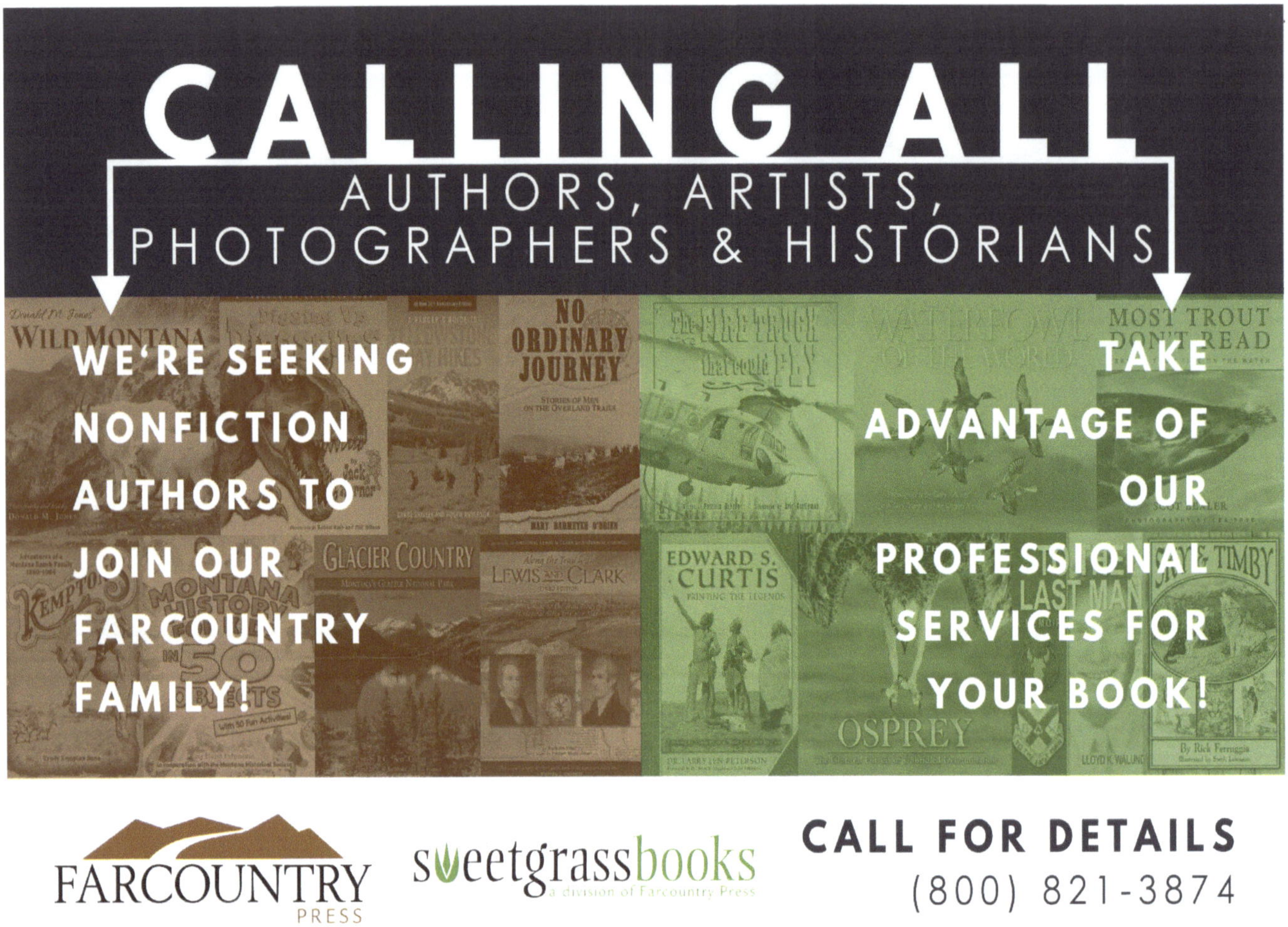

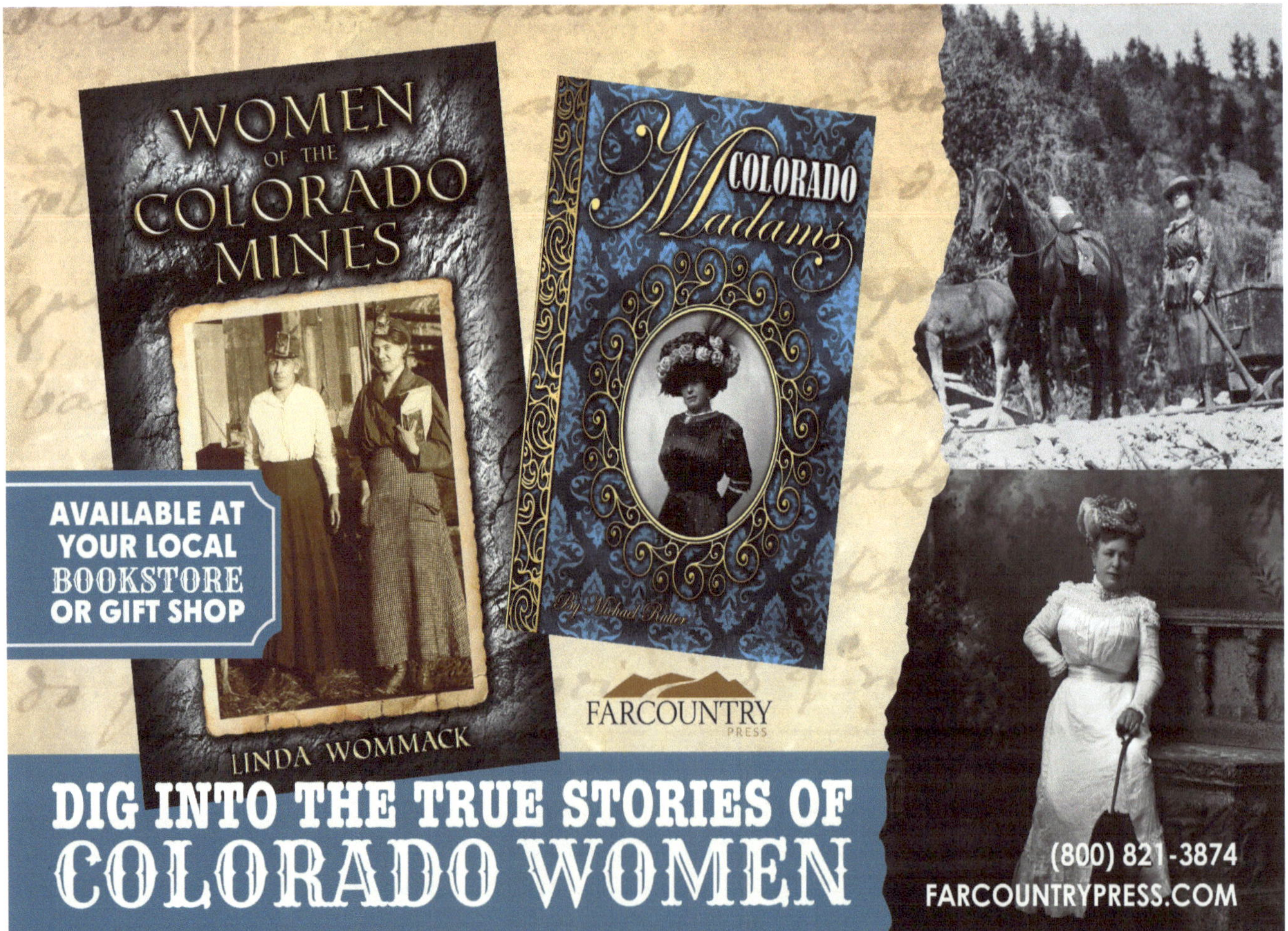

D.N. SAMPLE

THE PROMISE

A SHORT STORY

"Blessed Virgin Mary!" Katherine Quinn slapped a hand to her mouth. The broom she'd been holding thudded against the dirt floor. "Paddy! What's happened to ya."

Her husband, Padraig, swayed in the entrance to their one-room shanty. His left eye was swollen shut, the lid and surrounding socket already tinged with purple hues. Deep, jagged cuts, many still oozing crimson, marked his face. The bridge of his nose, once straight and narrow, had ballooned to four times its normal size and crooked a direction nature never intended. Crusty scabs formed crags around lips little more than pulp. His homespun shirt hung in tatters, revealing angry gashes while large, ugly bruises blanketed the muscular slabs of his chest and shoulders. Dried blood stained his denim pants. The hand locked onto the door jamb seemed all that kept him from collapsing. One gray eye stared at her, blinking almost as if wondering who she was.

He said nothing.

Katherine hurried to his side and dragged his arm over her narrow shoulders, hardened by the toils of daily life. Paddy sagged into her.

A quick glance past her husband. Nothing stirred in the street. Not that she expected folks to be out in the Shantytown section of Leadville. The joyful squeals of toddlers at play echoed from one of the homes across the way. Miners' children. A grim smile formed. How wonderful to be a child, oblivious to the worry pressing on the adults. A morning breeze ripe with the freshness of a recent Colorado fall rain flowed through the open door, rustling her skirts.

She supported most of Paddy's weight as together they hobbled the twenty feet to their bed along the back wall. After he dropped on to the thin rag-stuffed mattress, she helped ease him to his back, head resting on the frayed blanket that served them as a pillow. His feet hung six inches over the footrail. She brushed a shock of bright copper hair from his bleeding forehead and gently cupped his bruised chin.

"Paddy dear. Speak to me. What's happened?"

He groaned. "We were...." He stopped and took long ragged breaths through his mouth. "Attacked." More gasps. He felt his nose with fingers that hadn't straightened properly in at least five years. "Damned strike busters... from Missouri we heard." More wheezing gulps followed. "I got lucky."

"Lucky, ya say. Hardly looks like luck to me, 'less tis bad luck ya're speakin' of."

He reached out and engulfed her hand in his. "Twas surely luck." His face hardened. "A couple of our lads was killed. Lots hurt bad. No. I'll take the beatin'." He sagged, his hand released hers and his arm flopped over the side of the bed, knuckles grazing the floor. Breaths came harder than before.

"Paddy. Promise you'll not get your ownself killed. That you'll not leave the boys fatherless. Nor me a widow."

He took a few breaths through his mouth, then swallowed. Thoughts clear as the print on the newspaper crossed his face. He had fought for causes in the past. That was his nature—the reason they'd fled Ireland. Was she asking too much? Fear gnawed at her belly. She couldn't lose him. Deep down he was a scrapper, and he would fight now, too.

Everything would be fine, so long as he always came home.

But would he promise that? Could he?

He stared at the ceiling without answering.

"Please. I...." She couldn't say it out loud as if vocalizing it might make it happen.

He wheezed. His chest rose in stuttering steps before falling. This repeated for what seemed minutes—each breath a struggle. As his breathing settled into a smoother rhythm his face softened. His one open gray eye sought her gaze. The expression held his love for her—his devotion to his family. "I promise."

A hundred-weight lifted from Katherine. She patted his hand and, with a determined huff, stood. There was much needed doing. She hefted a kettle of water onto the arm of the fireplace crane and swung it over the glowing coals. As it heated, she gathered rags and the jar of salve the camp doctor had given her when Paddy was cut badly pulling men out of the mine during last year's collapse. That infection nearly cost him his leg.

By the time she finished cleaning and dressing his wounds, he dozed. The nose should be reset, but she refused to disturb him. Not that he slept well. Several times he kicked out. Muttered curses and unintelligible shouts filled the small room.

She slipped out, returning with a pail of water from the well that served Shantytown.

Katherine pulled a stool next to him and sat. She rubbed his chest and thought about the day they were married. Bastards trying to arrest Paddy had dogged their heels. All for complaining about English rule. Well, maybe he'd done a little more than complain.

The schooner *Suzzanna* had been moored at Foynes on the Shannon. They booked passage, lying to the clerk about being wed. On board they begged Captain O'Flynn to perform the ceremony. He'd done the deed as soon as they were clear of English law, and they'd spent the rest of the ocean crossing below decks.

The memory lightened her mood, and she tossed her head while running a hand through her hair. A mischievous smile crinkled her eyes and her cheeks warmed—the trip had indeed been memorable.

She returned her attention to her battered husband, contemplated asking Elizabeth, their neighbor, to fetch Father Baker, Saint Mary's priest, but decided against it. She missed Father Callahan. Growing up his mass had given her comfort amid the turmoil of life under English rule.

Father Baker was so stern, as if people should be perfect. Worse, he was English.

Katherine spat, her spittle forming a glob on the dirt. "Ah, girl. So, here's where your hatred's led. To spittin' on me own floor. As if we don't have more to worry about than a damned Sassenach priest. Ought a be ashamed of me ownself."

She withdrew her rosary from a pocket and fingered the beads as she prayed. Hours passed. Padraig sleeping, Katherine praying. On occasion, when sweat glistened on his skin, she stopped long enough to sponge him with a water-soaked rag.

Until the door banged open. The boys arriving from school. Laughter and shouts about things young lads love replaced the somber quiet.

Sean, nearly eight, wiry, and almost as tall as she, pulled up short. "What's wrong with Papa?"

Finn, just turned six and stocky built, was tight on his big brother's heels. He stared wide-eyed but said nothing. His jaw quivered. Large tears formed though he tried to fight them back.

"Papa was...." Katherine stopped. Was what? Beaten? Attacked? Yes, all of those things and more, yet she couldn't bring herself to utter them to his sons. They would just worry.

She glared at the bushel basket of potatoes in the corner opposite the stove. The community garden the wives planted had yielded enough for the next few months, but without cash money they'd not be able to purchase the other staples needed for the coming winter. Hiding concern from such tenderhearted boys seemed impossible. A week ago, Sean had offered to find work. Others his age worked—he would, too.

How could she tell these sweet, tender children about the violence that had visited their father?

Katherine choked back the sobs that threatened to burst forth. "Papa was hurt at the mine today."

"Like last year?" Little Finn's voice trembled.

Sean cocked his head for a second, then said, "The older boys said strike busters had attacked." His face screwed into an angry scowl. "Did they hurt Papa?"

Katherine gazed at her sons. First Sean, then Finn. She couldn't bring herself to lie. A slow nod of her head opened the floodgate of tears. She knelt in front of them and drew them into a mama bear's hug. Looking over their shoulders she vowed to keep them safe.

Supper that night was boiled potatoes. One each for the boys and Katherine. Paddy wouldn't eat. She fixed him a bark broth with wild mushrooms and onions. He sipped down most of it. The rest she set aside for later.

Darkness chased the final vestiges of light over the western peaks when William Doyle, the union leader and administrator, knocked on their door. Katherine opened it and he looked past her at Paddy. "How is he?"

"Breathin' some better. His body is one big bruise. I cared for him the best I knew, but he needs a proper doctor. Which we can't afford." Her cocked brow collapsed when faced with a wall of indifference.

Well, it's true what they say—every good Catholic mother knew how to apply guilt.

She swallowed hard and dug deep within herself. Pride was a powerful thing, but sometimes it had to be suppressed. Offering a silent prayer she'd be able to ask what needed asking for and say what needed saying. Katherine gripped Doyle's arm below the elbow. "Can't the union help? It's been over a month since we got anythin' from ya. We need doctorin'. And food. With the company store refusin' to sell to the strikers we've been forced to use the mercantile. Mr. O'Shea's been awful kind to us, offered us wives' credit when none a the others would, but yesterday he told us couldn't offer more 'till our men-folks get back to work. Without that we're hard put to

put food on the tables. Winter's comin' all too soon. Don't ya see, ya has to help us."

Doyle wasn't a tall man. She could almost look him straight in the eye. Halfway through Katherine's pleading he had turned his head away. He spoke without making eye contact. "We're out of money. The Montana union helped us for a while. Our national affiliate, too." He shrugged his shoulders. "That's all dried up."

He'd not ignore her so easily. Katherine drew herself up to her full height and fixed a glare on the man, willing his eyes back to her. "Yet ya found the money to buy a hundred Marlins to arm your men. While our families starve."

His brows rose ever so slightly, but he said nothing.

"At least ya aren't denying it even if ya aren't man enough to look at me." She paused to stab a finger into Doyle's chest. "Ya can't hide the truth from us. We wives hear things."

Exhaustion swept over her. This strike had been going on for months with no end in sight. Not working took a toll on a man. She'd seen it in her own Paddy. And in other men. Hollow expressions. Slumped shoulders. Sudden fits of rage. And fear covered the children's faces like a pox. And the wives. On her. That constant knot in the pit of her stomach.

She blinked back the moisture in her eyes. "Paddy took a frightful beaten'. An' he considers himself lucky. More men killed today. How many does that make? Families mourning the loss of fathers, husbands. What are those widows to do? How will they feed their children, now? Your union's no help." A tear spilled down her cheek, but she refused to swipe it away. "Ain't it time for this violence to end?"

Doyle's lip curled. "Those rich money-grubbers must be forced to pay proper wages. High time we workers got our due."

"To be sure, we could use the extra fifty cents a day, but is it really worth all this sufferin'? Why can't our men just go back to work?"

"And give in to those bastards? Never."

"What ya're askin' for can't replace our menfolk. Three dollars. Two-fifty. I'd rather the two-fifty if it means me boys'll have a father."

His lips parted and he seemed about to respond, but instead turned toward the door. As he walked out he mumbled something about her taking care of "him"—pointing to Padraig as if he'd forgotten the man abed's name.

Katherine closed the door behind Doyle. In her heart she'd wanted to slam it but refused to give in to that man. As the door latched, she spun to slump against it, her legs leaden and trembling. Her words had meant nothing to him. He cared as little for the miners as the greedy mine companies who wouldn't pay a penny more.

She slumped backward—the back of her head thumping on the door. How times had changed. In '87, when they'd first arrived in Leadville, Sean had been just a year old. Back then Paddy earned over four dollars a day, with steady increases as his experience and skill developed.

She closed her eyes. That was before the silver scare in '93. Prices plummeted. Owners forced hard rock miners like Paddy to take steep pay cuts or risk losing their jobs entirely.

What else could they do?

Katherine glanced at her husband. She knew him well. He loved her and his boys, but could he swallow his stubborn Irish pride and cross the lines? Some of the other men, desperate to feed their families, had done just that. The owners accepted them back with open arms. At two-fifty a day.

What were they to do?

⁕

Sleep eluded her. A ratty blanket made a pallet for her on the hard dirt floor beside their bed. She spent much of the night listening to Paddy's wheezing. Once he'd started choking. She held her breath. The fit dragged on until, in concern, she threw her covers aside. She'd just begun to rise when the gagging eased as if he'd finally cleared his throat. Paddy sucked in great gulps before collapsing back on the bed, resuming his regular, rhythmic breathing. Katherine's heart slowed to its normal pattern.

Wide awake, she fretted about the strike and weighed the cost of abandoning the cause. If she knew anything about her Padraig, it was that he would baulk at that thought. If the miners didn't stick together, they were done for. Yet how much longer could this go on?

At some point in the night exhaustion overcame worry, allowing her a few hours of blessed sleep. She woke to his grumbling about needing the outhouse.

"Lord A'mighty, I hurt. Those thugs did shore put a whooping to me." His hand tapped at the bed beside him.

"I'm down here."

"He'p me stand, please."

A shake of her head and she scampered to rise, then quickly picked up the pallet before he stepped on it. Once again Katherine lent him her strength. Between them he rose to unsteady legs, but when she tried to help him walk Paddy shook his head.

"I'll be damned if I'll allow ya to he'p me to the cro."

She shot him a skeptical glance, but finally nodded and stepped away. He wobbled for a long moment before gritting his teeth and tottered step-by-step to the door. Katherine fought the urge to rush to his aid. What dignity remained to him wouldn't thank her.

At the door, Paddy stopped, grabbed the inside edge of the frame, straightened, drew himself to his full height, pulled the door open, and marched through it.

Katherine waited, fearing the worst. The more time passed, the worse her imagination. Images of him stumbling, hitting his head on a rock, or strike breakers approaching him with clubs played out in her mind. She chided herself for not trusting him.

She waited.

The boom of a single gunshot shattered the early morning stillness.

Close.

From the direction of the outhouses.

Lumps clawed from Katherine's gut to her throat.

Another blast. And another.

Katherine froze.

One of the boys stirred in the loft.

"Mama. What was that noise?"

Sean. The first faint streams of light poked through the room's only window. He, too, would need the outhouse soon. She swallowed hard. "Nothing to worry yourself about." Had the tremble in her voice given away the lie? Oh dear. "Go back to sleep. It's not time to get up just yet."

"Okay, Mama."

A sigh escaped her. How long since the last shot? Did she dare go out. If Paddy was hurt, he'd need her. But if the shooters lingered, she risked being shot.

What would become of her boys, then?

Muffled voices. She strained to hear—to understand what was being said.

Her torso rocked as she stood staring at the door.

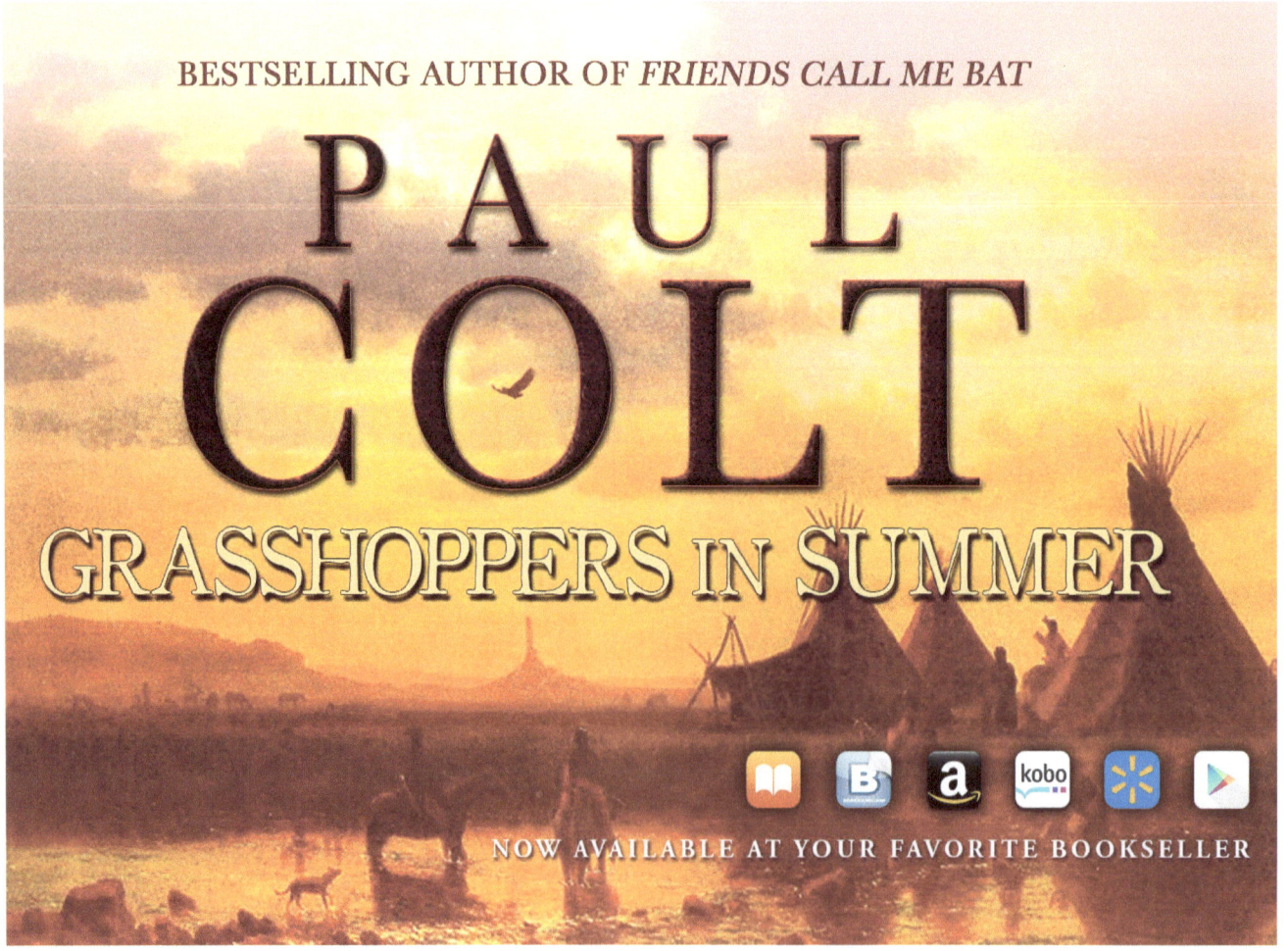

The door creaked open. Paddy. Fresh blood stained his undershirt. Heartbeats seemed drums in her ears. Quick steps carried her to him.

"You're hurt."

"Just me nose bleeding again."

"What's happening? The shots?" Deft hands felt along his body for any evidence of a new wound. Nothing. "Ya sure ya ain't hit?"

He tried shooing her away as he closed the door and slipped deeper into their home. "I'm fine I told ya. Doyle's boys are about. Shot at some busters coming up the road. The rat bastards' comin' back to finish the job. Well, there'll be hell to pay now." His gray eye blazed.

"What are we to do?" For the first time since the strike began Katherine allowed full rein to the despair and fear that filled her soul. She buried her face in Paddy's strong chest, tears staining the already bloody fabric.

He rested his hands on Katherine's shoulders, at first holding her, then pushing her away. Not to be deterred, she encircled his waist, clinging to him until he at last engulfed her with his embrace. "It'll be okay.

I . . .." His body shook with a rage she'd not seen in him before. His arms tensed around her and against her back she felt his hands curl into fists.

Tears dried as suddenly as they'd formed.

"Paddy?" No answer.

Katherine pressed hands to his chest, to push away so she could look at him but now it was he who refused to disengage, instead pulling her tighter.

"Paddy?"

The only answer was a snarled curse.

What was he thinking? She feared he was considering something rash. Something bound to end badly for them—all of them. "What's going on in that lumpy head a yours?" Her voice rose, sharpened. Now was not the time to be nice. She had to talk sense to him. This time she pressed both hands to his chest and pushed with all her strength, insistent.

At first, he held on, crushing her against himself. But then his resistance disappeared. She grabbed at his arms, to drag his face to hers, but he spun away toward the door.

"No. Stop."

He ignored her. Reached for the latch.

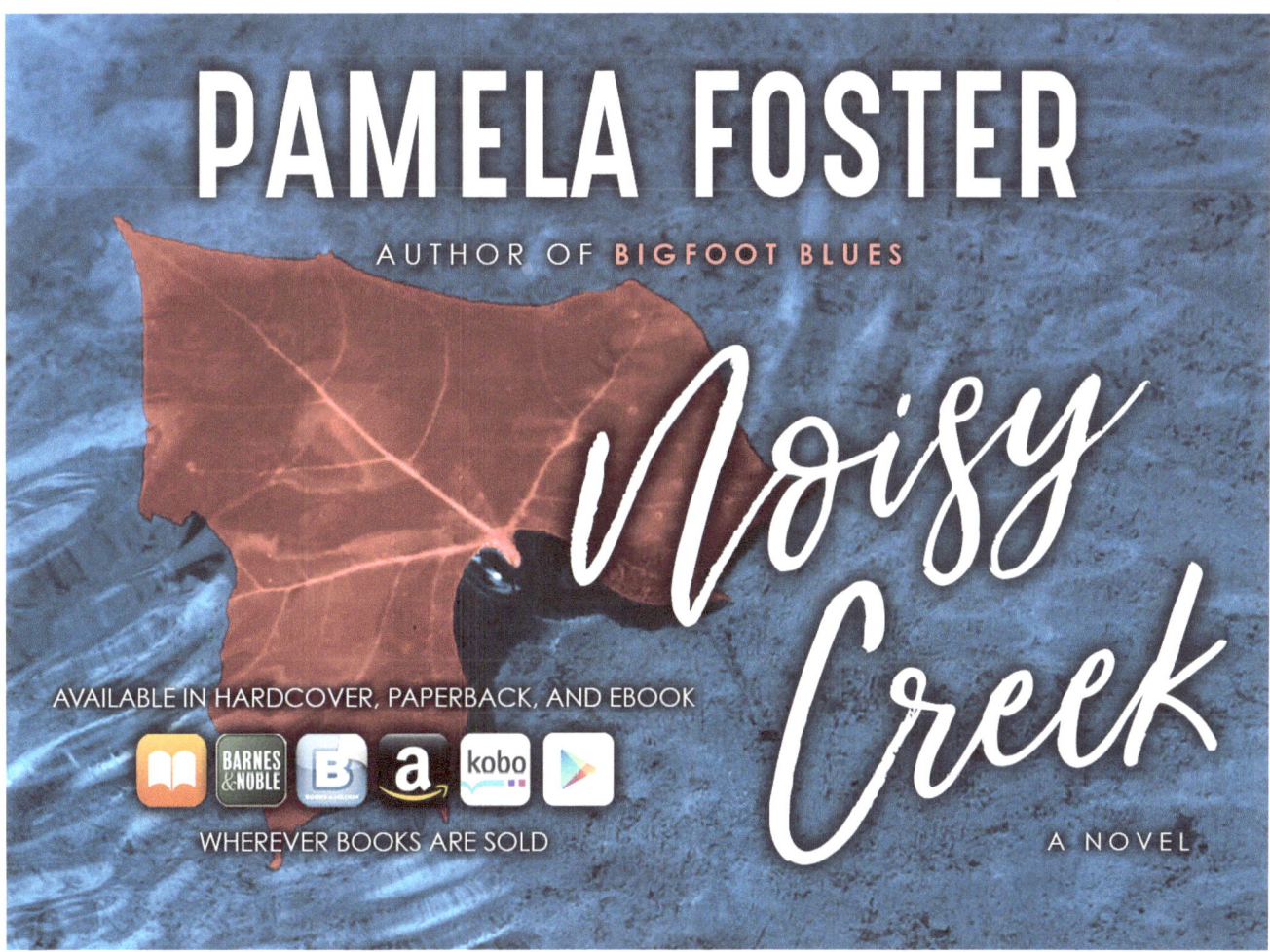

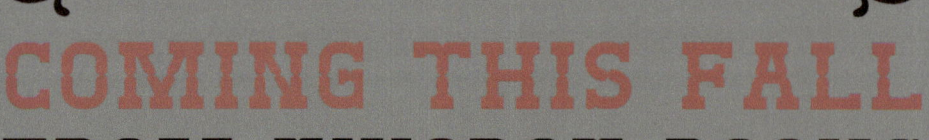

COMING THIS FALL
FROM TWODOT BOOKS

Tilghman: The Legendary Lawman and the Woman Who Inspired Him

By Chris Enss and Howard Kazanjian

October 2024
978-1-4930-4606-5
Paperback • 224 Pages • $26.95

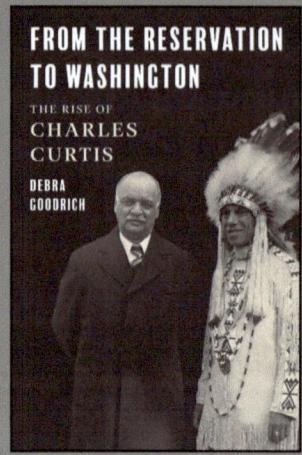

From the Reservation to Washington: The Rise of Charles Curtis

By Debra Goodrich

October 2024
978-1-4930-7535-5
Hardback • 296 Pages • $29.95

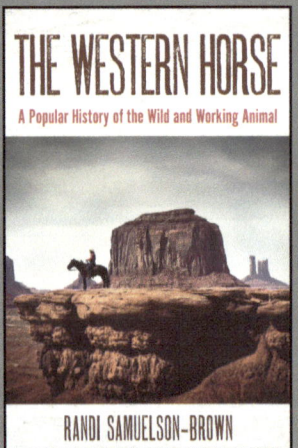

The Western Horse: A Popular History of the Wild and Working Animal

By Randi Samuelson-Brown

September 2024
978-1-4930-7384-9
Paperback • 208 Pages • $22.95

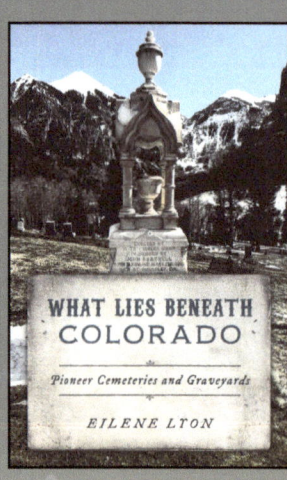

What Lies Beneath Colorado: Pioneer Cemeteries and Graveyards

By Eilene Lyon

September 2024
978-1-4930-7618-5
Paperback • 224 Pages • $22.95

AVAILABLE FOR PRE-ORDER NOW!

AVAILABLE NOW:

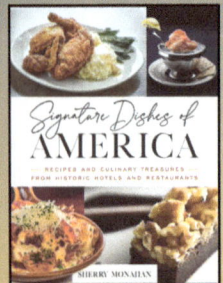

Signature Dishes of America

The Amusement Park at Sloan's Lake

Red Cloud and the Indian Trader

TWODOT®

Katherine scampered to get around him and block his path. "No, ya don't, Padraig Quinn. Not 'till we've talked." Fear snakes coiled and slithered in her gut. With her hip she bumped his hand off the latch. She wormed between him and the door. The metal handle bit sharply into her back but she pushed the pain aside. Her finger stabbed into his bruised chest. Panic overrode any regret his wince elicited.

"Out a my way."

"No. Not 'til ya tell me what ya're gonna do."

"Just never ya mind. Better ya don't know." His gruff yell took her by surprise.

"Padraig Aidan Quinn! I'll not be dismissed so easily." Katherine took a deep breath. "I'm your wife, not some cur to kick aside." She paused. "I want to know what's going on in there." With some stretching on her toes she managed to thump his head above the ear.

His good eye flashed, then a sheepish expression crossed his face. He hesitated, as if to say something. He remained silent for a long moment. When he spoke, his voice was gentler. "I'm gonna get me one a Doyle's Marlins and join the group going to fight the damned strikebreakers. Time we settled this."

"And what a your boys? If ya don't come back, what then? Just last night ya promised you'd not leave them fatherless nor me in widow's black. Are ya suddenly anxious to break your word now?"

Paddy said nothing for several seconds. Katherine raised her eyebrows, begging for an answer, yet afraid of what it would be—as if she didn't know.

At last, he pasted a forced grin onto his bruised face and shrugged. "I'll be back. There'll be a hundred of us with guns. Many more with clubs and picks to back us up. The owners'll have to listen to us."

"Because ya're threatenin' 'em with guns? Ya think they'll be havin' any a that? An' which a ya has ever fired a gun before? You?"

That he avoided looking at her answered her questions. Of course, she'd already known the answers. "Exactly what I thought. Don't ya think they've prepared for such as you've got planned? Ah. Ya're fools for goin' against the owners like that."

"It's them came against us. Those busters this mornin' were coming to finish the job they done on me. Hadn't been for Doyle's men they'd a caught me coming out a the cro. What then?"

"That damned pig-headedness a yours. Ya could go back to work. The owners took O'Connor and Fyrth back."

"Not for the wages we're askin'."

"But they're workin'. Their families have food on their tables. These owners can afford to hold out. We can't. We don't have enough saved to get us through the winter. Doyle made it clear last night the union has nothing to help." Katherine's voice turned bitter. "But they found the money to buy them guns. Your family can no eat guns nor the lead in 'em." She desperately wanted to add and will have nothing to eat if you break your promise, but refrained.

"Enough." His shout startled Katherine. She froze. With a gentleness contrary to the tone he'd just taken with her, Paddy nudged her aside, opened the door, and slipped outside.

Katherine followed him into the street. "Don't ya forget your promise. I'm holdin' ya to it." His step faltered but he kept walking. She started to call after him again when she heard the creak of the ladder from inside.

⁘

With the boys off to school, Katherine set about the morning's tasks. She'd planned a foraging trip into the forest, but dared not wander far while Paddy was out with Doyle and his lads.

Instead, she joined some of the other wives at the stream to do laundry. The constant chattering of gossip and stories normally helped the women pass the tedium of the work. Not today. The dull thud of rocks on fabric mirrored the somber mood. Hollow, worried expressions stared back at her. Blood stained the water—her husband hadn't been the only man injured in yesterday's confrontation.

Later, as she hung the clothes to dry on a line strung across the only room of their hovel, a single tear moistened her eye. No word yet from the strikers. She swallowed against her dread. Doyle's guns could only bring trouble. Damn the mine owners' greed. Damn Doyle for getting the boys' father mixed up in this. Damn Paddy for being a fool-headed lout.

Shortly before noon, booms of shotgun blasts erupted from the direction of Fryer Hill. Rifle cracks followed. Katherine raced outside. Shantytown's women milled on the street, staring toward the mines. Worry etched every face. Fifteen minutes passed—the gunfire slowed. Another fifteen and it stopped except for an occasional burst. What had just happened?

A chill wind rose from the northwest. The women retreated inside their homes. The Quinn's shanty grew crisp enough to be uncomfortable despite the small fire in the stove—or was it her dread?

Clothes came off the line. Still no word.

The gnawing in Katherine's stomach intensified. Hours had passed. They should have heard something by now. Perhaps the owners decided to sit down with the union and talk.

She forced herself to stay busy, but every household task required twice the time and energy. She hauled water. Ironed and folded clothing. Washed already clean dishes. Katherine gave up work for pacing. Another hour passed. She practically wore out her rosary but felt as though the Blessed Virgin was ignoring her. Occasionally she poked her head into the empty street. No news came. She contemplated going to the mines. But what would that accomplish?

School let out and children, including her own two, scrambled to their homes. Still no word. At least getting the boys busy with homework kept her mind off whatever was happening. There'd been no more gunfire for hours, but what that meant she had no idea.

"Oh, Paddy. What have ya gone and done?"

Sean looked up from working his sums. "What do you mean, Momma? Where's Papa?"

Katherine clapped a hand over her mouth. Had she said that out loud? She didn't know how to answer Sean because she didn't know herself. When they'd arrived home, she'd told them their father was attending to union business. Not a lie—exactly.

"Nothing. I . . . .." She shouldn't have said anything, but it was too late for that. "Get back to work

on your sums." Katherine touched the rosary in her pocket, but the prayers wouldn't come. She gave up. A hundred times she stared at the door, willing it to open and her Paddy to be standing there. A hundred times—nothing happened.

Darkness fell. She'd refused to allow the boys outside to run with their friends. Instead, they played draughts at the table by the glow of the lamp. Watching them kept her distracted—some. She held supper, hoping they could eat as a family.

A knock at the door broke the silence. "Who is it?"

"'Lizabeth." The voice was tired, flat—trembling. Elizabeth Shannon lived in the hovel next door. She and her husband, Oisin, had arrived in Leadville from Ireland six months prior. Newlyweds. No children yet, although Katherine suspected the neighbor might be pregnant, though nothing had been said. She opened the door.

Katherine stared at the woman slumped against the doorframe. Red, puffy eyes, tear-stained cheeks, and a grimace started the fear-snakes writhing again. The question formed, but dread made her hesitate. The need to know forced it out. "News?"

The single word hung for a long minute, pressing its weight on her shoulders. So heavy. The neighbor nodded, tears bursting from some well, flooding her cheeks. Katherine drew the gaunt woman into a firm but gentle hug. Elizabeth clutched at her as if desperate for human contact. Huge sobs wracked her body. Katherine began to weep with her. Whatever had happened, it had to be bad. Very bad.

"Boys, jump down. Let's get Mrs. Shannon into a chair."

Finn looked down at the neighbor. "What's wrong with her?"

"Hush. Just do as Momma says." Bless Sean for stepping in. Acting so much older than his years.

Several minutes passed and Katherine sat next to her, letting the woman cry onto her shoulder. She was anxious to know what had happened but wasn't sure she wanted her sons to hear it, especially not from someone other than herself.

"Boys, why don't you go get ready for bed."

"But where's Papa?"

"He'll be along soon enough." Katherine hoped she was right, but the woman sobbing on her breast gave her little confidence. Damn it, *where* was Paddy?

When the boys left for the cro, she pressed Elizabeth. "What's happened?"

A SHORT STORY

JAILBREAK

J. B. HOGAN

The younger woman struggled to control her anguish. After several deep breaths she sputtered an incoherent sentence. She gulped another breath. "My Oisin… was killed. Doyle just brought the news." Sobs returned.

Katherine hugged the woman harder. It wasn't lost on her that the union boss hadn't stopped by her home.

Did that mean Paddy was okay?

She allowed hope to rise.

If Paddy had been killed, Doyle would have come here next after the Shannon's. Relief flooded her soul. He'd kept his promise and would walk through the door any second.

Katherine exhaled a deep sigh, then pulled the widow closer, ashamed for her own joy in the midst of Elizabeth's tragedy, yet unable to stop it.

The door burst open and Katherine started, then sighed—just the boys.

"Off to bed with you both now." They scrambled up the ladder to the loft. All would be well in their world.

Elizabeth finally released her hold on Katherine. Sitting up, the neighbor woman scrubbed at her eyes and wiped moisture from her cheeks. "I'm so sorry. I've burdened you with my trouble. I didn't know who else to turn to."

"It's fine, dear."

"Have you word of Padraig?"

Katherine couldn't bring herself to tell her friend that Paddy was fine, so she settled for shaking her head. It wasn't a lie—there had been no news, yet, but she knew in her heart.

Elizabeth choked back a sob and swiped at a tear. "That lunkhead of yours will probably walk in himself soon enough."

Katherine took her friend's hand and patted the back of it, then drew her into another hug. Just then a knock rattled the door.

It took a second to disentangle herself from Elizabeth, but she managed and stepped to the door. She flung it open.

Doyle stood on the other side.

Katherine blinked.

Doyle?

He just stood, not speaking. She took in his torn and disheveled clothes. His grave frown. His downcast eyes.

A widow's wail broke the silence. ♘

THE AUTHOR

D.N. Sample *comes by his love of storytelling naturally. From his paternal grandfather, a Wesleyan Methodist preacher who sprinkled his sermons with stories only–cough, cough–mildly exaggerated, to his maternal grandfather–a crack shot who could shoot a dancing tick off the back of a racing deer at a hundred yards–exchanging fish stories with friends over a game of draughts, to Sunday dinners where the whole family gathered to enjoy Mom's cooking and exchange humorous family anecdotes, he was raised to spin yarns and tell tall tales.*

Born in western New York, he moved his wife and young son to the Saint Louis area via Conestoga wagon–or a Dodge Shadow–in '93, where they still reside.

Like many of the Old West's characters, Sample's trails in life have been many. He shepherded a flock as pastor of a church, rode night herd over 250 rambunctious young men as a college resident hall director, corralled young soccer stars as both referee and coach, wrangled with the IRS as an Enrolled Agent, and rustled grub in his fifth wheel on the road with his sweetheart and a pair grub-hogging pups of questionable heritage.

THE WRITER'S DESK
CRAIG JOHNSON
BRINGING WALT LONGMIRE
TO LIFE ON THE PAGE AND THE SCREEN

In Wyoming's expansive, often unforgiving landscapes, New York Times *bestselling author Craig Johnson has found the perfect backdrop for his unique brand of crime fiction.*

STORY BY
GEORGE "CLAY" MITCHELL
PHOTOS COURTESY OF CRAIG JOHNSON

With a penchant for the noir genre, Craig Johnson sought to break free from its conventional constraints by situating his stories in the least populated county of the least populated state—setting the stage for his celebrated protagonist, Walt Longmire. This choice not only refreshes the genre but also challenges the limits of its narrative possibilities.

Through the lens of Longmire's experiences, from his days as a young man to his reflective moments in Vietnam, Johnson explores the enduring questions of character and justice. As Johnson crafts tales that straddle the line between mystery and the deeply personal journeys of his characters, he invites readers and authors to step beyond their literary comfort zones, championing the idea that good storytelling transcends genre boundaries.

THE LONGEVITY OF WALT LONGMIRE

Johnson wanted to take on the crime fiction noir as a writer. He wanted to get away from the tradi-tional points of the genre. So, he decided to have it occur in Absaroka County, Wyoming.

"That sort of setting gives you a very different character and environment, and the difficulty it would entail. How many can you kill before it becomes ridiculous?" Johnson chuckled. "By the second book in this series, I figured out that if the protagonist is good enough, I could branch Walt out to other Wyoming counties or states.

"I could also go back in time and tell stories of Walt's life before we meet him in the first book. Rediscovering and researching the Vietnam War was just fun for me. It allowed me to explore how he became who he is and not impact the stories I already told."

Johnson covered Walt's and Henry's journey from college to Vietnam. He said the characters had very different ideas when they were 22. That Walt was "a different breed of cat. Exploring their lives at that time is just as compelling to me as I'm doing right now."

BOOKS SHOULD BE 'TRIGGER MECHANISMS' FOR THE IMAGINATION.

CRAIG JOHNSON

It's All About Character. Australian actor Robert Taylor as Walt Longmire on the hit television series *Longmire.*

Johnson said he doesn't put himself in a specific box when he writes but aims for the reader who wants more. He also added that there's a danger in getting stuck in a rut if you only read one kind of book (genre) and that the reader or the writer should challenge themselves with different ones. "When you read other genres, it will be a constant training ground for you."

"I'm kind of a crow, flying around all over the place, picking up shiny things and bringing them back to the nest that's my book. I firmly believe that genre is only a sales term the publishers use to pigeonhole books into marketable packages. There are only two genres: good books and bad books. The trick is reading the good ones and avoiding the bad. I like writing the books in layers, attempting to reach readers in every way possible."

WHO IS WALT LONGMIRE?

Characters are often an extension of the author, but Johnson said that he and Walt are nothing alike except for their sense of humor. Johnson added that humor is difficult to write but manages to get it across with Henry's dryness, honesty, and Vic's sarcasm. However, writers should take caution because even if you find something funny, someone else may not.

"I'm not Walt, but I travel along with him. I don't always agree with him, but he's honest and has a lot of things that I like about him. I'm fortunate that I don't have the kind of drama in his life... his tragedies. He's got advantages, and I know how to cripple him. His strengths are tied to his weaknesses, and that's a direct reflection of their strength. You must consider those things when you put [your characters] together.

You like them for their virtues, and you love them for their faults. It's all interconnected.

CHALLENGE YOUR READING

Johnson grew up reading the action adventures of Louis L'Amour, Robert Louis Stevenson, and what he calls "young boys' literature." He also explored worlds created by Zane Grey and the prose of John Steinbeck.

"I enjoyed reading those... *Canary Row, East of Eden, Tortilla Flats, 'Grapes of Wrath.* Those tackled social issues and seemed to be more aware of what's going on than just storytelling," said Johnson. "It's the kind of literary fiction that is lost, and those were beautifully done."

He talked about meeting one of his literary heroes, John Hillerman. "I asked him many questions about writing, and he said, 'Don't forget to tell a good story. I sat enough around campfires telling stories, and you must have a beginning, a middle, and an end.' I took that to heart."

Johnson added that books should be "trigger

Character Actors. Longmire's longevity stems in part from the show's cast. This includes Katee Sackhoff as sharp-tongued Deputy Victoria "Vic" Moretti, and Lou Diamond Philips as Walt's best friend and partner in crime, Henry Standing Bear.

mechanisms" for the imagination. He said this was one of the advantages books had over Hollywood, which often compromises the story to make it work for television or film. "With books, you don't have to worry about budgets, locations, and stars. Hollywood can't compete with that."

CREATING CHARACTERS

When writing a long-term series like the *Longmire* novels, Johnson doesn't see any way that there aren't new characters in each book. Each character has to be as interesting and compelling as the main character. "It's not like I'm re-inventing the wheel, but each [book] has to be different from those previous," Johnson said. "For me, the support characters must be just as interesting and compelling and capture your imagination. They inevitably turn back up, which is one of the joys of writing a larger tapestry than a single book. Having readers suddenly realize that they were introduced to a character a couple of novels ago is a blast."

Johnson said you mustn't reinvent the wheel to maintain characters beyond one book. Find a way to challenge the characters and the readers. He said to seek out interesting plotlines that will pull at the character's resources. Also, look at where your characters are at in their lives and what they are involved with. "That will help create conflict and pull them from their comfort zone."

This even extends more to the antagonists that Johnson pits against *Longmire.*

"The Northern Cheyenne have a saying, 'You judge a man's strength by his enemies.' I think the challenge is finding antagonists strong enough to go up against Walt, but also believable and relatable enough for readers to find them as compelling as *Longmire*," said Johnson. "I love it when readers write to me and say that they may not have liked a character, but they understand why it is that they did what they did. I think the antagonist has to be properly motivated, and as my ol' buddy Tony Hillerman used to say, 'You have to sit in all the chairs.'"

THERE ARE ONLY TWO GENRES: GOOD BOOKS AND BAD BOOKS. THE TRICK IS READING THE GOOD ONES AND AVOIDING THE BAD.

CRAIG JOHNSON

Making It Real. Johnson kicks his feet up behind Sheriff Walt Longmire's desk on the set of the hit television series *Longmire.*

DESIGNING THE PLOT

Johnson outlines his books. He breaks everything down by characters, chapters, and scenes before he begins writing.

"My ideas tend to get harebrained and psychological. Even while I'm working on the outline, something will happen, and I'll go in a different direction," said Johnson. "That's really your subconscious mind. The conscious mind does all the prep and the outline, and the subconscious is the backseat driver. When you start writing, the subconscious starts throwing something over the seat. Some writers don't want to let go of that outline and hold on to it like a life preserver. We should get more relaxed with our writing and have an improvisational moment that lures us onto thin ice. It can lead to powerful writing, and we must be open to that."

He also said that writers should play fair when designing a mystery. It helps to be well-versed in the genre to "see what's been done before."

"I don't write period pieces, and I really can't ignore what's going on in the country," Johnson added. "If I'm going to be honest and contend with those issues, I need to make sure that I understand the message I'm trying to get out."

Johnson seems content to keep Walt in Wyoming, the Big Horn Mountains, or other wilderness areas. So, we won't find Walt trying to solve a murder mystery in New York, L.A. or deal with international terrorists. Johnson laughed at the prospect of Walt being stuck on a cruise ship. "He'll never set foot on one." But "never say never."

"A strange thing happened to me a while back. I got a VIP treatment on an aircraft carrier. There were some actors, other writers, politicians, and I thought, 'My god, it's like an Agatha Christie novel.' In one of my books, Walt knows someone who was one of the Doolittle pilots, so it's there to happen. I even asked the NCIS liaison what would happen

Writing What You Know. If Absaroka County is as much a character in Craig Johnson's novels as Walt, Vic, and Henry, it's because he writes from experience. Here Johnson stands beside the city limits sign of Ucross, Wyoming, where he lives and works in the shadow of the Big Horn Mountains.

if there was a murder on the carrier and a VIP was killed. He set up a scenario that I could use Walt to solve the murder. It would be different. He was a marine investigator, so he had some experience on a Navy ship. The question would be how much difficulty would it be for him. Who knows?" Johnson laughs at the idea.

WORKING WITH A PUBLISHER

Johnson said that his publisher was responsible for getting *Longmire* to the screen, and he's happy that his character and, by extension, his books found a new audience. Even though the series last aired in November 2017, Johnson said he continues to meet people who have just discovered it.

"They don't put pressure on me. I can do whatever I want. They would ask me for a synopsis when I started writing the next one. The only directive I

get from them is that it must be a mystery and have Walt Longmire," he added. "They have faith in me to provide them with a product they can sell. For me, it's about writing a good book for them. It never hurts to have a bestseller. I feel like I've done good work for them for 20 years, and they give me the freedom to go in any direction. Penguin has been pretty wonderful. The fans still enjoy it and still read the book. It was a wonderful thing to happen, and everything fell into place early on. I think it was the attraction of Walt himself... he's intelligent, funny, and fun to be with. I have no complaints, and he's good company."

'BLUE COLLAR WRITER'

Johnson has written 25 novels and ebooks and has released at least one a year since 2009. He doesn't plan on slowing down anytime soon. He'll

*Getting to Know Your Character.*Johnson shoots the breeze with Robert Taylor during a break in filming on the set of *Longmire*. As an executive consultant and sometimes writer on the show, Johnson helped his characters make the often-difficult transition from book to screen.

write for four hours a day. He'll spend up to a year getting a new Walt Longmire story ready, and by the time he sits down to write, Johnson is "chomping at the bit." He also enjoys the research aspects of preparing for a novel and will try to find ways to weave in some of the history he's learned into his stories. "I'm a blue-collar writer. I write all day, evenings, and weekends to finish it."

"It's a challenge to set something in reality. It's important to give honesty to the geography and the people to provide the reader with an honest portrayal of the book. That's what they'll respond to," Johnson said. "Even when I'm writing, the research continues, but I will look it up when I'm not writing. I tell students to disconnect from the internet, or you can spend all day looking up different aspects of the Navajo."

"The best way I start writing is by reading what I wrote the day before. I will sometimes have to fix it if I find something wrong. Otherwise, it's going to haunt me or stop me from writing. I know it's not perfect, but the best way is to find what works for you and get your creative juices flowing. Everyone approaches it differently. I enjoy the process of writing. Write on that empty page and see where it will go. I would be in rough shape if I didn't have Walt. It's a joy I have to be able to write, and you should allow yourself to get carried away. You should be having fun when you're writing. Every opportunity to write is a godsend."

Johnson's latest Longmire book, *First Frost*, is on sale now.

George "Clay" Mitchell *is an award-winning reporter and photographer, a founding partner of* Saddlebag Dispatches, *and Executive Vice President and Publisher of its partner company, Roan & Weatherford Publishing Associates*

THE VICTORIANS

*Western Historical Romance
at it's Finest.*

Tyra's Gambler

Rowena's Hellion

Wilda's Outlaw

Find Them All Today on Amazon

VELDA
BROTHERTON

WILLA Award Winning Author of The Montana Series

GARY RODGERS

OLD GOLD IN COLORADO

A SHORT STORY

old air rushed through the open door as I stepped inside the eating house. Tables lined the walls on both sides and angry faces turned to express their displeasure with me holding the door open. I smiled at the typical reaction. Ugly looks from people who tend to keep quiet when they see me, mainly because of the tied down Colts on each hip. But the long, shaggy hair, and unshaven face seemed to add to my unpleasant appearance.

"Don't be a jackass, stranger. Close the door. Our food is getting cold. Charlie keeps a table open in the back for your kind. If someone else is sitting there, you and them can work it out," a female voice came from a table on the left side.

Something about the voice sounded familiar. I closed the door and made my way with slow steps to the table where the lady sat. When I saw her, I recognized the familiar voice and smiled.

"The Maggie Tobin I knew in Hannibal, Missouri, wouldn't talk to me that way. Unless she had a pocket full of rocks, that is."

"The only folks who would know me that well would be one of those knot-headed Rawlins boys. And I didn't expect any of them to live long enough to grow hair on their face. Which one are you?"

"I'm Jake, Miss Tobin. Them was my younger brothers you and your brothers used to wrestle and throw rocks at. I was done grown and gone to work when you came along. But I remember you from trips I made back home to see Ma."

"It's *Mrs.* Brown now, Jake. But I'd rather you call me Maggie. Would you like to join us? My husband will be here shortly."

"No thank you, Maggie. You were right about a table for my kind in the back. No offense taken," I added, when I noticed her cheeks redden. "Folks ain't as accustomed to seeing men like me as they used to be."

"I understand, Jake. But please come by Daniels and Smith dry goods before you leave town. I work there and would like to hear more about your brothers. If you have time."

I tipped my hat, like a gentleman should, my senses alerting me to the well-dressed man and his friends at the front table. They were paying too much attention to me. I'd seen their type many times and knew what to expect. So I made my way to the table in back and took a seat where I could see the entire room and the door. A pistol rested on my lap as I ordered food and coffee.

A week without coffee and a hot meal left me short on patience. The front door opened, and I noticed Maggie wave at the man entering. His smile told me he must be her husband. Then a big man at the front table rose and followed him till Maggie's husband took a seat, then continued toward my table.

I didn't appreciate his attempt to use her husband for cover. I moved the pistol from my lap to the table, keeping one hand on it as I sipped my coffee with the other. The big man hesitated, then came on.

Without looking up at the man's face, I growled, "Not interested."

"Mister, the boss sent me over here to…"

"If your boss has something to ask me, or talk to me about, he can come over here himself. But if

Charlie brings me the steak I ordered, I won't be in a talking mood. Now, it took you twelve steps to walk over here. I suggest you make it back in eight." I turned my eyes up from my coffee to meet his gaze. Something in my eyes set his feet in motion and he made it back to his boss in seven steps.

Charlie came from the back with my steak, and Maggie stopped him. She took the platter and made her way to my table. Without getting between the men in front and me, she cut the steak into bite-size pieces.

When she finished, she whispered, "Take care of how you deal with this man and his gunmen. Rumor has it they've been stealing claims. But nobody has come forward to prove it."

"Thanks, Maggie. I'll come by the store after I eat. But you and your husband might want to leave. I intend to remain peaceful if they let me. If not, I don't want innocent folks getting hurt."

She nodded, and I watched as she and almost everyone else in the café made their way out into the cold air of early spring. With one hand on the pistol, I devoured the steak and potatoes with my other, never taking my eyes off the men staring me down from the front table. It was the best steak I'd had in months. I meant to let Charlie know it, but he seemed to have left with all his customers.

The boss in the suit rose from his table and started my way, smiling, then turned into the back room where Charlie had disappeared. I waited, wondering how long he told his men to wait before approaching me. When the boss came out of the back with the coffeepot, I have to admit, I was surprised.

Our eyes met as he poured my cup full and filled one for himself before sitting the pot down and taking a seat. My eyes shifted back to his gunmen at the other table.

"Don't worry about them. I can tell them to leave if it will put you at ease. But they'd just stand outside shivering, waiting for me to tell them what to do next." He laughed.

Up close, the man I earlier believed to be a few years older than me showed signs of someone twice my age. Gray hair hid under the derby hat he wore. The wrinkles around his eyes and the hair growing out of his ears and nostrils, told me this man was well into his sixties.

"They can stay. I don't expect us to be talking for long."

"Men like you don't come to Leadville unless

someone pays them to, or they're looking for work. And by work, I *don't* mean working in the mines."

"I'm not doing either. I'm on my way to Oregon. All the passes are closed, so I came to Leadville to hold up till they thaw." Part of my statement was true.

"Well, you have about two, maybe three weeks' time before then. We got some late snow this year. Perhaps I could interest you in making some money while you're here."

The old man didn't waste any time making small talk. But I needed to let on like I wasn't interested.

"Mister, I don't even know your name. I'm Jake Rawlins. If you've heard of me, then you know I don't work cheap. I've been through the pass long before most people would try it. So, I won't be in town long."

"The name's Morgan Hayes," he offered his hand, and I took it.

"And I knew who you were when you walked in, Mr. Rawlins. I have businesses in Denver and Kansas City, as well as smaller mining towns all over the west. I have an office across the street from the assayer's office. You give it some thought, then come see me. I can pay whatever price you ask if you find the man I need located."

My unwillingness to react to his offer didn't appear to have any effect on Morgan Hayes. When he stood up, saying nothing else, I knew he had experience in dealing with hard men. The kind who took care of the unsavory work Hayes preferred to keep his hands clean of.

He and his men left, following a brief conversation. After another cup of coffee, I put six-bits on the table, checked my pistols, and made my way out into the cold. The sun, having broken through the clouds, added warmth to the air. Smoke drifted from chimneys, stinging my eyes, but smelled better than the harsh aroma of lead from the mines.

I knew Hayes would have a man watching me. A walk down to Molly May's on Fifth Avenue wouldn't seem out of place for a drifter like me. If I appeared eager to take Hayes' offer, he might get leery of me.

As I ambled down the boardwalk, I noticed one of Hayes' men watching me from the other side of the street. Having his men follow me wouldn't do. The assayer's office was in the opposite direction of Molly's, but I needed to let Hayes know I worked alone. And I wouldn't stand for him having his men follow me around town, or anywhere. I turned and headed for Hayes' office.

———— •··• ————

Back at Molly's, I met Angela in her room. We met two weeks earlier in Denver, where she convinced me to help find her grandfather. The man Hayes wanted me to find sounded like he might be her grandfather. Not all my jobs required there being a bounty on someone.

"I remember Papa saying he found the white half-moon, and the gold wouldn't be far from it," Angela said as she pulled her dark brown hair up in a bun. "But the only other landmarks he mentioned all pointed him to Leadville. He never mentioned having to get a grubstake from Mr. Hayes."

"You told me your grandfather was looking for gold he believed Conquistadors buried in the mountains," I said. "Did you ever see the map he was using?"

"No. It was on rolled leather he kept hidden. I can't remember him leaving it lying around for anyone to see. But I read some of the writing on part of it because Papa couldn't read well. The language differed from what he knew, but I'd learned from nuns at the mission school, and I could make out parts of it."

Old leather maps with strange markings and writings would be little to go on if a man was treasure hunting. An old man, alone, in the mountains of Colorado all winter would have to be hickory tough to survive. I couldn't destroy Angela's hopes of him still being alive. In our time together over the last two weeks, I'd grown fond of her. I didn't know if she felt the same way.

From what I'd learned when Hayes made his offer, the old man survived Hayes' men looking for him. My mistake was thinking the old man got involved with Hayes while looking for someone to help him find the lost gold. But Hayes and his men were nothing but thieves. I might be hasty in thinking my days of being a bounty hunter were behind me.

"Angela, I need to go see Maggie. The lady I told you about from the café. Is there anything else you can remember from your grandfather's map or whatever it was?"

"The only other thing I remember was something about where the crows gather. It made little sense to me or my grandfather. Can I go with you? I worry Molly will tire of me using a room here."

"Molly owes me a favor from her days in Deadwood. She said you can stay as long as we need. With Hayes' men watching me, we don't want them finding out who you are. They could use it against us."

I could see the worry in her beautiful brown eyes. "I'll find someplace else if being here bothers you. The gentlemen Molly entertains haven't been bothering you, have they?"

"Oh, no. Molly doesn't tolerate any of them even talking to me. She has teased me about my looks being worth a small fortune, but she only does it to keep my mind off Papa."

———— •··• ————

Outside of Molly's, I noticed one of Hayes' gunmen watching me from across the street. If he wanted to follow me to the dry goods store where Maggie worked, he would find more trouble than he wanted there.

Customers occupied Maggie and the man behind the counter when I entered the store. I made my way back and started looking at blankets and home items. They were close to the dresses hanging along the wall. Angela could use a new dress. She'd left most of her things in Denver, where we met. The only thing I'd left were the two men following her around. They might live, but they wouldn't be on anyone's trail for a long time.

"Jake, I'm glad you came by," Maggie said. "I mentioned the man you were looking for to Mr. Daniels after we talked yesterday, and he thinks he knows the man. He didn't tell me his name, but Mr. Daniels wants to help you. He agrees with me. You need to be careful dealing with Morgan Hayes."

A blue dress with white flowers caught my eye, and I held it up to Maggie to compare the size. "I'm known as a dangerous man myself, Maggie. But if you could take this dress to Molly's and leave it for a girl named Angela, I'd appreciate it. After we talk to Mr. Daniels." I smiled.

"I need to meet this Angela if you're buying her a dress," Maggie teased. "I've made curtains and sewn some dresses for Molly's girls, and I don't remember any Angela."

"I'll write you a note to take with the dress. She can tell you what she wants you to know."

"You're just as knot headed as your brothers. Come on, I'll introduce you to Mr. Daniels."

An older man with graying hair at his temples didn't fit what I expected from the store owner. I expected a younger man. Mr. Daniels was at least sixty, maybe older. When he smiled with less than

THE THRILLING NEW WESTERN SERIES FROM
THE AUTHOR OF LUNGER: THE DOC HOLLIDAY STORY

PAUL COLT

WINNER OF THE WILL ROGERS MEDALLION AWARD

WANTED: SAM BASS

THE GREAT WESTERN DETECTIVE LEAGUE

AVAILABLE AT ALL YOUR FAVORITE BOOKSELLERS

half his teeth remaining, I knew he would be a man with experience and knowledge.

I looked around to see if my shadow might have slipped in before speaking. "Mr. Daniels, I'm Jake Rawlins, and I'm looking for a man by the name, Francisco Gallardo. They might call him Frank."

"Call me Thomas. Does the man you're looking for have a scar running from his right ear to his nose?"

Angela had told me about the scar. "Yes, he does. Got it in a knife fight in Juarez when he was young. You wouldn't know where he is, would you?" It couldn't be this easy.

"I haven't seen him since late fall. He talked to an old trapper at the Silver Dollar one night, then said he was going to see his granddaughter in Denver. Worked all summer for me at the Monarch Mine. He's a hard worker for a man his age."

"Do you know what they talked about?"

"Frank was telling us he heard about there being gold where the crows gathered, but it didn't make any sense to him or us. This trapper heard him talking and laughed, said he must have his places confused, just like all of them other folks years ago."

I waited for Thomas to continue, but he seemed to relive the event in his mind. "Did he explain the confusion, or offer any direction to Frank?"

"It took a few whiskeys to get him to talk, but then he said..."

I held up my hand to stop Thomas, then slipped over to the door to find Hayes' man with his ear to the wall. Before he could react, I pulled the Arkansas toothpick from my belt and sliced off a sizeable chunk of his ear. Well, his whole left ear. His screams brought Maggie and Thomas running outside.

"I hope it ain't far to a doctor. Seems this fellow needs one before he bleeds to death. Doc won't be sewing your ear back on, though. I'm taking this to Hayes. He needs to keep his men out of my business."

Maggie had a roll of cloth from the store pressed to the gunman's head. "Was that really necessary, Jake? I'll get him to Doc Baker down the street. You and Thomas finish up your business." A wink as she herded the man away told me Maggie was acting a sight angrier than she was.

"That won't make Hayes happy," Thomas said. "But I have to admit, it's good to see someone who still

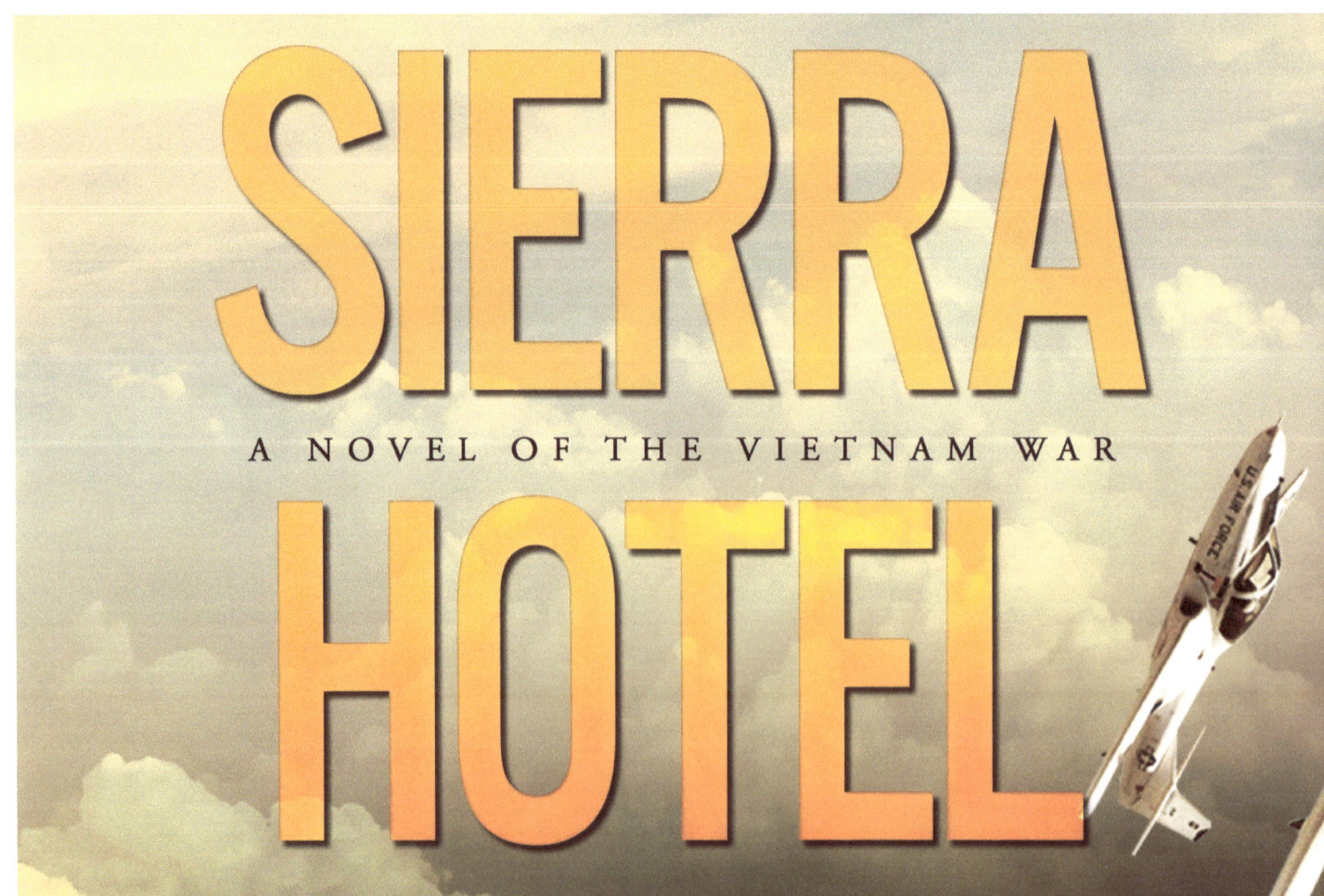

understands the old ways. Takes too long for the law to show up and deal with troublemakers these days."

I nodded. "I can't wait for the law to get anything done. Now, about what that trapper had to say..."

"That trapper said the real meaning of the saying came from old Spanish. It should be interpreted as 'where the chiefs have gathered.' Back before white men came into the area, the chiefs of all the plains and mountain tribes would gather every spring and fall in the eastern foothills. Somewhere near the headwaters of Ute Creek. But nobody's found any gold to speak of there. The only gold I've heard of is down by Colorado Springs."

"Ute Creek? Isn't that north of Denver?"

"If it's the same place. But there's a Ute Creek east of here on the old trail from Colorado Springs to Denver. Folks stopped using it after landslides filled all the passes. I think they call it Black Springs now."

An old memory flashed through my mind. "Have Maggie take the dress I showed her to Molly's tomorrow, would you? I need to pack my horse and tell someone where I'm headed. Thank you, Thomas. This gives me a direction to go looking in." We shook hands. "Oh, and do you have a small box I can put this ear in? I'll need to make one more stop."

I hurried to Hayes' office, only to find he had gone to the Silver Dollar. It would be a perfect place for me to put him on his heels.

I found him seated with his other gunman, eating a steak. Placing the box Thomas gave me in front of him, I removed the lid so he could see the ear I'd cut off his man. "I told you I work alone, and I do things in my time. I'm headed into the mountains the day after tomorrow to find Gallardo, or his remains. If I find you or your men on my back-trail, I will send all of you back in pieces. Do you understand?"

"Where's Clayton?" the gunman asked.

"If he's alive, he's at Doc Baker's. This is the only warning I'm giving you, Hayes." I turned and walked out of the saloon.

It took longer to get to Molly's, stopping every block or two to make sure someone wasn't following me. Angela wouldn't be happy with me leaving her in Leadville, but I couldn't take her with me. I hadn't expected Maggie to be there when I made it back to Molly's. One woman arguing with my decision would

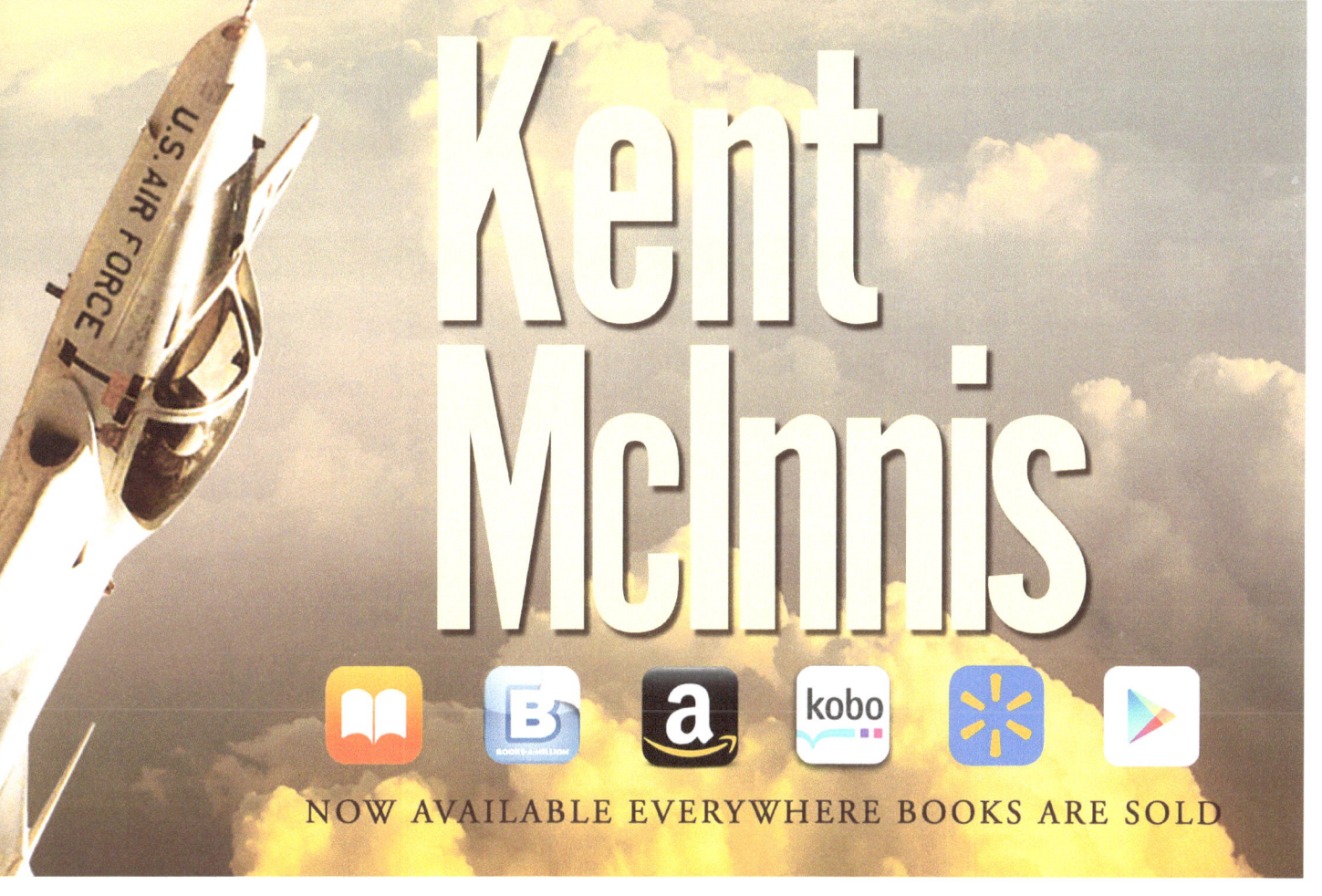

THREE TIME SPUR AWARD WINNING AUTHOR

DUSTY RICHARDS

with VELDA BROTHERTON

IN THE HEART OF **TEXAS**, LAW AND CHAOS
COLLIDE IN THE ULTIMATE **BATTLE** FOR **JUSTICE**.

TEXAS WILDLING

COMING TO YOUR FAVORITE BOOKSELLER WINTER 2024

have been enough, but *two* made me think seriously about catching the next train west and disappearing.

After a lot of explaining and arguing with Angela and Maggie, I said, "Angela, I want you to catch the train back to Denver in two days. If I find your grandfather, we should meet you there in a week or two. It all depends on the snow in the passes and what, if anything, we bring with us."

"I'm scared to get on the train by myself, Jake. If Hayes or his men know about me, it won't be safe."

"My husband and I can travel with you," Maggie interrupted. "I've wanted to go to Denver for some time now. I can get Mr. Daniels to write a letter of credit for me to buy sewing materials for the store."

After a short discussion, an agreement was reached. Angela would travel with Maggie and her husband, and I would meet Angela there in a week or two. The only person uncertain of the plan was me. If Francisco was where I planned to travel, it didn't mean he would welcome me, or that he'd be alive. I hoped to stay alive myself.

"It'll be night soon. I need to get my horses packed. Hayes will have someone try to follow me. I can lose them in the dark easier." I wrote a note with instructions for Angela and let Maggie read it. "This is where I will meet you in the next week if possible. If I'm not there in two weeks, go to the marshal in Denver and tell him what you know."

I turned to leave, and Angela threw her arms around my neck. Tears streamed down her cheeks as she kissed me on the lips. "Thank you for the dress, Jake. You find Papa, then both of you come back to me in Denver, or I'll never forgive you."

I smiled, took her in my arms and returned her kiss, then hurried out the door. Women beat anything I ever dealt with. I had too much to worry about for my feelings to be lassoed by a woman. But it might be too late to avoid that.

Three days later, I was looking at a large, crescent-shaped white quartz mysteriously lodged on the side of a mountain above Black Springs Canyon. I knew of its existence thanks to a trapper I met in Deadwood years earlier. He'd told me the Indians said the Si-Te-Cah placed it there to ward off evil spirits. When I asked him what a Si-Te-Cah was, he said they were red-headed giants that used to live in the area but had moved south into Utah or Nevada.

Red-headed giants sounded like evil to me.

The familiar report of a Sharps rifle reined my thoughts back in. It didn't sound too far away, but there weren't any trails leading toward the sound, only the granite-like walls of the canyon. I rode close to the wall and began looking for the opening the trapper had told me about. Beside a clump of cedars, I found it. Even though it was large enough for a man on horseback, I left mine tied off to the cedars and carefully weaved my way along the trail. It would be near impossible for a man to find this place without knowing about it or falling into it from above.

A hundred feet later, the trail opened into a valley a mile long and half as wide, with a stream flowing from a pond on one side. The stream disappeared into a cave on the east side where I could see a horse and two pack mules grazing on the new spring growth. A light tendril of smoke told me someone was in the cave.

"Hello, the fire," I shouted. Hoping it wouldn't draw a shot from the Sharps I heard earlier.

"Over here," came the reply from my right. "Nobody at the fire. If you're here to rob me, the least you can do is help me get this meat back to my fire, so I don't starve."

I made my way through the scrub brush and cedar, pistol drawn, in case this was a trap. When I spotted the old man, I figured it had to be Francisco.

"I'm not here to rob you, mister. If you're who I think you are, I'm here to take you to your granddaughter. My name is Jake Rawlins."

"Afraid I might never leave this place, stranger. Broke my leg a few weeks back and couldn't get on my horse to get out of here. Ran out of food a few days ago. This cougar was slipping up on my horses and I shot it. I've heard cats are good eating. I mean to find out."

"Let's get you back to your fire and check your leg out. I'll cook you up some fresh meat while we do. Even if you aren't Francisco Gallardo, I couldn't leave a man out here to starve."

"Did my Angie send you to find me?"

"Angie? I guess the girl I know as Angela is your Angie. I met her in Denver when a couple of men, hired by Morgan Hayes, followed her into the hotel where I was staying. They'll be in the Denver jail now, if they healed up enough to get out of the hospital."

"Hayes wants the gold I found. He'll send more men after me. I met him at the assayer's office in Denver when I took some of the gold to be appraised.

I told Angie about him before I left Denver, but one of his men followed me. He died in a rockslide not far from here."

Getting Francisco settled back in the cave, which was much larger than it first appeared, I brought my horse into the valley. With grub ready, I began packing the mules with more gold than I'd ever seen.

"We need to get to Denver before Hayes figures out I gave his men the slip. They're headed north of Denver, but they may make it back before we do. I can leave you at a rancher's house I know outside of Denver."

"Will you steal my gold when you leave me, Jake?"

I wanted to be offended, but considering how much gold he had found, I understood his concern.

"No, Francisco. But if she will have me, I might steal your granddaughter.," I smiled.

"Then we should get me on my horse. I don't want her alone in Denver if Hayes will be there. I risked my life to find this gold so Angie could have a better life. And because my ancestor was one of the conquistadors who hid the gold here."

"My brother is a deputy marshal in Denver, and I sent word for him to be watching for Angela. Besides, some other friends are traveling with her. Let's get you where you can get healed up. I'll deal with Morgan Hayes when I get to Denver, or I'll bury him in Leadville if he heads back there."

———————————

With Francisco settled in at the Rooney Ranch, I rode into Denver with one purpose. I wanted to know where I stood with Angela Gallardo. Even if she had feelings for me, would they change when she found out how rich she was about to be? Besides, a woman like her deserved better than a man known as a bounty hunter and tracker, even if my reputation included bringing them in alive. Could I settle in to being tied down in one place?

"A man can be an easy target riding around with his head in the clouds, brother."

Jess, my younger brother, interrupted my thoughts as I rode toward Angela's hotel. But he was right. I needed to get my mind back on the business at hand. As I swung down from the saddle, I heard Angela's voice.

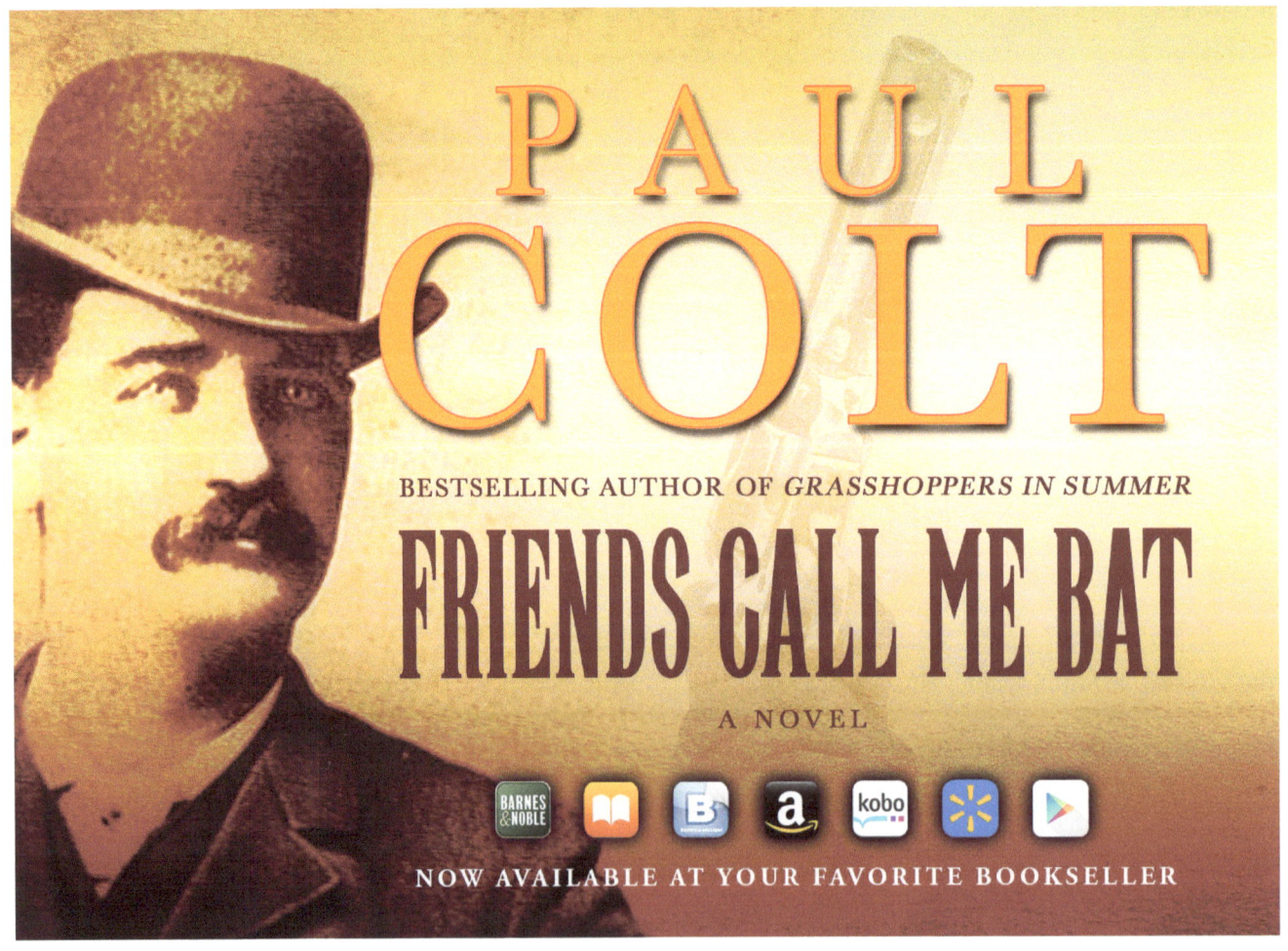

"Jake. Thank God you're alive." I turned as she ran off the boardwalk and threw her arms around my neck. "Did you find Papa?"

I held her close and looked into her eyes. "Yes. He's at a friend's ranch, healing up from a broken leg. His gold is there, too. You and your grandfather will be rich, Angie."

"Papa is the only one who ever called me Angie. But I could get used to hearing you call me that," she said with a smile.

"I could get used to saying your name every day. But I have little to offer a rich lady like yourself. Besides, I need to finish this business with Hayes and his men."

"Hayes is dead, big brother." Jess interrupted.

"Dead? What happened?"

"Our old rock throwing friend, Maggie, and her husband went back to Leadville a few days ago and told the sheriff what was going on. When the sheriff went to confront Hayes, he found Hayes dead and his safe cleaned out. It looks like his men got tired of doing all his dirty work and robbed him."

"I suggest you and the sheriff in Leadville look for a man with one ear. He might have decided Hayes owed him more than he was getting paid."

"Enough talk of Hayes and his men. Take me to see Papa." Angie smiled. "Please. I need to tell him I found the man I want to spend my life with. And Jake, if you agree, Papa and his gold can join us in finding that ranch in Oregon you told me about."

Her remarks set me back on my heels for a moment. I wanted to settle down on a ranch and leave the dangerous world I'd grown accustomed to, but until now, it hadn't included a woman being a part of it. But now I couldn't picture my life without Angie in it.

"We can find a ranch anywhere, Angie. Oregon, Montana, wherever. As long as it's with you, I will have found a place to call home. And yes, your grandfather is welcome to join us."

"So, you would be okay with California. Some place where I don't have all this snow to deal with?"

"California will do just fine. But I want you to see the ocean. Who knows? We might find a ranch with a view of the ocean."

"Papa always said he wanted me to see the ocean. Our kids will love it."

I had to admit to myself, being lassoed and branded felt better than I expected it to. ♘

THE AUTHOR

Gary Rodgers *grew up in rural Arkansas in an age when children were expected to be seen and not heard. As a result, he learned the art of tall tales and lively storytelling at the feet of his grandparents and many uncles, aunts, and cousins.*

After a tour in the Army, then a job which took him to all fifty states, all provinces of Canada, and Jamaica, he retired to his rural Arkansas roots. Gary lives with his wife, writer Kimberly Vernon, and an assortment of rescue pets.

Gary has won numerous awards for his stories, some of which have been published in anthologies and magazines.

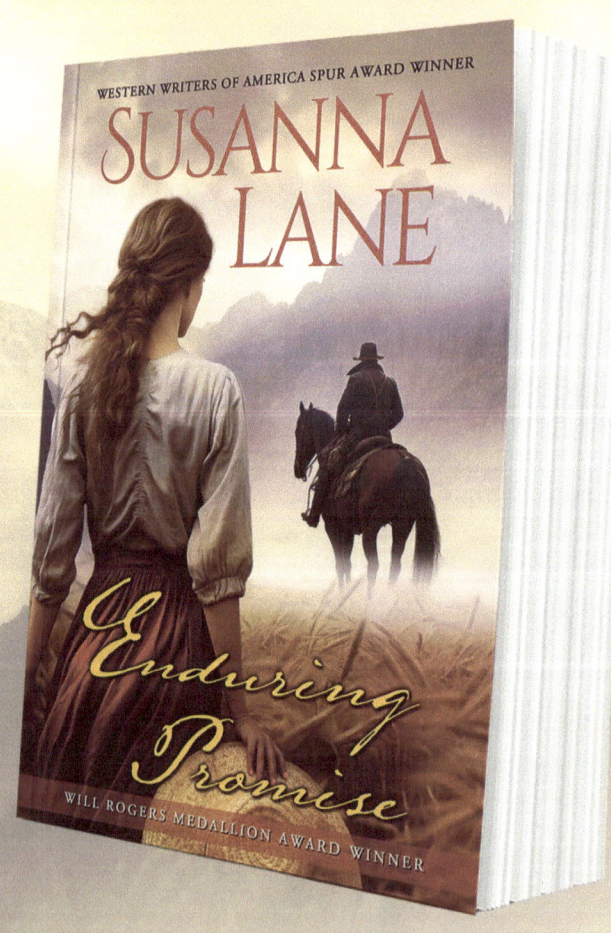

DON MONEY

LILY BILLY & THE SUNFLOWER KID

A SHORT STORY

"Cleve Watson, you make a right pretty sunflower," Billy Bransford said, laughing at his friend.

Cleve retorted with a smile, "Better looking than you in that fancy flower get up."

The two cowboys laughed together in the alley behind the Tabor Opera House at their idea that had been born the night before in the Lucky Strike Saloon.

"Well, I bet we both make a big impression on our visitor," Billy said. "You hit on the best idea with these costumes."

"Oh, I can't take all the credit," Cleve replied, " I read that the people in this traveling show like to use floral emblems, but I believe it was the drinking that truly brought this idea together."

"Whiskey will be for sure what takes the blame if it blows up in our faces," Billy added.

"One way or another this will garner plenty of laughs when we show up to tease the man when he gets onstage," Cleve said.

The event that brought about the planned mischief was the arrival in Leadville of Oscar Wilde on the South Park train that morning. The Irishman was traveling the country on his 1882 American Aesthetic Movement lecture tour and had made a stop in the booming Colorado mining town.

Both Cleve and Billy worked cattle for the former Texas war hero, Charles Masters, at the Piney Creek Ranch. Masters was a good tempered man but held a disdain for the visit by Oscar Wilde and the Aesthetic Movement. He would get worked up about what he heard about the movement.

"Sounds like hogwash," Masters would say.

"Those folks believe life should be all about having a life full of pleasure and nothing else. That doesn't match up with life in the west, life here is full of hard work and harder times."

Cleve and Billy took their boss's sentiment as an opportunity to give everyone a good story to laugh at. Maybe even earn a pat on the back from their normally stoic boss. Early in the morning Cleve and Billy had visited Ellie Mae for some assistance. The hostess at the Silver Rose brought the men's vision to light in creating the costumes.

Now, hours later, and fully sober, the two men were questioning just how their friends in the crowd would react to seeing their appearance. Cleve, the taller of the pair, was a sight with his face painted green and a halo of yellow petals fashioned out of a cotton dress sticking out and ringing his head. Billy, stocky and wide in the shoulders, looked equally out of place with rings of flowers draped in multiple rows of necklaces spilling colorfully down his shirt and woven into his wavy brown hair and beard.

"I don't know about all this, Billy. You know the boys down at the saloon are gonna give us heck for doing this." Cleve snickered, "If we have to throw some punches to get some respect back, it'll be worth it, don't you think?"

Billy rubbed his forehead, "Yeah, but that's a guaranteed busted lips and a broken nose."

Cleve laughed out loud. "Dog gone it, boy, you ain't never backed away from the chance to get into a good fistfight."

Oscar Wilde was scheduled to take the wooden stage and begin his lecture soon. The cowboys had rid-

den their horses into the alley behind the opera house to get into costume a half hour earlier and remained hidden out of sight, lest someone spoil the surprise.

"Are we still doing this?" Billy questioned.

Cleve looked around. "No one has seen us yet. I was thinking, though, Mr. Tabor might not take too kindly to us disrupting the proceedings."

Billy sensed his friend's hesitation and sought to seal the abandonment. "And if Tabor gets mad he may send Marshal Duggan to deal with us."

Marshal Mart Duggan, an Irishman himself, believed in a strong arm of the law tactic to keep the people of Leadville in line. The marshal was quick with his temper and quicker with his gun. Not a man to cross the cowboys determined in silent agreement.

"Probably for the best," Billy said. "The joke might have been on Mr. Oscar Wilde, but the two of us would be living it down for the rest of our lives."

Cleve looked at the flowers draped around Billy and laughed. "They would be calling you Lily Billy."

"Slow your horses there, Sunflower Kid," Billy retorted. "You would have heard it just as bad."

Before the two could doff their ridiculous costumes several shots rang out from Front Street. A man ran past the alley yelling, "They're robbing the National Bank!"

"Mr. Masters was going to the bank," Cleve said as he pulled his Colt 1851 Navy Revolver from its leather holster.

Billy slid his Winchester rifle from the saddle scabbard levering in a round. "Let's go."

The bank was near the end of the street and the cowboys could see the chaos spilling out of the front door. Four men were emerging from the bank, all of them wearing long dusters and dark hats with bandanas pulled up covering half their faces. Two of the men were firing revolvers to keep people ducking for cover. One of the others waved a double-barrel shotgun around looking for anyone coming against them. The last man, carrying a Winchester rifle in one hand, held a large heavy-laden burlap bag in the other.

Cleve and Billy ran down the street and sought cover behind a row of barrels stacked in front of the general store near the National Bank. Gles Havner, one of the dozens of lawyers that had descended on Leadville when mining claims started up, cowered in the store, peeking out the window. His eyes couldn't quite believe what they were seeing. In the middle of a storm of bullets flying down the street, two men that looked like they might have just crawled out of the Garden of Eden, were aiming their guns at the bank.

Cleve saw Gles and nodded his head, yellow sunflower petals bouncing up and down as he did so. "Stay down, Mr. Havner, we'll sort this out," he called to the lawyer. At the moment Cleve caught his reflection in the window glass realizing what a sight the pair of them must look.

Billy took aim at one of the pistoleros with his rifle, firing off a shot that caught the outlaw in the neck and dropped the man to the boardwalk in front of the bank.

"Nice shot," Cleve began, but his congratulations were cut short as two of the other bank robbers turned their attention to where the two cowboys hid.

A boom from the shotgun and the pair could feel the buckshot hammering into their wooden barrier Cleve and Billy knelt behind.

Drifting down from his head, a piece of the cloth sunflower petal landed on Cleve's leg. "Dang blast it," Cleve said, "they have gone and shot off one of my petals."

A short lull in the gun battle came and Cleve and Billy looked over the barrels. A fifth bank robber was pushing his way out of the bank and holding Mr. Masters in front of him as a hostage.

"Can't shoot, we might hit the boss," Cleve said. "Fire over their heads and get them to duck. I'm going to run across to the saloon."

"Not the best time for a drink, Cleve," Billy replied.

"Are those lilies too tight around your neck? I'm going to run through the building and out of the back to try and get around them on the side."

Sensing the idea was the best they had Billy loosed a round of shots as fast as he could over the outlaws, and Mr. Master's head. Cleve darted across the road, his yellow petals blowing in the breeze.

The distraction allowed Charles Masters an opportunity also. He pulled free from the man behind him and snaked the revolver out of the holster of the man holding the Winchester. Curving around, Masters fired a round into the man that had been using him as a shield. The shot caught the man in the chest and he fell back into the bank. Unfortunately, his momentum sent Masters toppling to the ground.

The second robber with the pistol drew a bead on the downed man and jerked the trigger grazing Masters in the thigh. Before he could fire off another round, Billy shot him in the side of the head.

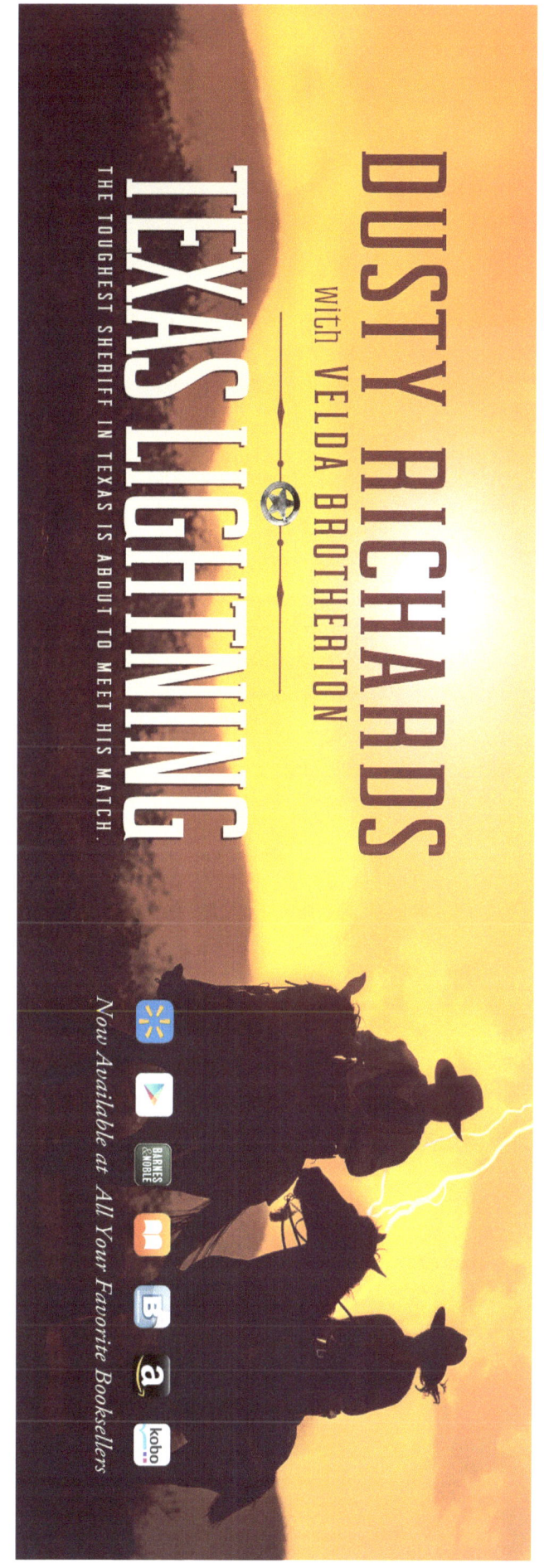

"Crawl out of there, Mr. Masters," Billy shouted.

Masters looked over and could not understand what he was seeing. One of his cowboys, Billy Bransford, was firing his rifle at the outlaws that were trying to escape, dressed like a flower in the process.

The two remaining bank robbers, not liking the odds they now faced, lit out in a run around the corner. No sooner had they made it halfway into the alley, a tall sunflower charged right at them out of the back door of the saloon. "Drop you guns or I'll shoot."

The bagman recovered at the shock first and tried to raise his Winchester with his one hand to get a shot off but wasn't quick enough as Cleve Watson fired twice. One hit the man in the arm, forcing him to drop his rifle. The second shot punched into the man's gut and folded him over.

The last outlaw squeezed off a trigger pull from the shotgun, pelting Cleve with a shot across his torso. Cleve cartwheeled backwards hitting the ground hard. The bank robber was reloading and planning to finish off the only obstacle left in his escape.

A shot rang out, wood splintered in the wall beside the outlaw as Billy rounded the corner with his rifle up. The bank robber ducked around another corner heading to where the gang had tied up their horses. Billy dropped down next to Cleve to check on his friend who lay there trying to sit up on his elbows.

"Looking rough there, Sunflower Kid." Billy kneeled and assessed Cleve's injuries. "You caught what looked like five pieces of shot, but I don't think anything major got hit."

Mr. Masters stumbled around the corner. "My lord, I did see what I thought I saw." He said looking down at Cleve and Billy. "I've got plenty of questions for you two, but that can wait. I'll get Cleve to Doc Abrams. Billy, you go get the one that got away."

Billy nodded and sprinted around the corner. Four horses remained tied up to the fence. He approached them cautiously. "Which one of you is going to let me ride you?" he asked as if expecting an answer.

A brown Morgan turned and took a bite out of the flowers hanging down the front of Billy's shirt. "You'll do," Billy said and swung up on the horse.

A quick nudge from the stirrups and they were back on Front Street. The bank robbery had rattled everyone's nerves, but the sight of the cowboy draped in flowers was almost beyond the pale of the day. People stood staring at the sight until Billy broke the spell.

"Which way did the robber go?" Billy asked.

A teenaged boy pointed down the road leading out of town and Billy sent the horse bolting in pursuit. Either he had a better horse or the man he was chasing was a poor rider because he quickly closed the gap.

Looking over his shoulder, the outlaw saw a strange-looking pursuer catching up to him. The man fired over his shoulder but the distance was too great for the shotgun to matter. Billy brought his rifle up as he rode and let loose a shot that went true. The man in front tumbled from his saddle and was quickly overtaken. The bullet had caught him in the right shoulder and taken the fight out of him.

Billy cantered past the man and caught up with the fleeing horse. Bringing the riderless mount under his control he turned back to take the outlaw prisoner. With his Winchester pointed at the man's back he followed him into town.

As they drew near Billy could see the townsfolk appearing to be lining the streets talking about the robbery attempt and the two odd heroes that stopped it.

Deputy Cal Barnes walked up to the approaching riders. "Marshal Duggan is out of town, but he will be mighty appreciative of what you men did stopping the bank robbers."

Billy nodded his head and turned his prisoner over.

"If I might ask," Deputy Barnes said, "What in the tarnation is this get up you are wearing?"

"Another time," Billy replied.

Seeing Mr. Masters and Cleve sitting on a bench outside of the Tabor Opera House the flower-covered cowboy rode down to them, relieved to see the doctor looking over his friend.

"He'll make it," Mr. Masters said as Billy slid down off his borrowed horse.

A man began to clap and walked forward from the assembled crowd. Oscar Wilde waited like the performer he was and drew everyone's attention. "Ladies and gentlemen, let us cheer for our well-dressed heroes of the day, Lily Billy and the Sunflower Kid."

Mr. Wilde walked over to the two cowboys and stood before them. He made a big show of it, shaking both of their hands and leaning in lowering his voice. "I heard you men talking in the alley earlier when I stepped out for some air before I went on stage."

Cleve and Billy looked at each other.

"Guess we got to see you in those costumes, after all." ♄

THE AUTHOR

Don Money was born and raised in rural Arkansas. He spent the majority of his youth exploring the woods around their family farm or with his face buried in a Western novel. After graduating high school he joined the United States Air Force and traveled the globe as a Nuclear, Biological, Chemical Weapons Defense Specialist. After ten years in the service, Don returned to his roots in Arkansas and now teaches Language Arts to sixth graders. He holds Masters and Bachelors degrees in Education from Arkansas State University. Don is an active member of the White County Creative Writers group and enjoys writing fiction across multiple genres. He has sixty short stories published in a variety of anthologies and magazines. Don resides in Beebe, Arkansas with his wife Sarah where they are the proud parents of five children.

REAVIS Z. WORTHAM

ANNIVERSARY

PART ONE OF THE EXCLUSIVE SERIAL NOVELLA

A SHORT STORY

James Anderson lifted his foot from the accelerator of his new Ford Bronco. With the flick of a finger, he hit the turn indicator to signal his intention to exit the southbound lane of Interstate 90. His wife, Katie, looked up from her phone and confirmed the exit number.

An electronic voice with an artificial British accent filled the car. *"Turn left in four hundred yards."*

Katie lifted her light brown hair to cool her neck with a very feminine motion. "That is, turn left after you stop. No need to ruin a perfect anniversary trip with a traffic ticket."

Around them, Crow Agency in Montana, was a wide open, rolling landscape of hills and ravines covered with an inverted bowl of blue stretching to the distant horizon. The busy highway led past neat buildings surrounded by white plank fences and long lines of scraggly trees which broke up the view on both sides.

Driving with his wrist hanging over the steering wheel, James waved his fingers to paint the landscape around them. "I wish we could have seen this country back when it was wide open."

Knowing her husband's penchant for history, she fed his enthusiasm. "It would have been different. That's for sure."

"Imagine what it looked like when the Sioux owned everything as far as you could see."

She laughed. "I bet I know what it looked like when Custer thought everything as far as you could see were *warriors.*"

He chuckled. "You're coming along. Five years ago, you wouldn't have thought like that."

"Five years ago, when we got married, I didn't much care for history."

"The perks of being married to a history professor. You know why I wanted to come out here today?"

She'd done her homework. "I do. It's June 25, the anniversary of Custer's Last Stand, and I'm wondering if you planned for us to get married on this date when we were trying to decide."

"Well," he threw her a puppy dog look. "This all worked out just fine. The summer session ended at just the right time, and I didn't teach the second semester so we could take this trip. It seems like we're charmed. Everything else worked out perfectly."

Katie wasn't overly enthusiastic about Custer and the Battle of the Little Big Horn but understood her husband's fascination with history.

He glanced at the little brunette in the passenger seat. "I know this doesn't excite you, but I can't wait to see the battlefield." He squeezed her knee. "I think you're gonna like this stop."

"The jury is still out, buddy." She leaned over and kissed his cheek. "I hope this place is as interesting as you said it was. I'm not much on battles and wars."

"It'll be fascinating." He switched to what he considered an announcer voice. "And as a bonus, you get to pick the night's dinner venue, how about that?"

She laughed as the car trailed along the road leading to the visitor center. He found an empty slot in the busy parking lot then killed the engine. She opened the door and stepped out. A light breeze ruffled her long hair as she came around the car then took James' arm.

"Come on, big boy. Lay a little history on me."

Their anniversary trip—planned to celebrate five years of marriage—began in Texas and drifted through the Rockies to the Grand Teton and Yellowstone National Parks. A longtime outdoorsman when they married, James introduced her to the Rocky Mountains to their west. Energized by the majestic scenery and the solitude on the backcountry trails, Katie had taken to camping and backpacking like a natural.

Years earlier, he'd eased his new bride into the outdoors one step at a time. He knew better than to make the disastrous mistake others made with novices. He gave her a light backpack on their first trip and led her carefully through the wilderness, opening it up as a wonderful experience with nature, not a survival course.

Now completely compatible in the outdoors, they'd spent two weeks in the adjacent parks of Yellowstone and the Tetons, and finally emerged, tired but happy. From there they traveled to the Custer Battlefield sixty-five miles from Billings, Montana.

She took his hand as they stepped onto the sidewalk, knowing from past experience how two hours could stretch to four. James at the national monument would be like a kid in a candy shop. "We're doing this only on one condition. Since you picked this stop, I get to select the hotel for tonight, too. Deal?"

"Lordy, you drive a hard bargain for somebody who ain't no bigger'n a minute." James nodded his shaggy head and rolled his eyes, knowing the arrangement would come with considerable cost.

Katie's idea of comfort included king size beds, spa, pool, room service, and a large expensive meal. "You know the only hotels that'll suit me begin with an H. Hilton or Hyatt, either one."

She roughed it like a champ in the backcountry, but this particular young lady believed very firmly in her comforts.

Katie hoped the park service at the battlefield site would provide something more interesting than hokey dioramas or paper mâché hills and toy soldiers. She didn't mind real artifacts, photos, or clothing, but reading display cards barely kept her attention, and Lord knew there had been plenty of those over the past five years.

With a wide grin, James took her arm to lead her through the glass doors of the National Monument's

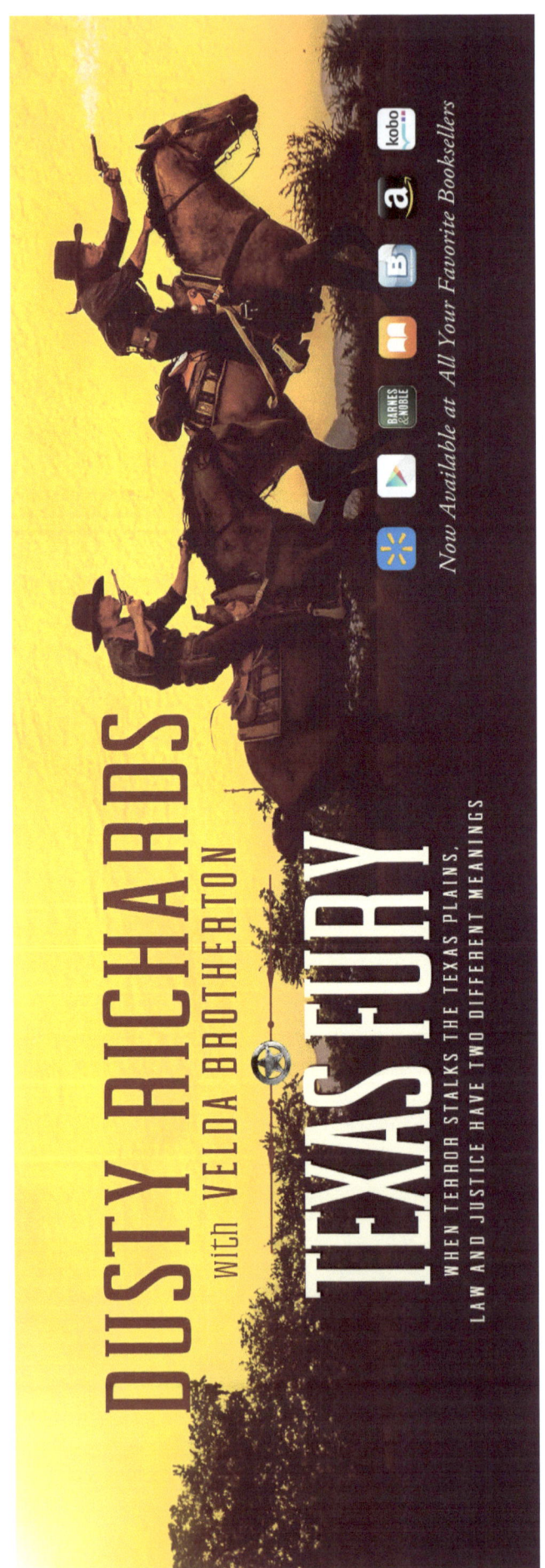

Visitor Center. Beyond the facility, a line of clouds built up dark and blue on the horizon. She hoped it wasn't going to rain. Then, with a flash of guilt, she thought if it did, they wouldn't have to stay outside to walk the battlefield inch by inch.

He stopped just inside the entrance to study a large painting on the wall depicting the 1876 battle between Custer's men and the Sioux. While he stood spellbound by the painting, she drifted over to browse the selection of books, maps, and battlefield purchases. A bright display of coffee table books caught Katie's attention. "Look at this."

She held aloft a large book featuring a ramrod straight Custer completely surrounded by his blue-clad soldiers attempting to cover and protect their beloved General. Custer's long wavy hair flowed from under his campaign hat as he and a small group of soldiers fired toward a mass of mounted, brightly painted and feathered warriors "I've seen this picture of Custer's Last Stand somewhere before."

James glanced at the cover, barely acknowledging the illustrator's efforts. "Let me show you what he really looked like." James motioned with his arm, leading her back to the painting she'd ignored at the outset. "Take a look at this. It's probably a more accurate picture of the battle than that cover."

Katie slipped her arm around his waist. "It doesn't even look like General Custer. His hair is too short."

"You're a victim of Hollywood." James pointed to a figure near the center. Wreathed in gunsmoke, a short haired man leaned over a fallen horse and aimed a revolver through the haze. "Custer'd been busted to Lieutenant Colonel, so he wasn't a General. Second, he'd cut his hair because he knew the June weather would be hot and dusty. Long hair was too much of a bother in the field."

He was already on a roll and had seamlessly reverted to his teaching voice and mannerisms, so she knew better than to ask too many questions. It would only serve to fertilize his attention, and before long, it would be an in-depth class on the Custer campaign.

A noisy tour group moved through the center, following a diminutive guide dressed in buckskins who stood less than four feet tall.

Dwarf.

As soon as the name popped into her head, Katie's face reddened. In this day and time of political correctness, it didn't seem like an appropriate term. But the man really was a dwarf.

She watched from the corners of her eyes so as not to stare at the buckskin-clad gentleman punctuating his comments with a short black cane.

Caught in his own thoughts, James kept talking as if he were in a lecture hall. "The only thing the artist on that book got right was Custer's last name. He shows him wearing a blue uniform, but on the most of his campaigns he wore buckskins. They were more practical than the hot, heavy woolen uniforms. None of them carried sabers like those, either. Not that day, anyway."

She rolled her eyes in mock frustration. "Take all the fun out of everything, would ya?"

Holding his gnarled black cane by the gray metallic head, the nearby guide used it as a pointer to draw attention toward a glass display of artifacts collected from the battlefield just outside. Light from the large windows on their left reflected off the cane's head, almost glowing like fire.

St. Elmo's Fire.

Katie frowned when the name occured to her. *Probably thinking that because it's coming up a cloud out there.*

James' voice trailed off and he stopped, eyes glazing as he stared in to the painting and beyond. The muscles in his craggy face relaxed.

Katie looked up into his slack expression. "Just kidding. I'm still listening, bub. You don't have to be so dramatic. Hey, you all right?" She punched his arm. "Quit horsing around, dummy, people are watching."

He failed to respond, almost catatonic. Her brow furrowed, and she gripped his forearm. "James?"

The buck skinned guide led his tour away, and the absent look in James' eyes faded. He scratched his short beard with a feeble, absent-minded motion. "What did you say, babe?" He blinked two or three times and massaged his forehead.

"Are you all right?"

"Yeah, sure. What's the problem? I just felt a little dizzy for a moment."

"You just vacated the premises on me, bud, and nearly scared me to death in the process."

"I just got lost in the painting, that's all. I felt sort of funny for a moment, though. I thought I smelled gun smoke for just a second. This guy's a good artist!" James grinned, his old enthusiastic self again. "Let's check out the museum."

He took her hand, then they walked into the dimly lit display area. Katie watched him, still worried.

They moved through the display area with James lecturing on each individual piece in the glass cases. His passion for history gained enthusiasm as they talked, and soon, a small group of listeners followed. Enjoying the opportunity to teach, he pointed out different items or photographs and even addressed the visitors personally. Most were learning more history from his impromptu discussion than if they'd simply walked through and read the small, typed cards at each artifact.

———————————

James talked on autopilot so he wouldn't worry Katie. His momentary blackout wasn't the first that day. For a fraction of a second, after turning onto the drive leading to the Visitor Center, the landscape had shimmered and become indistinct before clearing up again just as he'd put the Bronco into park. The experience had made him dizzy and cold.

The odd sensation repeated itself in the parking lot. His head swam for a brief moment at his first glimpse of the small white grave markers scattered on the site of what most folks knew today as Custer's Last Stand.

But when he caught sight of the tour guide's cane, the feelings resurfaced—faster and more intense. For a moment, the strange metallic head in the man's hand seemed to glow, and at the same time, the smell of dust and the sharp, acrid odor of gun smoke enveloped him.

The painted images became almost *real,* like some movie where cartoons come alive. Standing there, James felt as if he were being pulled into the fighting, and for a brief instant, he could almost hear the pop and rattle of the soldiers' guns and the screams of dying men coming from a great distance. His stomach clenched as a deep, terrifying fear made him feel he was about to die in the most violent way imaginable.

A horse shrieked, and a man's terrified scream cut off when Katie placed her hand on his arm. The familiar, comforting sound of her voice yanked him back into the present, and it took a long second for his mind to re-focus on their surroundings.

They stepped from the dark museum into a lighted art gallery. James stopped and allowed his informal assemblage to disperse when they realized there would be no more. Several tourists thanked him for the tour, and he figured they thought he worked for the park service because of his short beard and shirt that only vaguely resembled those worn by the rangers.

Katie watched his face with a worried frown. "Are you sure you're all right? You don't look too good right now."

He managed a grin. "Sure, I'll be fine in a minute. Just a little headache. I'll take some Tylenol when we get back to the Bronco, and everything'll be all right."

"Well, little headache or not, you sure gave me a scare back there. I thought you were going to pass out or throw up or something."

"Me, throw up on history?" James laughed. "Maybe on a class of freshmen, but never on Custer, even though he was an arrogant dumbass." With one arm he hugged Katie, then they stepped through the gallery's doors onto a covered walkway.

A light breeze cooled the air under the shade of a portico, while the June sun pounded the landscape. The approaching line of dark clouds hung over the ridge, but it didn't seem to be moving, merely resting on top of the trees.

The tiny guide dressed in fringed buckskins lectured to a group of assorted tourists about the Custer massacre. Most were captured by the speaker's rendition, others by the man's appearance. Two men walked past James, and he overheard snatches of their conversation.

A balding man of indeterminate age grinned at his friend in an aloha shirt. "Guy's not bad, is he?"

"He's a talker." Aloha Shirt sported knee-length shorts. Both wore black socks with sandals.

James made a mental note to forgo shorts after he reached seventy. He glanced down at his ever-present jeans and a pair of running shoes that should have been retired a year earlier.

He allowed Katie to pull him behind the crowd to an unoccupied bench. The dwarf speaker had completed the preliminary portion of his speech and was winding up to launch into Custer's last and most famous campaign.

The guide noticed James behind the scattered tourists and pointed his glossy black cane. "Welcome, sir, I heard a portion of your impromptu lecture inside. Well done. I'm glad you could make it for Custer's folly. As I like to say, his *final* folly."

James laughed. "I couldn't agree with you more. If he'd been a little less spontaneous and glory hungry, and more cautious, he might have survived this one also."

WILL ROGERS MEDALLION WINNING AUTHOR

MANUELA SCHNEIDER

THE SILENCE OF ECHOES

THE SECRET OF THE BIRD CAGE THEATRE

BUY YOUR COPY TODAY AT YOUR FAVORITE BOOKSELLER

The speaker tipped his hat. "A man after my own heart. You know your history then, sir."

"I should. I teach it day after day at the university level."

"Excellent! Then if I make any fatal misstep in this presentation, would you be so kind as to inform me? After I'm finished, of course." He added a wink toward the crowd to bring them into the conversation. They chuckled in response.

He replaced his wide brimmed hat. "Now, to begin. For the newcomers, my name is Ambrose B. Hollis, and it is my pleasure to take you on a journey through that fateful day of June 25, 1876. At the same time, I will try to clear up a misconception or two you may have picked up from the movies and television. You'll learn about the Little Big Horn, and the Indian campaign in general.

"Before we continue, yes, I am a *dwarf,* and it's the proper word, should the occasion arise for you to use it. If you speak Lakota, you might refer to me as *Canotila.* Native legends talk about *Canotila* who play pranks on their people. Those who look like me are said to sing just out of sight then hide when the People searched for the source of the music. Other, darker legends say little people love children and we would take them away from abusive parents to raise as our own. These legends varied from tribe to tribe, and depending on those legends, *Canotila* could be good, evil, or merely mischievous. Sometimes, they were said to be gods."

Like any good showman, he paused and continued with a straight face. "I'm here to set the record straight. I am all of those, and more, rolled into this cute little figure."

The crowd laughed at just the right time, giving Hollis the opportunity to limp to the edge of the portico, favoring a withered right leg James hadn't noticed until then. Hollis turned to face his audience of about fifty people.

"To begin, Custer was not the senior commanding officer during this particular campaign. That honor belonged to General Terry. Custer was in charge of his regiment though, and these men, numbering about six hundred, made up the 7th Cavalry which, by the way, still exists. They've distinguished themselves in both World Wars and most of the major conflicts since that time."

Hollis rested his cane over one shoulder and directed their attention to a framed movie poster be-

side him. His short fingers danced absently over the lead-gray, misshapen metal head of the walking stick. James noted the ferrule on the other end seemed to be made of the same material.

"Contrary to the popular belief generated by Hollywood, Custer had short hair on this campaign. This may have been one of the reasons that it wasn't until long after the battle the hostiles learned they'd killed the famous cavalryman here at the Little Big Horn. Sitting Bull himself admitted he knew nothing of the presence of Yellow Hair that day on the Greasy Grass."

———— ·--· ————

Katie looked at the smug expression on James's face and elbowed him in the ribs. She whispered. "Smart guy, huh?"

Although she hadn't said anything, she was still worried about what had happened back in the museum. James had never even spoken of a headache as long as she'd known him, and when he suddenly had one, he shrugged it off as inconsequential.

She unconsciously tuned out the lecture and gazed out over the treeless, windswept hill behind Hollis. A random pattern of small white marble headstones dotted the grassy hillside as if some giant scattered them by hand like so many seeds.

Many of the markers stood alone on the desolate ground. Others huddled together in twos, threes, and in large groups, connected by a meandering concrete walkway. They indicated the sites where members of the 7th Cavalry had fallen before the savage assault of the combined tribes of Sioux, Cheyenne, and Arapaho.

One of the closer markers stated "Unknown 7th Cavalry Trooper." Another bore the name of a trooper who'd been identified before burial. Katie glanced down at the Park Service pamphlet in her hand and read many of the fallen were never identified.

The pamphlet told her closer to the top of the hill, the markers became more numerous. It was there historians believed Custer and his men had attempted to gain the high ground and defend themselves against superior numbers. These markers were spaced closely together, where more men of the 7th Cavalry had fallen. Weeks after the battle, members of another unit hastily buried the dead in shallow graves. They later returned to re-bury the remains once the danger of further attack had passed.

Hollis rattled off volumes of information as her eyes followed the markers to the top of Custer Hill.

An iron fence enclosed an even larger group of white stones bearing the names of the men who fell in the immediate vicinity of George Custer during the last bloody minutes of the battle.

Above this enclosure stood a large granite monument, dedicated to the memory of the men of the 7th Cavalry, bearing the names of all who'd died at the Little Big Horn.

Hollis swept the large hat off his head and planted the ferrule of his cane to give himself more stability. "Now, if you'll follow me, we'll take a walk to the top of the hill where you can get a better feel of the troop movements. You will be able to see the hillside and ravine below from the defender's point of view and will hopefully get a feeling of what it was like on that fateful day when so many men lost their lives."

Hollis led the tour group into the hot sun, limping past a final glass display case containing rusty artifacts discovered on the battlefield. Most of the tour group gave the contents of the case only a cursory look as they passed. Katie glanced inside at the rusty guns, arrowheads, and other ancient relics as she trailed behind the shuffling group of tourists.

⁂

As James followed them into the sunshine, his gaze skipped over most of the items in one of the last cases on display before locking on a rusty knife blade. A sudden wrenching in his mind caused him to stop. He felt as if something inside his brain was pulling loose. Incredibly, he felt the smooth handle of a sweaty knife in his hand.

In his mind, his shaking hand worked the sharp edge of the blade underneath the edge of an empty shell casing lodged in the rifle.

Gotta get this out! Gotta reload! Damn those people who said these rifles were—

Nausea accompanied the tug on James' consciousness. The electric jolt shot through his head again. In the museum, he looked down into his empty hand, opening and closing on nothing. A large man bumped into James from the rear, tearing his attention from his palm and causing him to stumble.

"Sorry, mister, I didn't realize you'd stopped," the stranger apologized.

James glanced around. "No problem." He gave the man a weak smile and swallowed. The wave of dizziness that had nearly overcome him once again passed quickly.

the STORY

How Billy Thomas Learned the Importance of Being Honest

PHIL MILLS, JR.

with illustrations by JEAN ABERNETHY

Katie hadn't noticed the lapse. She merely assumed that he'd stopped to study the relics. She took his hand, the hand that actually *felt* the knife's bone handle only seconds before, then they followed Hollis toward the walkway leading to the top of Custer Hill.

James moved slowly, allowing the remainder of the group to walk ahead until he and Katie were at the rear of the tour. He forced himself to settle down as his stomach unclenched. He consciously straightened, realizing that he'd been slumped forward.

She looked at him in concern. "You still don't look good."

"I'm fine. This headache is just making me a little dizzy is all."

She frowned upward at him.

"I'll be fine when we get to the hotel. It's probably the sun."

"Let's go back."

"No way. We came here to see this hill." He pointed to the line of clouds that had finally moved closer. Turning green and ugly, they promised a storm soon. "It won't be long until it clouds up and cools off."

Insects hummed in the grass beside the path. Hollis favored his bad leg while limping slowly toward the first white markers beside the trail. He stopped and pointed with his cane in a southerly direction.

"No one knows exactly what route Custer took, since there were no survivors from his battalion. But from carefully interviewing the Indians who fought here, and by studying his original plan, we know he moved his troops from a southeasterly direction. Captain Benteen didn't march this far forward on the initial thrust. Major Reno accompanied Custer partway toward an Indian village in the valley where he then halted."

He turned and pointed his cane. "Reno and Custer then split up at the river below us, near what is now the Garryowen Post Office. It was there Reno made his initial engagement with the Indians. He tried to make a stand, but the overwhelming number of warriors who seemingly materialized from nowhere soon forced a retreat to the bluffs. It was a tactically better defensive position for his men, but it left Custer with no reinforcements close by."

James's head pounded harder. He and Katie walked farther uphill, past Hollis and his group. The slashing pain that made him think his skull was splitting in two became almost unbearable. The sharp edge of another wave shot through his head. He staggered slightly and leaned heavily on Katie's shoulder.

He groaned. In James' mind, the hillside below him shook as if they were experiencing an earthquake. The physical world shimmered and dissolved. Shapes and shadows moved at the edges of his vision. A strong feeling of *déjà vu* made his stomach flip.

A cold knot of fear clenched Katie's stomach in a frozen fist. "James, you've got to tell me what's wrong!"

"I don't know what's happening," he mumbled, his eyes closed. "I feel terrible all of a sudden." He met Katie's gaze. "No, not terrible. *Terrified.* What the hell's going on?"

Her hands clenched his biceps. James was twisted tight as a watch's mainspring. He trembled, and his knees sagged.

An older couple glared at the newlyweds with annoyance. They'd come to listen to Hollis, not someone's private discussion.

Hollis tilted his hat back, unaware of the developing crisis behind him. He again pointed back with his cane, this time to the north, almost directly at James.

"The remaining part of my discussion is mostly educated conjecture, much of it revealed by the great fire of 1983 that swept this battlefield when it uncovered a wealth of information about the combatants' movements and positions.

"Dreadfully outmanned, Custer had sighted the big Indian village in the valley. He sent a message to Benteen. It read, *'Come on. Big Village, be quick, bring packs. P.S. Bring packs.'* As far as we know, it was at this point when Custer engaged the enemy."

He waved his cane in a broad arc. "The Battle of the Little Big Horn began."

When the cane pointed directly at James, he stiffened, staring at Hollis down what looked for all the world like the barrel of a rifle. Behind the little tour guide, transparent shapes moved where none had been before. Hollis's gnarled cane straightened. The ferrule vanished into the maw of a rifle bore. The man himself shimmered, became transparent and then faded. The sun in James's vision grew murky and dim as smoke and dust obscured the bright summer light.

The savage pain again ripped through James'

head. With a sickening, audible tear, his mind pulled loose from its moorings. The markers vanished into a sea of grass. The crystal-clear hot June day turned to a haze, but not enough that he couldn't see the figures moving in a man-made cloud of dust pounded into the air by hundreds of horse hooves.

He could see them now. *Indians!* They were everywhere, moving from side to side, jumping up to run, fire, and fall to the ground behind long clumps of grass. But there was no sound.

Everything was silent. Horrifyingly silent.

James backed slowly uphill in terror, away from the oncoming horde. He no longer saw his wife, Hollis, or the tour group, only the men who would try to take his life. Horses ran through the dust and smoke, and men with terrified looks on their faces scrambled for safety as they fought for their lives.

Noise started to register. Quietly at first, the pop and crackle of small arms fire filtered through his consciousness. Like the volume being increased on a television set, it became louder and louder until he was consumed with the sound of battle.

James yanked his arm from Katie's grip. She stifled a scream when his face changed. His normally clear blue eyes clouded as if covered in cataracts. The man before her was unrecognizable as the skin on his face pulled tight. Those eyes that softened when they were intimate widened in what looked like confusion, then absolute terror.

Time stopped. Dreamlike, she found herself moving through thick water.

Only yards away, Hollis continued to describe the battle in great detail to the tourists gathered on the concrete pathway around him. The inflections in his voice made the imagination race as he described the Sioux's method of attack, and the futile efforts of the soldiers to rally and form an orderly retreat.

"Many of the troopers tried to help each other, I'm sure. Escape was now impossible." Hollis' voice was full of excitement, as if he were watching the events unfold around him. "Many of the men simply gave into panic and tried to escape before a tidal wave of warriors, fleeing toward the ravines and scattered brush. Others dismounted, and in twos and threes, tried to defend themselves from the attackers swarming from the village below."

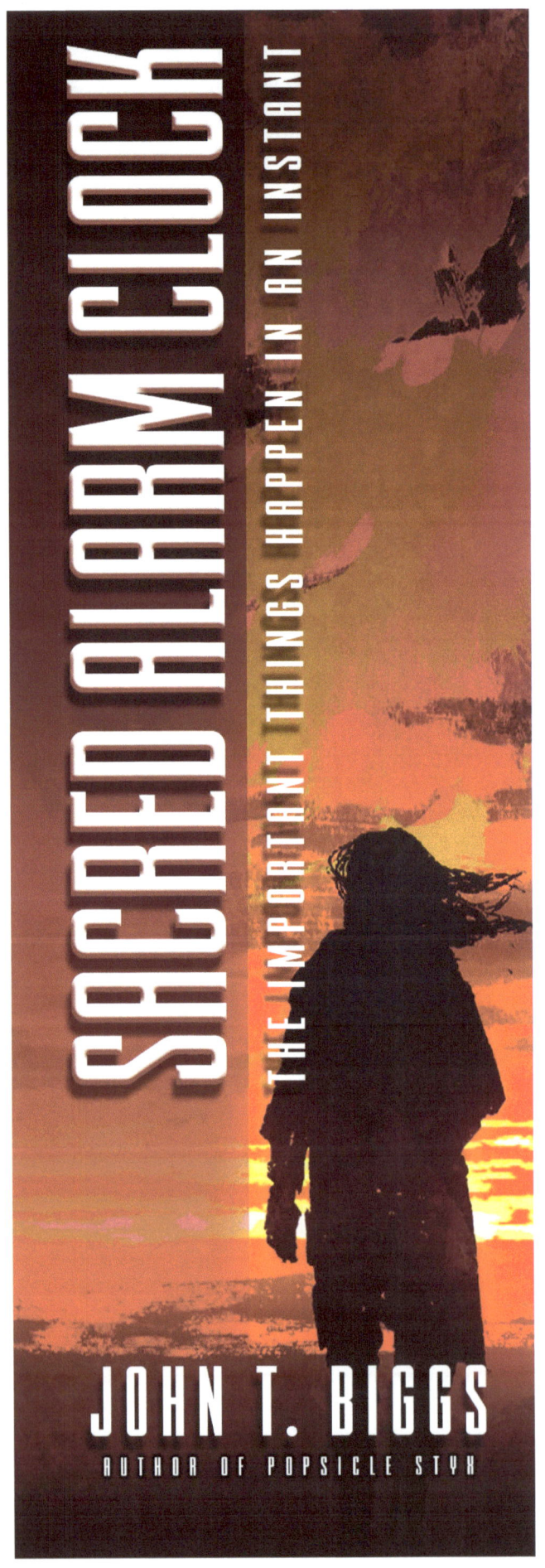

SACRED ALARM CLOCK

THE IMPORTANT THINGS HAPPEN IN AN INSTANT

JOHN T. BIGGS

AUTHOR OF POPSICLE STYX

Service revolver in hand, James backed up several more steps, tugging at the sweat-soaked bandanna around his neck. He'd lost his army-issued campaign hat somewhere, and the dry wind blew dust into his eyes, blinding him. In his left hand he held the leather reins of his terrified, bolting horse. With his right, he aimed the Colt revolver at the nearest warrior. Sweat, the sweat of fear, soaked his back and the dark blue cavalry uniform stuck to his skin.

Hollis continued, still not realizing James' dilemma. "Others dismounted, held onto their horses, and attempted a rally farther up the hill where, we assume, Custer was organizing a defensive line. Troops were scattered haphazardly over the hillside and the surrounding area you see here. Ragged skirmish lines decayed into every man for himself."

"Fall back up the hill!" James screamed, trying to control his fear-maddened horse and shoot at the same time. "My God, *look* at all of them!" His voice was filled with disbelief.

Hollis froze at the sudden shout. Cane pointed uphill, his next words were forgotten. The tour group stood in shock as James stumbled several more steps toward a trio of nearby markers.

Tugging at the collar of his sport shirt with one hand, his left fist rose above shoulder level and jerked back and forth as if by invisible strings. His right grasped at his waist for a moment, then clutched an invisible object, around which he alternately crooked his thumb and squeezed with his forefinger.

"What are you *doing?*" Katie shouted, less than a yard from her frenzied husband. The look in his eyes froze the next words on her lips. James stared completely through her and out into the distant valley of the Little Big Horn.

Two men started forward to take his arm. They stopped in shock at the crazed expression on the man's face.

Hollis limped closer to the animated man, being careful not to get within reach. "He's not having any type of seizure I've ever heard of. Hey lady, what's the matter with him?"

"I don't know," she sobbed, her hands held toward her frantically jerking husband. "He's never done this before."

James emptied his pistol. "Come on, Bill. Look out behind you!" He screamed as a Cheyenne warrior, clad only in a breechcloth and leather leggings appeared in the yellow cloud of dust and ran up behind the crouched trooper to cave in the back of his skull with a brightly decorated war ax.

Another cavalryman fought his way to James' side. With the horse's reins in his left hand, James holstered his pistol, jerked his newly acquired carbine from its scabbard buckled onto the saddle, and fired awkwardly at a warrior running toward him.

"Where's Custer?" the soldier shouted, blood running from a shallow wound in his cheek.

James barely heard him over the shrill screams of wounded horses, and the war cries from white and red men alike. "Last time I saw him he was moving up the hill."

"What do we do?"

"Head that way!"

Two Sioux seemed to emerge from the very ground before them and both men fired simultaneously. To their right, three of their companions crumpled in a hail of arrows and gunfire.

Hollis and the others stared at the raving man before them. "This is bizarre," he exclaimed as James swung to his right and gaped at an invisible object in the vicinity of three white markers nearby.

He shouldered an invisible rifle and squeezed with his index finger. To the observers, it looked like some type of odd mime in a stage play.

Voice full of fear, James screamed at the empty landscape and the stunned tourists. "They're all around us!" The veins in his neck bulged with unseen effort. He again made a levering action in the direction of the markers, fired what appeared to be an imaginary rifle, and stumbled backwards up the hillside, knocking two tourists to the ground before they could get out of the way.

"Custer, where's Custer?" James shouted into the still afternoon.

Astonished, Hollis watched as James looked to his right.

"Oh, my God, Tom's down! Sam, Tom's down!

Autie! Where...? Sweet Jesus. Where are they all *coming* from?"

Understanding struck Hollis with the intensity of a lightning bolt. "He's reliving the battle," he said in wonder. The hair prickled on the back of his neck and a shiver went up the man's spine as the cane's head warmed in his hand. "Today's June twenty-fifth. He's seeing and experiencing what happened on this hill over one hundred and thirty years ago!"

James dropped to one knee and shouldered his rifle once again, sighting down the Springfield's barrel at the nearest warrior. The availability of targets was no problem in the swirling melee. A man charged him, his long hair flying behind. James pulled the trigger and heard the dead snap of a defective cartridge. The brave knocked him to the ground, but another trooper killed him before the Arapaho warrior could strike a fatal blow.

James's horse reared, jerking him back to his feet with the reins wrapped around his left wrist. They were near the crest of the highest point around them where Custer and the remnants of his 7th Cavalry were making a desperate last-ditch effort. A writhing mass of howling braves moved through the dark haze of smoke and dust illuminated by a sickly yellow sun above.

Three troopers broke free from the melee and fled downhill in a full-blown panic. They disappeared under a swarming mass of warriors. Reins still in his left hand, James wiped the sweat with a dusty sleeve and led his horse at a run toward a knot of blue-clad soldiers.

Terrified and unable to comprehend James' actions, Katie followed her frenzied husband through the long summer-browned grass. Well off the concrete walkway, he aimed an invisible rifle downhill at a clump of weeds. His eyes widened in sudden shock. James glanced down at his clinched hands for a moment, then flew backward onto the ground.

His body slapped into the grass with a sickening sound. She rushed forward and knelt beside her fallen husband, sobbing until his contorting body miraculously jerked completely into the air by invisible strings. She fell back with a shriek as he rushed uphill, left arm up and behind his body as if he were pulling something along.

James looked back over his shoulder and shouted toward Katie. In the eerie silence of the hot day, his voice sounded pitifully alone. "Hurry Sam!' He dodged an unseen object. "We're almost there!"

Hollis limped after him, fascinated. Many members of the forgotten tour group turned and rushed for their cars, apparently afraid the affliction was contagious. A handful kept up with Hollis, watching the action with the morbid curiosity of those who stop to stare at the bloody aftermath of an automobile accident. Most were recording the scene with their phones.

"You," Hollis pointed his cane at a young man wearing a fluorescent blue *'Custer was Siouxed'* tee shirt. "Run down to the Ranger's office and tell them to call an ambulance." He spoke with authority, though he'd never seen the man before.

"Then tell Ranger Starnes to get up here on the double. I need someone I can trust for a witness. This needs credible witnesses, besides all this" He waved the cane at those recording the scene, then prodded the young man with the ferruled end. *"Hurry!"*

The teenager flung one last fearful look at the man who appeared to be play acting and streaked away, shouting to a milling crowd of curious newcomers that someone had gone crazy on Custer Hill.

Hollis turned back to Katie. He took her arm and helped the slender, nearly hysterical, young woman to her feet. Looking up at her, his eyes were bright, almost feverish. "There's nothing we can do until help arrives. Just watch. You'll see something no white man could ever describe. The actual events of Custer's Last Stand."

She jerked her arm away from the sweaty grip of the little guide. "Are you *crazy?*" Tears ran down her cheeks. "That's my husband, and he's sick! He's having some sort of seizure!"

"Yes, it *is* some sort of seizure. He's seized by *history,* woman. He's reliving the past." Hollis thought aloud. "Somehow he's experiencing the events of that day almost a hundred and fifty years ago, yet his body is in the present. Maybe he's psychic, or maybe a reincarnate."

Katie screamed as bright red blood blossomed through the jean material of James' upper thigh, though nothing visible had touched him.

The cane's head grew hotter in Hollis' hand. Holding the hand-carved walking stick by the wooden shaft, he glanced back and forth between it and James. "Or maybe *this* has something to do with it."

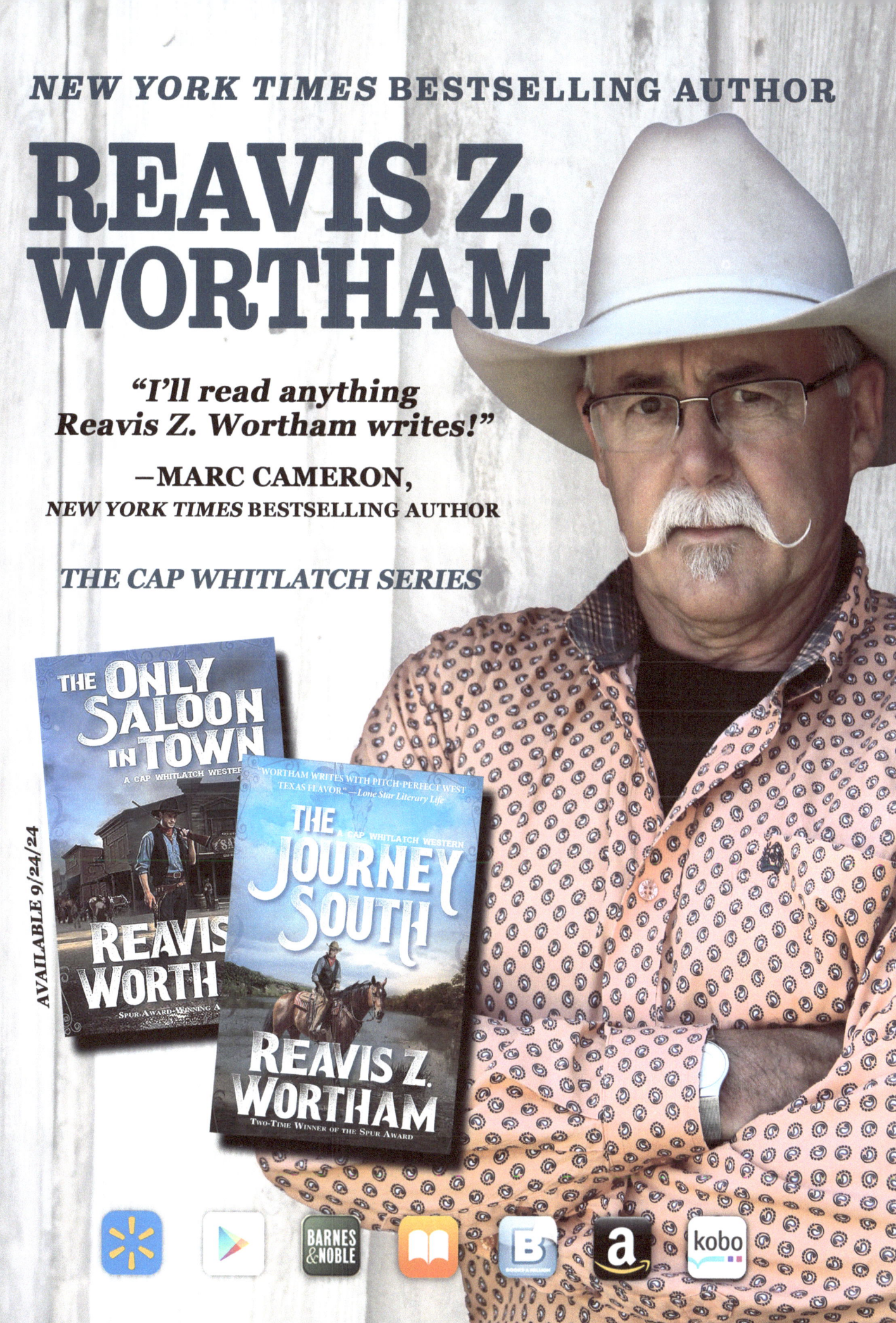

"Your cane?"

"The head is made from a meteorite. The shaft was made by a Sioux friend of mine."

James grunted as a steel-tipped arrow suddenly appeared in his upper thigh. The pain shocked him into immobility for a moment and he gasped for breath.

Deadly projectiles flew through the thick dust churned by hundreds of combatants. As the warriors fired arrows and bullets at the milling, nearly panic-stricken soldiers, horses and men alike screamed in fear and agony.

Most of the troopers around James were wounded. Many had been hit two or three times. Pulling the shaft free from his leg would gain nothing, so he concentrated on fighting for his life. Hissing from the pain, he crouched in the melee and reloaded the carbine. Levering a round into the chamber, James fired a quick shot at a warrior as he bent over to strike a downed soldier.

When he jacked the lever, the spent shell in his Spencer refused to eject. He snatched a knife from the sheath on his belt and worried the sharp edge under the hull.

"They have better weapons than we do!" One trooper shouted.

"Henry rifles." James looked down at his work. "My god, some of them are killing us with new rifles and I have *this!*"

A shot went off almost directly in James' ear. He went instantly deaf.

"He's making his way toward where Custer fell," Hollis pointed with the cane. The head had cooled somewhat, but felt strangely alive in his fist. "There, in the enclosure. They're completely surrounded now, with no hope for reinforcements."

He continued to hold Katie's arm to keep the sobbing woman away from her potentially dangerous husband. "The hostiles had complete control of this entire area," he said with an excited gleam in his eye. "By this time, most of the fighting occurred right here around us, but the battle was lost as skirmish lines fell apart and many of the men ran for their lives."

Katie looked down at Hollis with tear-filled eyes. "I don't know what to do." She pleaded with her eyes, breaking his heart. "I can't help him."

"At this point, nothing could help any of them," Hollis replied.

Thunder rumbled over the rolling hills in the distance. The wind freshened and the line of dark clouds finally approached Custer Hill.

Dead and dying men lay scattered over the hillside. Around him, the bluecoats went down before the relentless onslaught of red bodies as they butchered their victims. Sheer numbers allowed many of the warriors to stop fighting and count coup, the act of physically touching one's enemy. They began to strip the already dead soldiers.

He stumbled into the midst of the surviving 7th Cavalry soldiers. "Shoot the horses! Shoot the horses and use them for cover!" he shouted, firing into his mount's head, just behind the ear. The battle-maddened gelding dropped instantly into a heap. He dove behind the still trembling body. A bullet thudded into the animal's side and James felt the shock through the dead flesh.

Around the battlefield, the survivors shouted the same orders and killed their horses to use as barricades. Lying prone across the carcass, James looked back over his shoulder, trying to determine how far their defensive ring extended. He couldn't see anything but smoke and dust. It felt if they were fighting in a cyclone. Troopers stood, knelt, or sat, and fired their weapons from wherever they happened to be. Dead men and horses lay everywhere, their bodies bristling with arrows.

To James' left a young soldier crouched low behind the flesh barricade, frantically using his penknife to pry a stuck cartridge from the chamber of his carbine. The new 1873 Springfields were jamming on the defenders, causing a shocking number of men to die while trying to clear the fouled breech of their weapons.

Boston Custer raised up from behind a kicking horse and was slammed backward from the force of a large caliber rifle.

"Boston's down!" James shouted in grief and anger. Another good friend for many years was gone. "Where's George? He got us into this!"

"Boston," Hollis repeated after James. "He's talking about Boston Custer, George Custer's broth-

er. By God, if I only had the opportunity to speak to him for a moment. This man is a living textbook, right here before my eyes, and I can only see a minute portion of what's going on." He paced in frustration. "Will one of George Custer's men actually murder his own commander?" he asked more to himself than to anyone else. "James, where did Custer fall?"

Katie's voice was full of rage. "My husband's hurt and bleeding, you bastard, and all you can think about is *history?*"

"We don't know if he's really wounded or in any real danger," Hollis countered. "This may simply be some sort of psychic manifestation that will clear up in a moment. Right now he's watching those events unfold in what he perceives as real time!"

A national park ranger for fifteen years and the victim of too many fatty foods, Starnes puffed up the hill. He stopped on the hot walkway trying to regain his breath. "We've called the ambulance. It's on its way. What's happening up here?"

Hollis silently pointed his cane at the kneeling man on the hillside. Face tight with terror, James crouched in the grass amid the white markers, his blood-soaked leg stretched out before him. Dust drifted lazily from underneath his scuffed sneakers. His hair in disarray, leaning his left elbow on an adjacent marker, James sighted down an invisible gun barrel, and squeezed with his index finger.

"What's he doing?" asked Starnes in amazement.

"He's fighting alongside Custer," Hollis said.

"How'd he get hurt?"

"I suspect some kind of stigmata."

"You're crazy!"

"No, I'm not," Hollis answered and finally making up his mind, rushed up to James. He knelt before the man and watched in awe as James' blank eyes stared completely through his body. "Mister! Mister! Lady, what did you say his name was?"

"James," Katie answered numbly.

"*James!* Answer me! Tell me what do you see? What's happening?"

Hollis had the odd sensation that he'd somehow broken the third wall and talking to a television character while the action swirled around them.

Katie covered her face with her hands, weeping in fear and frustration. "Do something. Please, somebody help my husband!"

The onlookers continued to hold their phones out to record.

James' face was streaked with sweat and dirt. His eyes filled with tears from the acrid gunsmoke that lay like a fog amid the scrambling figures around him. It was all happening so fast.

Beside him, a trooper named Sam gasped with pain. James glanced at him and saw an arrow protruding from the man's side. Before he could do anything more than realize what had happened, a Cheyenne leaped over the horse and stabbed Sam with a home-made knife. With a grunt, James swung his empty carbine like a club against the warrior's head. The dying man fell over Sam's twitching body. James dropped beside them on the blood-soaked ground.

Members of different tribes surrounded the terrified men, pouring round after round into the area. Battle-hardened veterans of numerous fights, the Indians took advantage of every scrap of cover, even lying flat behind the bodies of fallen soldiers. They shot, reloaded and advanced as relentlessly as a flood.

It was every man for himself. James used his carbine as a club until the stock shattered. He pulled Sam's rifle from the ground beside his old friend and fired only one round before the weapon froze up. Sobbing from fear, he snatched Sam's revolver from its holster, knowing he was running out of time. He wished for one of the cutlasses they'd packed with the supplies, at the rear.

Something heavy slammed into his shoulder and he dropped under the force of the slug.

The crowd grew at the bottom of Custer Hill. Newcomers were quickly informed of the activities on the hill and speculation ran from demonic possession to an overdose of drugs. Two harried rangers down below kept everyone back while they waited for the ambulance. From their vantage point, the figure on the hill looked like nothing more than a small boy playing cowboys and Indians.

However, amid the cluster of marble markers, James fought for his life.

Katie tried to console her husband, but he didn't acknowledge her existence, nor that of the other two men with her. He leaned on the ground and ducked his head occasionally, dodging some unseen person or projectile. Tears poured from his eyes, making muddy streaks in the dust on his face.

Suddenly he turned uphill, towards the monument and its small clump of markers enclosed by the iron fence. He half stood, swinging both hands in an arc, much like that of a person swinging a baseball bat. He sagged to the ground. With a violent wrench, he flew onto his back. The three observers saw a gout of blood erupt from his side.

James doubled over with pain and swung his fist against an invisible opponent.

Hollis nodded. He knew what was happening. "The fighting has become hand to hand. The end is near."

The lone figure pulled himself up to one knee, picked up an invisible object from the ground, and lunged around in a short arc. "Oh, Sam," he said in a whisper. James recoiled, screamed like a panther, and fell amid the long grass.

The firing on the hillside had become sporadic. Most of the troopers were down, dead or dying. A few made a desperate break for the ravines, pursued by groups of warriors. Their end was brutal and bloody. Only a handful remained as a cohesive unit, all of them grouped around Custer, near the crest of the hill. As each soldier died, the warriors increased pressure on the surviving defenders.

James lay still amid the grass, surrounded by dead horses and men. The attackers advanced, then moved past his bleeding body to fire upon the last remaining cavalrymen. He tried to move his left arm, but it hung limply at his side.

He pulled himself to one knee and picked up the

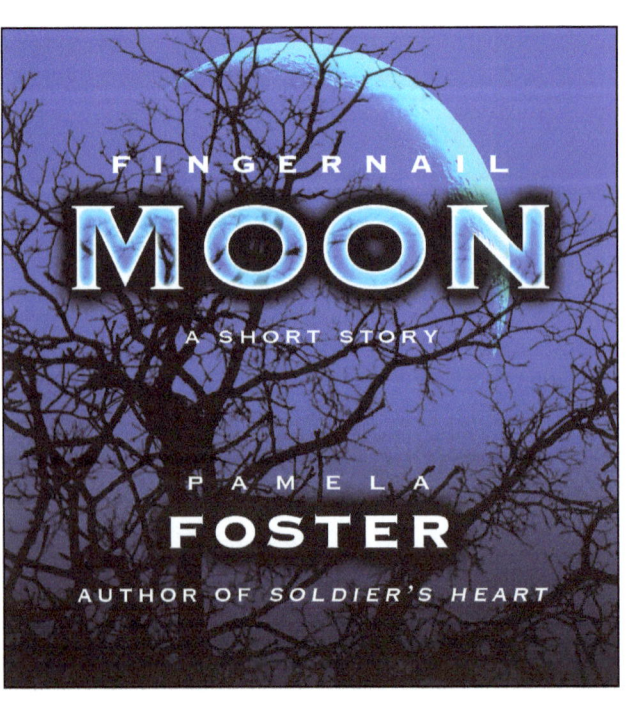

only weapon nearby, a fallen arrow. A Cheyenne warrior launched himself at the wounded man with a shrill war cry.

James swung the arrow in a short, vicious arc, catching the Indian in the abdomen. Someone hit him in the back and the force of the blow turned James around in time to see George Custer's head jerk from the impact of a bullet.

"*Colonel!*" he shouted, knowing now that all was lost. From the corner of his eye James saw the man who would kill him. The painted Cheyenne rose from behind the body of a cavalry horse and raised a shiny Henry rifle to his shoulder.

A thought flashed through James' mind. *This has been going on so long that some of them had time to put on war paint.* Again seated on the ground and wounded for the third time, he was weaponless. He raised his head slightly, staring into the huge black bore. Gunsmoke blew across the ground like a fog.

"Oh, no."

———— • ••• • ————

On her knees beside her husband, long hair flying and in sweaty tangles, Katie alternately sobbed and shouted at him. "Jimmy, honey, just be still. We'll get help soon."

James sat up.

Hollis had given up trying to calm the hysterical woman. He moved forward for a closer look at the man heaving for breath. James was covered in blood and dirt. No wounds were visible under the wetness, but pain caused James to hold his left side and thigh.

"The battle is almost over," Hollis said, leaning on his cane. "See how calm he's become. They are almost overrun, and he sees his own death. James, what happened to Custer?"

"Colonel!" James shouted, looking back toward Custer's marker.

Hollis recoiled from the sudden shout and stepped back. "He sees him," he whispered in elation. "Custer's still alive at this point." He pointed his black cane at the markers on Custer Hill. "How did he fall, son? By his own hand?" He had to know, and mercilessly prodded the wounded man who heard or saw nothing in their world. "Please tell me."

"Leave him *alone!*" Katie turned, furious.

"Oh, no," James whispered, eyes staring into the past. "Oh, God...."

With a convulsive jerk, his head snapped back and he landed hard on the ground, hitting a marker with enough force to snap it in two. Katie shrieked and fell back into the grass. Her husband lay like a broken puppet, unmoving, on top of the white stone turning red from the blood pouring from his wounded chest. Though no discernable wound was in view it covered his shirt, and formed a puddle in the dust beneath him.

Katie went to pieces. In horror she threw herself across the still body and held her dead husband's face in her hands. Sightless eyes stared at the clear blue Montana sky.

"The battle is over," Hollis concluded. His shoulders slumped at the realization that his questions would never be answered.

———— • ••• • ————

The sound of gunfire had almost completely died away. The victorious warriors looted and stripped the bodies of their victims. They slashed saddlebags open and pawed through their contents. Many of the victors donned the bloody clothes of their enemies and shouted their excitement to the sky.

Captain Thomas B. Weir led an advance company of reinforcements to the top of a hill a mile downstream and halted his column. They sat atop their blowing mounts in shock at the sight of so many hostiles. The firing had stopped, and they could see nothing of Custer and his men. They were soon joined by Reno and Benteen.

The columns had no more than merged when they too were attacked by a large force of hostiles. Reno ordered a withdrawal, and the seven companies fought their way back to entrench themselves under the riverbank for a long siege. There would be no help for Custer and his men.

It had arrived too late.

The Indians' fury was so intense that instead of simply killing Custer's troopers and scalping them, the maddened warriors mutilated the dead after stripping them of their bloodied blue clothing.

James' nude body lay where it had fallen, surrounded by dead horses, and the bloody bodies of his former comrades. Indian women, newly arrived from the massive village below, moved amid the carnage. They emulated their men in the mutilations of their enemies, chopping and hacking at the naked white bodies until their fury abated.

Clutching a white man's trading knife, an elderly Sioux woman moved toward James' as-yet un-touched corpse.

The hillside quieted in the late summer evening. The long grass waved in the freshening breeze. Two grim-faced Montana state troopers question Katie not far from her husband's still body.

Hollis stood, watching the trio that turned away from the blood-soaked corpse. He looked down at the body. It rested on an overturned marker which simply read, *Unknown 7th Cavalry Trooper.*

Thunderheads blocked the sun. Lightning frac-tured the boiling clouds and thunder rumbled across the low hills. A rain-cooled wind rushed across the grass threatening to snatch Hollis' hat.

He pulled it down tighter and watched as Starnes turned his back on the dead man. Hollis frowned. "I wonder if this was really some form of psychic pro-jection, or a man experiencing the most horrible form of reincarnate memory?" he mused, more to himself than to his coworker.

Kneeling beside James, the paramedics opened their cases of equipment. One ripped his shirt open, looking for the source of the blood while another attached leads, though the man's eyes had already glazed and were starting to dry.

"I don't know, I'm just glad it's over." Starnes shook his head. "That poor woman."

"They need to get her farther away from here, ac-cording to what all I've seen here today." Hollis said.

"Why?"

"Because up to this point we've witnessed a faith-ful reproduction of what happened on this day."

"So?"

Hollis looked up in disgust at the man standing nearly six foot six. "You really should read the his-tory books you sell, Starnes." Lightning flashed and thunder rumbled closer, washing over them. "Now the mutilations begin."

Fat raindrops made small explosions in the dust. It splattered and steamed on the hot walking trail. More and more drops fell, spotting Hollis' hat.

Hollis took Katie's arm, surprising the troopers. "Believe me when I tell you this. You need to come with me now, and don't look back."

"I can't leave him."

"He's gone, and I beg you to come with me."

The oldest of the two troopers shook his head.

"We're not finished talking with her buddy. You need to stay out of this."

The Sioux woman handed the butcher knife to her husband, who had lost his own sometime during the vicious fight. He held it to the clearing sky and asked his spirits to watch him take this symbol of his tribe's victory over the white man. The wind blew threw his long hair and brought the scent of death to his nostrils.

He knelt to take the scalp to hang in his lodge. She would do the woman's work.

As the wind tousled James' shaggy hair, his cooling body suddenly jerked from side to side. Starnes stumbled back in terror. The usually cold, hardened paramedics froze. Hollis looked up at the three white faced men as Katie screamed in horror.

Thick red blood flowed from beneath James' shaggy hair. His limbs rose into the air as if by magic to fall limply to the ground. Of its own accord, the body rolled facedown.

Then, his head raised up and bent completely backward, his mouth hanging open.

Hollis turned and walked slowly downhill to his car through the increasing rain. He knew what was next.

He didn't have to watch.

Katie's horrified scream welled from deep within her soul. Starnes turned and ran as if the very hounds of hell were on his heels as the paramedics stumbled back in horror.

"Jimmy!"

And the blood, the blood flowed with the rain once again into the thirsty Montana ground.

**LOOK FOR
REAVIS Z. WORTHAM'S
"SECOND ANNIVERSARY"
ONLY IN THE DECEMBER ISSUE
OF *SADDLEBAG DISPATCHES***

THE AUTHOR

New York Times *bestselling author* **Reavis Z. Wortham** *is the recipient of numerous Will Rogers Medallion Awards, the Western Writers of America Spur Award, and the Independent Book Publishers Association's Benjamin Franklin Award. He has been a newspaper columnist and magazine contributor since 1988, penning over 2,000 columns and articles, and has been the Humor Editor for* Texas Fish and Game Magazine *for the past 26 years. When he's not writing, Reavis is also an avid outdoorsman, loves to travel, camp, canoe, backback, hunt, and fish. He and his wife, Shana, live in Northeast Texas.*

the Silver Dollar

I swing the doors expecting a waft
of stale beer and rancid sweat; shabby,
not shiny like a new brass spittoon.

But the Silver Dollar Saloon fairly gleams.
It's the place to be seen for all the wrong reasons,
iniquity's playground, an outlaw's oasis.

Yet, empty it echoes—a hollow shell and
vacant vessel of dreams deferred where
trouble dogs each patron's steps,

my steps as well. Alone, I sit at piano
plunking out notes, a scrap of a song I
cobbled together those nights I barely slept;

a shadow of why I came west.
It's my shot at redemption—showcase
my talents, find purpose banging out

tunes for miners, scofflaws, women
of the night. Rumors tell of epic fights
and gunplay is a given.

"Mr. Harris?" A lady enters—all business.
"Yes," I say, embarrassed, standing.
"Can you start tonight?" She asks,

not probing for training or skill. "Sure!"
I stammer, thrilled until I spot the sign, and
it's clear why I've just been hired at a glance.

The reason for my swift election is manifest.
"Please don't shoot the piano player," the sign reads,
"He is doing his best."

poetry by

DAVID CAMERON

Elizabeth McCourt "Baby Doe" Tabor

A MATCHLESS BRIDE

Elizabeth McCourt—better known to history as "Baby Doe" Tabor—has been called the original "Gold Digger." The truth, however, is far more complicated... and tragic.

STORY BY
CHRIS ENSS

A shabby-looking prospector emerged from the dark, weathered entrance of the Matchless Mine in Leadville, Colorado, and straightened his stooped shoulders. He dropped his pickax beside a rusty ore cart and rolled and lit a cigarette. His weary face was set in a scowl as he surveyed the mountains rising precipitously around the well-worked diggings. The smoke from the chimney of a nearby shack rose into the air and drifted toward him. As he watched the smoke swirl and evaporate into a vibrant blue sky, an elderly woman charged out the building into the cold. Seventy-five-year-old Baby Doe Tabor was dressed in layers of torn, threadbare garments that dragged along the ground as she walked. The woolen hat on her head sat just above her azure eyes, and she wore a ragged leather boot on one foot and a cluster of rags bound by a strip of material on the other. As she made her way toward the miner, a slight smile stretched across her hollowed cheeks. "What did you find?" she asked him hopefully. The man shook his head.

A flash of irritation erupted in her eyes but quickly dissipated as she scanned the colorful horizon.

Baby Doe's late husband was Horace Tabor, the Silver King. He made and lost a fortune in mining. At one time the country around her was swarming with workers who pulled millions out of the diggings where she lived. It had been more than thirty years since the mine had yielded anything but dust and rock. Baby Doe stayed on the property because of a deathbed promise she had made to Horace. "Never let the Matchless go if I die, Baby. It will make millions again when silver comes back."

She had implicit faith in her husband's judgment and in the Matchless, but she was alone in her belief. The only men who would agree to venture into the mine in 1929 were drifters or one-time hopeful prospectors. Baby Doe persuaded them to dig in exchange for shares in the potential find.

The disheveled miner looked around, gathered up his few belongings, and tramped through the snow out of camp. Baby Doe's eyes followed the prospec-

Baby Doe Tabor was born Elizabeth Bondual McCourt in 1854 to an Irish immigrant family of modest means in Oshkosh, Wisconsin. She was one of 14 children.

Baby Doe's first husband, William Harvey Doe, Jr., was heir to a wealthy mining dynasty. They divorced in early 1880, after she delivered a baby boy that was rumored not to have been his.

tor until he disappeared into a grove of pine trees. "Hang on to the Matchless," she whispered to herself. "Horace told me it would make millions again."

The poverty and degradation that Baby Doe experienced in her last few years on earth were in direct contrast to the time she spent as the wife of a mining mogul. Born Elizabeth Bonduel McCourt in 1854 to a family of moderate means in Oshkosh, Wisconsin, she maneuvered her way around Colorado's high society until she met a man who would liberate her from her lackluster background. Her parents were Irish immigrants from County Armagh who had escaped the turmoil in their own country and initially settled in Utica, New York. They had fourteen children, many of whom died in infancy.

Elizabeth's angelic face, golden locks, and striking blue eyes set her apart from the other children. Her father, a tailor and the owner of a clothing store, doted on his daughter. Often, he brought the child to work with him, and customers raved about the little girl's beauty. On more than one occasion, businessmen would ask if her father wasn't afraid "someone

would steal her away." Baby Doe thrived on the attention of the male clientele and learned at a young age how to manipulate them into giving her whatever she asked for.

Elizabeth's stunning looks continued to improve as she got older. At fifteen she was five-foot-two, with long, blonde hair, a robust figure, and sun-kissed porcelain skin. Men of all ages hovered around her like frantic bees at a hive. She received several marriage proposals but refused the sincere suitors in favor of pursuing a career on the stage. She was also determined to wed a man of great wealth.

The bold teenager dismissed the admonitions of her brothers and sisters to behave sensibly, abandon the notion of acting, and settle down. Although there were a few respected actresses in the late 1870s, for the most part women thespians were considered to be a slight step above soiled doves. Elizabeth didn't care what "polite society" thought of her. She was driven by an independent spirit her father had nurtured and her dreams of fame and money.

In December 1876, Elizabeth participated in a

skating contest hosted by the Congregational church. Boldly sporting a skirt that revealed her calves, she gracefully twirled through a routine, exciting the male onlookers and enraging female audience members. At the end of the competition, Elizabeth had captured a first-place ribbon and the heart of handsome socialite Harvey Doe.

Elizabeth was attracted to Harvey for a variety of reasons, not the least of which was the fact that he was heir to a wealthy mining dynasty. William Harvey Doe, Sr. owned a substantial number of mining claims in Colorado.

Doe also owned a lumber business in Oshkosh and had returned with his son to check on his investment at the same time the skating event was being held. Harvey was quite smitten with Elizabeth, and her parents found the young man charming and personable. Mrs. Doe, however, objected to her son spending time with a girl she considered to be a "daring exhibitionist." Harvey disregarded his mother's complaints about Elizabeth's parents' financial standing and her view of the girl as a "social climber." Instead, he proclaimed his love for Elizabeth and proposed marriage.

Elizabeth's recollection of Harvey's proposal was that it was the first such invitation that had "moved her deeply." According to what she shared with a friend in the 1930s, Harvey was different from the other men in town who sought her affections. "He would come over to play the piano for all my family in the evening, seeming to love us all. He would join in the general fun without trying to monopolize me, like other men."

On June 27, 1877, Harvey and Elizabeth were married at her parents' home. Immediately after the ceremony the couple boarded a train bound for Denver, Colorado. Harvey Doe Sr. planned for his son to take over the mining property in nearby Central City.

Once the newlyweds had finished honeymooning they would embark on a life in the gold fields of Pike's Peak. Elizabeth's father-in-law made arrangements for her and her new husband to reside at a posh hotel called the Teller House. The inn was elegant and decorated with the finest European furniture and rugs.

Due to her stunning good looks, men of all ages hovered around Elizabeth like frantic bees from a hive. She became adept at manipulating those attentions at a very young age, and was a woman who generally got whatever she wanted.

Elizabeth was enthusiastic about her new home, and the luxurious living conditions were precisely what she had envisioned for herself. She was also enchanted with the activity at the Fourth of July Mine where Harvey worked. The sights and sounds of the miners descending into the diggings and reappearing with chunks of earth that might be gold stirred her desire for outrageous wealth.

At the time Elizabeth believed the opportunity to amass a fortune could only be realized through Harvey's efforts. Doe Sr. wanted his son to earn his profits and reputation the same way he had, by working in every area of the mining development, from collecting ore to operating the stamp mill. Harvey, however, wasn't interested in manual labor and preferred anyone else to do the work. Elizabeth was far too ambitious to leave the future of her financial status to a lazy husband and quickly took command of their property and limited income.

After moving their belongings out of the expensive hotel where they had been living and into a small cottage, she organized a crew of Cornish miners to work at the Fourth of July Mine.

Some of the prominent town leaders with whom Elizabeth was acquainted advised her to have a shaft dug into the mine before winter fully set in. Joseph Thatcher, president of the First National Bank, and Bill Bush, owner of the Teller House, were two men whose opinion she respected the most. They urged her to do the digging herself if necessary.

Motivated by his wife's drive, Harvey finally bent to her will and joined in the work. The first shaft the pair sank proved to be unsuccessful as there was no high-grade ore in that section of the mine. Elizabeth was not going to give up. She convinced her husband and their employees to drive a second shaft. Dressed in one of Harvey's old shirts, a pair of dungarees, and a cap, Elizabeth toiled alongside the men.

For a moment it seemed that Elizabeth and Harvey were striving together for a common goal. The pair diligently worked their claim, leaving the mine only to collect supplies in town. Historians speculate that it was during one of those trips when Elizabeth acquired the name by which she would be more commonly known. Rough,

outspoken miners congregated outside saloons and mercantile, talking with one another and swapping stories about their prospecting adventures. As Elizabeth passed by the men on her way to purchase food and various odds and ends, one man called out, "There goes a beautiful baby." The handle suited her diminutive frame and delicate features, and from that time on she was referred to by most as "Baby Doe."

Despite their valiant efforts, the Fourth of July Mine never yielded the gold necessary to fund continued diggings. Harvey borrowed money to keep the operation going, but it was ultimately shut down. He went to work for another miner and abandoned his dream of striking it rich. Baby Doe held onto her aspiration of becoming a "woman of great means." She was determined to realize that dream with or without Harvey.

Baby voiced her disappointment to Harvey about his lack of business sense and drive and he drank a lot as a way to cope with her criticism. They spent a great deal of time apart, he at the saloons and she at a fabric and clothing store called Sandelowsky-Pelton. Baby's father-in-law returned to the area to try to help the pair get beyond their financial difficulties. He sold the Fourth of July Mine and settled their outstanding debts, but it couldn't save Baby and Harvey's relationship. By the summer of 1878, the two were leading virtually separate lives.

Baby spent a great deal of time with Jake Sandelowsky, the distinguished and handsome co-owner of the store she frequented. Her actions scandalized the town and infuriated Harvey. She defended Jake to her husband, making mention of the financial support the businessman had given her.

She wasn't shy about reminding Harvey that what she wanted most in life was financial independence. Desperate to save his marriage, Harvey worked extra shifts to provide his wife with a quality of life that would make her happy. Jake seized the time during his absence to shower Baby with attention. He was her

"THIS IS THE FIRST INSTANCE WHERE A LADY, AND SUCH SHE IS, HAS MANAGED A MINING PROPERTY. THE MINE IS DOING VERY WELL AND PRODUCES SOME RICH ORE."

—OCTOBER 1878 NEWS ARTICLE ON HARVEY AND ELIZABETH DOE'S COLORADO GOLD MINE

frequent escort to a local theater and saloon called the Shoo-Fly. Jake tried to persuade her to leave Harvey and marry him, but he didn't possess the riches Baby hoped to make her own. She decided to remain married to Harvey until a truly better offer came along.

News that gold had been played out in Central City rapidly filtered through the Shoo-Fly clientele in November 1878. Silver veins had been located around the area, however, generating a surge of eager mine investors. Among the men with the capital to sink numerous shafts and extract the mineral was Horace Tabor. He had become rich with similar mines in Leadville and hoped to duplicate his success in Central City. Baby knew of Horace and had caught sight of the entrepreneur at the Shoo-Fly but had not been formally introduced. Before the possibility of a meeting was realized, Baby learned she was pregnant.

For several months Harvey was nowhere to be found and could not be told that he had a child on the way. There was some speculation that he had sneaked away to a nearby mining camp to avoid the humiliation of his wife's questionable behavior with another man. Harvey Doe, Sr. located his son and brought him home to Baby.

On July 13, 1879, Baby gave birth to a boy. The child was stillborn, and both parents were crushed. Harvey was further devastated by the rumors circulating that the child might not have been his. Baby was discouraged by Harvey's inability to pay any of the medical bills or make arrangements for the infant's burial. Jake Sandelowsky came to Baby's rescue and took care of matters. The Does divorced in early 1880, and Baby left Central City for Leadville with Jake.

Jake and Baby lived at separate hotels. Although he had planned for their relationship to blossom, Baby had other ideas for her life. Everywhere she went in Leadville she heard stories about Horace Tabor. Tales of his wealth and how he achieved it, his benevolence to average citizens, his term as first mayor and postmaster of the city, his time as governor of Colorado, and his reputation as owner-operator of the Leadville Bank excited the industrious beauty from Wisconsin. She set her sights on meeting and befriending Horace. Jake would be a means to an end.

"He must be close to fifty," a friendly Leadville resident shared with Baby when she asked to know more about Horace. "They say he's worth $8 million and likes to play poker in the saloons around town after the theater lets out. He was one of the early prospectors out here, came in an ox-wagon across the plains in '59. An awful easygoing sort of fellow."

Baby listened intently to every detail of Tabor's life that the talkative local shared. She learned that the mine owner panned out his first millions in the gold stampede on Colorado's Gregory Gulch, that he grubstaked two miners who discovered a wealth of silver at the Little Pittsburgh Mine, and that he used the money from his investments to buy a claim called the Matchless Mine. She ignored the details about his longstanding marriage to a refined woman who possessed a considerable strength of character and focused instead on the name of the restaurant Horace frequented. It was not a coincidence that she ended up at the same establishment the "Silver King" visited during intermission at the Opera House.

"He was over six feet tall with large, regular features and a drooping mustache," Baby recounted years later to a young woman who spent time with her at her famous mine.

Known as the "Silver King," Horace Tabor was not only Leadville's founding father, but one of the richest men in the world during the 1880s. He would marry Baby Doe in 1883.

Leadville's famed Matchless Mine made Horace Tabor a wealthy man. It would also, one day, be his ticket back to the poor house. The shack Baby Doe Tabor lived and died in following his death can be seen in the foreground.

"Dark in coloring, at this time his hair had begun to recede a bit on his forehead and was turning gray at the temples. Always very well dressed, his personality seemed to fill any room he stepped into."

Horace noticed Baby almost from the moment he entered the eatery. They exchanged polite glances, and eventually one of his business associates invited Baby to join them at their table. Horace ordered champagne and regaled the captivated Baby with tales of his ventures west. "It was the merriest night of my life," Baby later confessed. By the end of the evening, she was convinced she was in love with Horace and he was equally as infatuated with her. He promised to support Baby monetarily, and, as his first order of business, he wrote out a check for $5,000 to help ease Jake Sandelowsky's soon-to-be broken heart. Funds were also provided for Baby to purchase herself a new wardrobe.

Within twenty-four hours of meeting the businessman and appointed governor, Baby had become Mr. Horace Tabor's mistress. They tried to keep their relationship a secret. Tabor would sneak away from various civic events to spend time with Baby at her hotel room, and when she appeared in public with him, she hid her face under large hats and long veils.

When Horace moved his mining offices from Leadville to Denver, Baby followed him. Friends and business associates aware of the scandalous romance tried to persuade him to end the affair for his family's sake and for the sake of his political future. Horace refused. The longer their relationship lasted, the bolder their behavior became. They traveled back and forth to Leadville together in private railcars and openly attended parties at various stops along the way.

Horace had a special box for Baby at the Opera House he had built. According to Baby Doe, at the opening of the Tabor Grand Opera House on September 5, 1881, she and Horace eyed one another fondly during the performance. Horace's wife, Augusta, was eventually made aware of the affair, but refused to divorce her husband; she considered divorce a social and moral disgrace. After close to two years of pleading and negotiating with Augusta, Horace decided he and Baby Doe would exchange vows regardless of what Augusta did or didn't do.

On September 30, 1882, Baby Doe and Horace

rendezvoused in St. Louis, Missouri where they were secretly married by a justice of the peace. Although Baby was grateful that Horace had taken her to the altar, she was disappointed they weren't married in a church. "To me, a marriage was only binding when it had been sanctioned by the church and performed by a priest," Baby Doe recounted to a friend.

In January 1883, a few weeks prior to the senatorial election, in which Horace Tabor was a candidate, Augusta agreed to a legal divorce. The specifics of the settlement and circumstances leading up to Augusta's decision were front-page headlines. The highly publicized affair detracted from the real issues of the election and ultimately cost Horace a seat in the Senate. He was, however, asked to stand in for the winning candidate for a month until the newly elected official could take over his duties. It was with a heavy heart that Horace accepted the responsibility. Although he was disappointed in the vote, he found solace in the fact that he would soon be married in a church in Washington, D.C.

On March 1, 1883, Baby Doe was escorted down the aisle of St. Matthew's Catholic Church, wearing a $7,500 wedding dress and beaming at the attendees, including President Chester A. Arthur and the secretary of the interior, Henry Teller. Most of the wives of the political figures who were guests at Horace and Baby's wedding refused to be a part of the ceremony in any way. They spoke out against what they called an "unholy union" and considered it poor taste that the "shameless mistress" sent invitations at all.

Elated by the fact that they were now legally and finally married and optimistic that Horace's political career would be rejuvenated, the newlyweds returned to Denver. They moved into the Windsor Hotel and entertained celebrities and Civil War heroes in their suites. They traveled about the state, making stops at various mining camps in what the two secretly discussed as a precursor to a much larger tour coming their way once Horace became president of the United States. "First Lady of Colorado. Hell!" Horace told his wife. "You'll be first lady of the land."

In between making their elaborate plans for the future, the Tabors purchased the first of two grand, brick homes. The house featured fine furnishings, ornate verandas, driveways to the stables, and hundreds of live peacocks. An army of servants attended to the couple's every need. On July 13, 1884, Horace and Baby Doe brought their first child into the luxurious

setting. The little girl's nursery was complete with an expensive layette and a sterling silver rattle. Employees at the Matchless Mine sent the child a gold-lined cup, saucer, and spoon. Horace sent small gold medallions to many of Denver's most prominent citizens to announce the birth of his daughter.

Regardless of the opulent living conditions and numerous attempts to obtain good standing in the social community, Baby and Horace were, for the most part, ostracized. Unable to find grace and acceptance within Denver's elite, Baby decided to focus solely on Horace and his mining claims. The Matchless Mine earned the Tabors more than $1 million annually and his other investments made more than $4 million. Horace used a substantial portion of the family's income to support the Republican Party in Colorado. He had hoped the hefty contribution would help him win a nomination for governor. Baby was frustrated with the treatment he received from the party, which in her opinion had no intentions of placing his name on the ticket. "They took his money and denied him any recognition," Baby lamented.

In his quest to become a man of unlimited power, Horace invested in mines in New Mexico, Arizona, Texas, and Latin America. He purchased forestland in Honduras and he and Baby spent $2 million developing the property. Many of his risky ventures, including the Honduras project, lost millions.

Ten years after Horace and Baby were wed, the bottom fell out of the silver market, and overnight the Tabors lost all the wealth they had accumulated. "It seems incredible that it should have all happened so quickly," Baby later recalled, "but with one stroke of President Cleveland's pen, establishing the demonetization of silver, all of our mines, and particularly the Matchless, were worthless."

The Tabors were stripped of their possessions a little at a time over a six-month period. By December 1893, all that remained of their vast fortune was the Matchless Mine, and even that had to be shut down because the market would not support its yield. At sixty-three years old, Horace went to work as a regular laborer at a mine he had once owned. Baby tried to manage the minimal funds her husband brought in and cared for their two daughters. (In 1888 the Tabors had a son who lived only a few hours after his birth. Their second daughter would be born in December 1889.)

When the Tabors were unable to pay their electric

THE TABOR GRAND OPERA HOUSE, DENVER, COLO.

and water bill, workmen came to the house to shut off their utilities. Baby was livid and let her feelings be known.

"Just wait until Congress repeals the ridiculous law about the regulation of silver and the Matchless is running again," she told the workmen. "Then you'll be sorry you acted like this."

The Tabors moved into a small home on the west side of town. Denver's socialites gossiped about Horace and Baby's relationship, speculating on its

longevity now that Horace was broke. Baby heard the rumors and insisted to all who would listen that she and Horace would stay together through the difficulties and rebuild their lives on the renewed success of the Matchless Mine.

According to Baby Doe, in late February 1898, she met with Colorado senator Ed Wolcott and pleaded with him to help her and her family. Wolcott knew Baby from her days in Central City and Leadville, and he and Horace had squared off politically on several

Horace Tabor had a habit of flaunting his wealth and social status, as evidenced by his construction of both the Tabor Opera House in Leadville and the Tabor Grand Opera House in Denver. He also seemed to have enjoyed flaunting his other possessions, as well, building a special box for Baby Doe in the Tabor Grand where she could attend performances while he sat with his wife, Augusta.

hold onto the Matchless Mine. Cards and letters of condolence poured in from national and state political leaders. Flags across Colorado were ordered to be flown at half-mast. Out of respect for the years Horace had spent as a political servant in the state of Colorado thousands of mourners lined Denver's streets to see Horace's funeral procession. Seems odd that the couple descended into poverty, and he ended his career as a minor civil servant, then his death resulted in an outpouring of public grief, as if he were a major celebrity. After a graveside service, Horace was laid to rest at the Calvary Cemetery. He was later moved to the Mount Olive Cemetery when the Calvary Cemetery was dissolved.

With Horace gone, the grief-stricken Baby decided to focus her efforts on finding investors to back the reopening of the Matchless Mine. Having been unworked for many years, the mine was filled with water and initial funds were needed to pump the liquid out, stabilize the tunnels, and purchase new machinery. After an exhaustive search, Baby located a businessman who fronted her the capital to begin operations. Baby moved her fifteen- and nine-year-old daughters, Elizabeth Lillie and Rose, to Leadville where the Matchless Mine was located, and she went to work hiring help to support the dig. She encouraged her children to learn all the aspects of running the mine, from swinging a pick to hauling ore to the surface, but her eldest daughter refused to ever have any part of it.

When the Matchless Mine failed to produce any significant gold, the investor withdrew his support, forcing Baby to search for other backers. This scenario was repeated time and time again. She refused to give up or sell the property outright, and for three decades she steadfastly maintained that riches were buried deep within the walls of the mine. Her children grew up and moved on, but Baby remained in Colorado in a dilapidated cabin located at the site. "I shall never let the Matchless go," she told a banker she was asking to back the mine operations. "Not while there is a breath in my body to find a way to fight for it."

occasions. It was because of Senator Wolcott's efforts that Horace was appointed as Denver's postmaster. The job paid $3,500 a year and helped restore a modicum of dignity to Horace's life. Baby was overjoyed. She believed it was an indication that their luck had changed and that their old life would soon be restored, but harder times were yet to come.

On April 3, 1899, Horace died from an acute appendicitis attack. Baby was at his side when he passed away. With his last breath he encouraged his wife to

Last known photograph of Baby Doe Tabor, standing in the door to her shack at the Matchless Mine in 1933. She would freeze to death in the same shack during a blizzard in February, 1935.

When the money ran out, Baby worked the mine alone. Occasionally she sold off a few of Horace's valuables (such as watch fobs, and cufflinks) to buy food and clothing. Both of her daughters, tired of their mother's obsession with the Matchless, distanced themselves from her. Elizabeth Lillie married and moved to Wisconsin; Rose ("Silver Dollar," as her mother called her) drifted to Chicago where she was murdered at the age of thirty-five. With the exception of a neighbor and benevolent mine engineer and his daughter, Baby Doe lived the life of a recluse, visited by no one. The journal she kept in her later days describes how lonely she was and how much she missed Horace and her children. An entry she made on April 19, 1925, reads "Holy Thursday. Dreamed of being with Tabor, Lillie, and Silver and seeing rich ore in No. 6 shaft."

In 1932, a movie about the life and career of Horace Tabor, entitled *Silver Dollar,* premiered in Denver, Colorado. It generated new interest in the Tabor legacy and in his affair with Baby Doe. Press agents and historians sought out Baby to interview her and persuade her to tell her story in exchange for a fee, but she refused. She maintained that any money worth making, the Matchless Mine would ultimately supply.

On February 20, 1935, Baby Doe Tabor, the woman once known throughout the West as the "Silver Queen," died. A severe blizzard blanketed Leadville with snow and ice, and Baby, who was suffering from pneumonia, was unable to keep a fire going in her cabin. Her neighbors became concerned about her when they didn't see any smoke emanating from the chimney. Her frozen body was found lying on the floor of her rundown cabin, her arms outstretched at her side.

Funeral services for Baby Doe were held at a church in Leadville, and her remains were then taken to Denver to be buried next to Horace. The headline across the front of the *Rocky Mountain News* read, "Baby Doe Dies at Her Post Guarding Matchless Mine." The article that followed reported on the squalid conditions of her home and noted that only a "small cache of food and a few sticks of firewood" were found on the premises.

Among the personal belongings she left behind were seventeen trunks filled with a variety of memorabilia, including scrapbooks, old newspapers, and a silver Tiffany tea set. Sue Bonnie, the daughter of the

The 1932 Edward G. Robinson film Silver Dollar about the life and career of Horace Tabor generated new interest in Baby Doe's relationship with the late Silver King.

mine engineer who called on Baby from 1927 until her death, used Baby Doe's scrapbook and journal entries, along with their documented conversations, to write a series of articles. From January to May of 1938, the articles about Baby Doe and her recollections of life as a miner and her marriage to Horace Tabor were published in *True Story* magazine.

Baby Doe Tabor was eighty-one years old when she passed away. The onetime heiress to a vast silver empire had remained faithful to her husband's parting advice for thirty-six years. Baby Doe was buried next to her husband at Mount Olivet Cemetery in Jefferson County, Colorado.

Chris Enss *is a* New York Times *bestselling author who has written about the women of the Old West for more than thirty years. She's penned more than fifty books on the subject and been honored with nine* Will Rogers Medallion Awards, *two Elmer Kelton Book Awards, an Oklahoma Center for the Book Award, three* Foreword Review Magazine *Book Awards, and the Laura Downing Journalism Award.*

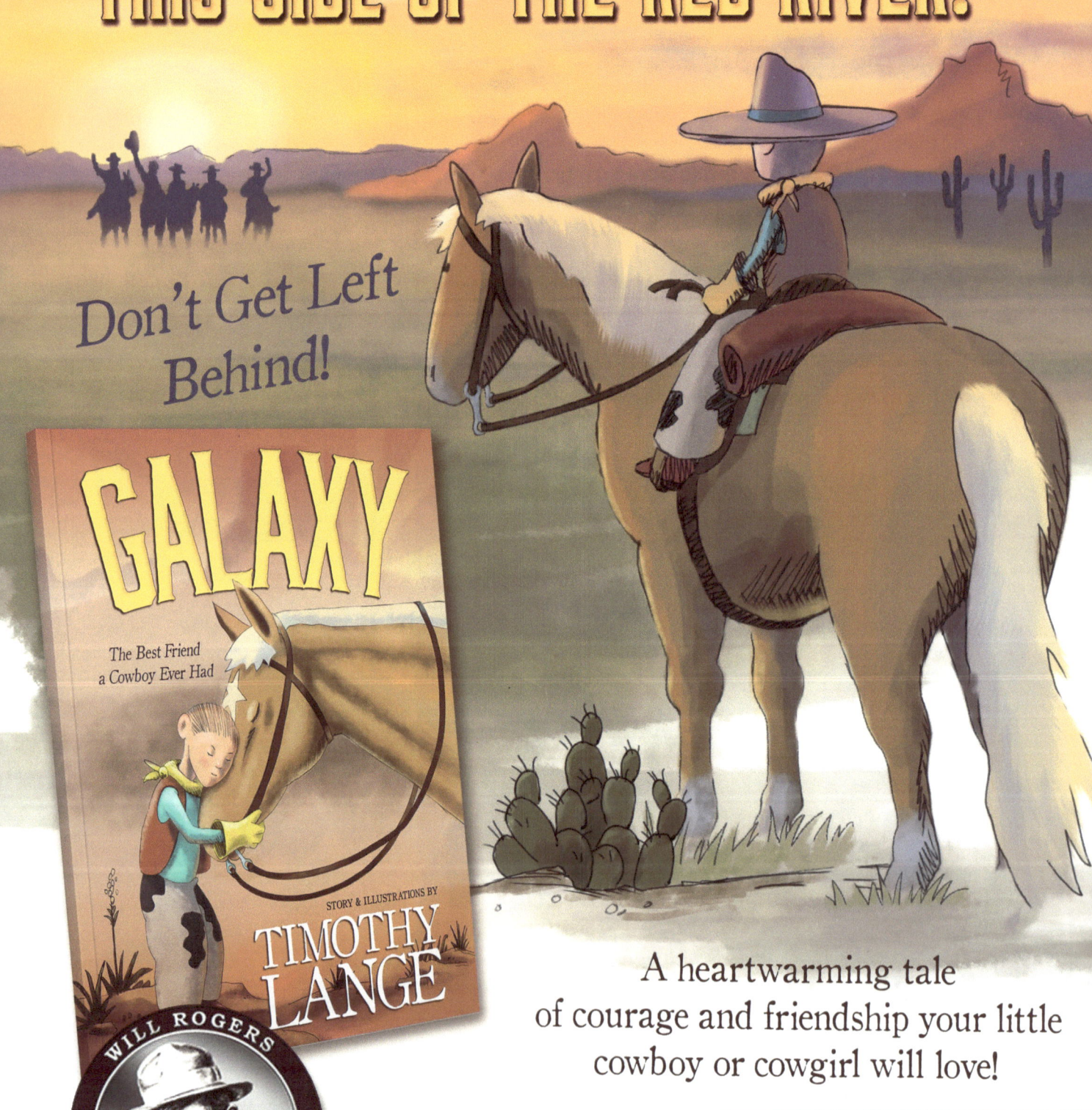

KIMBERLY BURNS

FORTUNATE MAN

A SHORT STORY

Broken Nose Scotty reclined against the bars of cell #3 of the Lake County jail. Both his mouth and his head felt clogged with cotton. He wasn't sure how or why he had ended up spending the night in jail. He and about thirty-five of the town's citizenry currently resided in the eight cells located in the basement of the new Harrison Avenue courthouse. Actually, prisoners occupied only seven of the cells, as cell #8 was haunted by the ghost of a man who'd hung himself there earlier in the year.

He patted his pockets, empty as usual. No doubt he'd be fined for public drunkenness. He had no idea how he'd pay for it, but he wasn't worried. Something would come up. Scotty was an optimist at heart.

Looking around at the three fellas sharing the cell, Scotty didn't recognize any of his new roommates. However, he decided time would pass more quickly with friendly conversation.

"When," he began because Scotty did not think in discouraging terms such as 'if.' "When you find that fat vein of silver, what's the first thing you are going to do?"

"The only thing I've found lately is a fat run of bad luck," said a fellow named Gus who occupied the bunk across from Scotty.

"Luck can change in the blink of an eye," Scotty answered. He had seen it happen. Here in Leadville, a man could be a down-and-out prospector one day and a millionaire the next. Fabulous riches just waited to be plucked from the earth. It was only sensible to anticipate prosperity. "It behooves a man to plan for the possibilities and opportunities that will come with wealth."

His fellow inmates, in various stages of sobriety, mumbled and muttered.

"I'll tell you what I'd do," said the ragged man sitting on the floor in a back corner of the cell. "I'd buy a new suit of soft wool tailored to fit me just right." Old Benny shot his arms out of the frayed cuffs of his current outfit, a coat that might have been a Union blue years ago. The brass buttons were long lost.

"How about you?" Scotty prompted the third cellmate, a skinny kid with a whiskerless face.

The youth, whose name was Henry, said he'd send money home to his sainted mother as she was a widow with five young ones still at home.

A twinge of guilt shot through Scotty. His wild ways as a youth had nearly caused his own mother to pull out her hair. He would add "Send home a supportive check" to his list of things to do when his fortune arrived.

Another cellmate attempted to roll over on the small bunk above Scotty's head. The mattress was so narrow that Big John could only turn halfway over before shifting his weight to the side or risk rolling out of bed. His feet hung over the end. "I'd book a fancy room at the Clarion Hotel, one with a big ol' feather bed where a fella can stretch out."

A voice from the next cell over chimed in, "I'd go to the Shoo Fly Saloon and get me a pretty gal to share that bed." Laughter rolled through the jailhouse.

"I'd head to the Tontine Restaurant and order the biggest beef steak they had," said a man from across the corridor of cages. The crossbar buddies were warming to Scotty's game.

"I'd get a shave and a haircut," said a man with the unfortunate, but well-deserved name of Stinky Pete. Scotty nodded. He too enjoyed the restorative effects of a bath, a shave, and a trim.

"These are all fine ideas. Myself, I will celebrate my good fortune with a dram of the very finest whiskey fair Scotland has to offer." Although his name was Scotty, Broken Nose shared none of the traits of that tribe, known for their frugality and pessimism. James Daniel Ellis earned his nickname when he broke his nose while drinking his favorite Scotch whiskey. It didn't deter his fondness for the brew of his homeland, which he much preferred to Irish whiskey or the native rough stuff called Taos Lightning.

A cheer went up. "Hear, hear." Everyone in the Lake County jail would join Scotty in a toast of gratitude should the opportunity present itself.

"James Ellis, you have a visitor." The sheriff strode into the lockup followed by a small, well-dressed man wearing a stylish bowler hat and carrying a fine leather satchel. "Which one of you is Ellis?"

Broken Nose Scotty raised his hand and approached the bars. No one had called him by his Christian name in years. Curious inmates crowded around.

"Mr. Ellis, I have a business proposal for you," the little man said. "You own a claim on Breece Hill abutting the mine of my client."

Scotty staked that claim a good while back but gave up after a back-breaking week trying to dig through hard rock which resulted in little but calluses. Since then, drinking had been his main occupation.

"My client needs more land to expand the operations at his mine." The businessman continued to talk about an adjoining shaft to house pumps to keep the water out of the main tunnel and creating small, horizonal drifts to circulate air. "He doubts there is any valuable ore to be found on your claim; however, he is prepared to offer you $30,000 for it."

"Done." Scotty stuck his hand through the bars for a handshake to seal the deal before this sucker got away.

"I've already spoken with Judge Harding, and he will release you without a hearing if you plead guilty and pay the fine from the funds I have with me." The business agent patted the leather satchel. "If you agree..."

"Agree? Hell, yes I agree," Scotty said. Thirty thousand dollars was a fortune. "I am so agreeable that I'll pay everyone's fines."

"Hip, hip, hooray," cheered the inmates.

"Now hold on a minute. It ain't that easy," Sheriff Tucker said, adjusting his pants a little higher around his comfortable middle. "The drunk and disorderlies can pay a fine and go, but I got claim jumpers and fighters and bunco men and pickpockets in here. I can't let them out. They have to stand trial."

"He could post bail," someone hollered. Shouts, whistles, stomps of agreement reverberated throughout the jail cells.

During previous bouts of incarceration, Scotty had known the sheriff to be a practical man who recognized that keeping order in the chaos of a mining boom town was akin to holding a tiger by the tail. Sometimes it was best to make adjustments to the law. "Add it up, Sheriff. I can afford it."

Several verses of "For He's a Jolly Good Fellow" were sung while Sheriff Tucker calculated the cost to empty the jailhouse.

"I do have one small request," Scotty told the business agent as they signed papers and he took ownership of the fine leather satchel and its contents. "Would you please take half of the money and wire it to my poor, dear mother back in Scotland?" She could live in grand style for the rest of her days on $15,000. The agent agreed with a shrug.

"You best head straight to the bank with the rest of that loot," the sheriff told him. "This can be a rough town."

Lightheaded with exuberance, Scotty could only grin at Sheriff Tucker. He would not be sobered by the lawman's wet blanket. He was the luckiest fella in town and surrounded by nearly three dozen new friends who wished him only the best. What could possibly go wrong?

Many hands clapped Scotty's back as the merry miscreants marched out onto the streets of Leadville, all expressing their boundless gratitude and offering undying friendship. "Gentlemen, nothing in this world can lift a man's spirits like a fresh shave and a haircut. That will be my first order of business. Following that, I'm going to purchase a fine new suit, one befitting a respectable gentleman. Then I'll enjoy a nice dinner at the Tontine Restaurant. I'll finish the evening with libations at one of Leadville's drinking establishments."

"With all that money you can have a drink at all

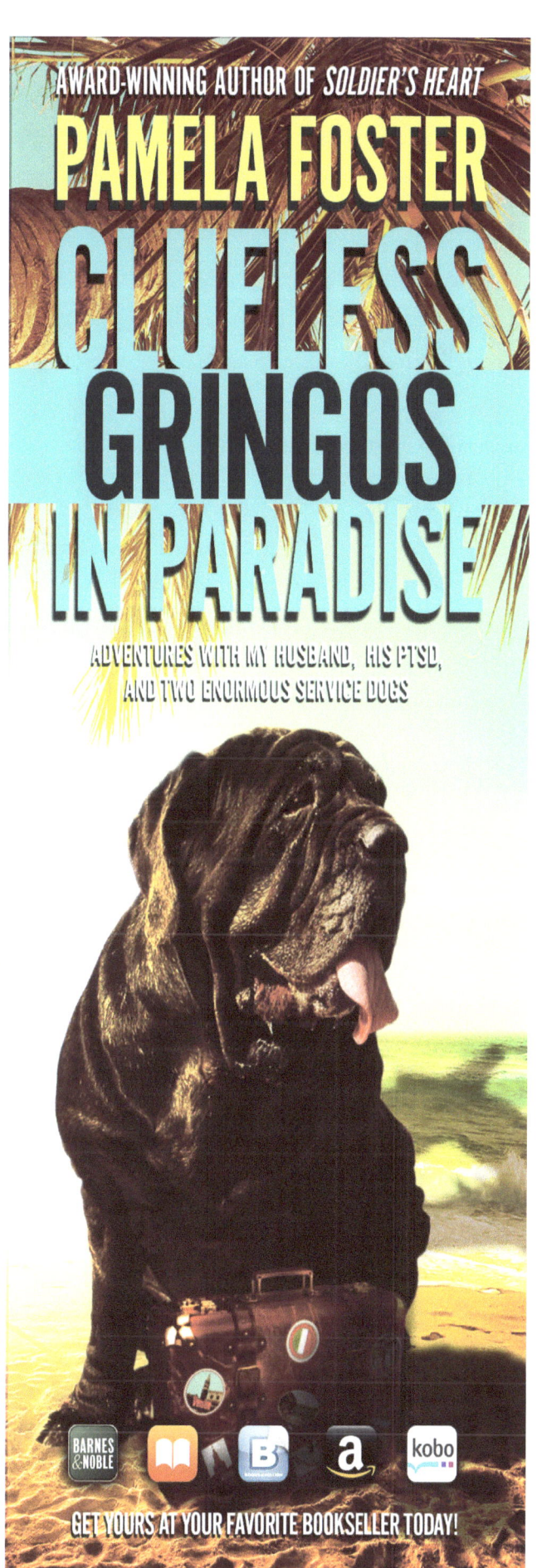

of Leadville's saloons," suggested a man whose eyes and nose were veined in red.

"How many saloons do you think there are?" Scotty asked. He had visited many but not bothered to keep count.

"Oh, about a hundred, I'd say," was the tippler's answer.

"An admirable goal. Who's with me?"

A whoop went up. Scotty thought these were the most agreeable men he'd ever known. "New clothes and haircuts for everyone." The new man of means led Stinky Pete, Gloomy Gus, Old Ben, Young Henry, Big John, and a parade of ne'er-do-wells down Harrison Avenue to the nearest barber shop. It was conveniently located next door to a haberdashery.

Scotty explained his philanthropy plan to the owners of both businesses. The proprietors insisted on being paid in advance and their prices seemed a little steeper than usual. But Scotty felt it would be miserly for a man of his stature to haggle, so he dipped into the leather satchel and pulled out the required banknotes.

As the barber shop was a two-chair affair, the group split up. While Scotty and Pete enjoyed a warm lather and shave, several others went next door to pick out new ready-made suits and try on hats. The remainder of the fellas waited on the bench outside the barbershop, shooting the breeze and waiting their turns.

"Give Pete an extra shot of that nice smelling hair tonic." Scotty gave the barber an extravagant tip and a wink.

A man Scotty didn't recognize quickly took his place in the chair, and Scotty stepped out into the bright sunshine, aiming for the clothing store.

"It's getting mighty hot out here," said one of the fellas holding down the boardwalk in front of the shops. "We are working up quite a thirst while waiting our turn." The old rummy wiggled his eyebrows suggestively.

"A sip of whiskey is just what is called for on this most auspicious afternoon," Scotty agreed. He tossed a twenty-dollar gold piece to a passing boy and instructed him to run to the saloon and bring back as many bottles as he could carry of the finest whiskey he could buy. Another ten-dollar gold piece would be waiting for the kid when he completed the errand.

It turned out the boy was stronger than he looked and could carry several bottles. There were no glasses available, so the bottles were passed from one eager mouth to the next. After all, they were friends.

A few drinks later, Scotty made it to the haber-dashery. A dozen or so men had already picked out ready-made suits, white dress shirts, stiff new collars and silk ties. The shopkeeper's wife and daughter were frantically pinning and sewing hems in pant legs and jacket sleeves, while the owner suggested the perfect accessories for each outfit.

Old Ben stood in the center of the room caressing the arm of a lovely dove-gray jacket make of soft worsted wool; Scotty was so impressed he ordered one like it.

As the new coat was slipped over his shoulders, Scotty cooed, "Tis fine, really grand." He turned to the store owner, "It fits perfectly. I look like a million bucks. Or should I say thirty thousand bucks?"

Everyone, including the formerly gloomy Gus, laughed at Scotty's great wit. He spotted the efficient errand boy lingering at the doorway. "Fetch more whiskey, boy. Take the money you need out of the satchel."

The shopkeeper placed a new bowler on Scotty's freshly clipped head and handed him a cane topped with an intricately carved pheasant head. He studied Scotty for a moment before snapping his fingers, "Of course, cufflinks." He pulled a matched set of large golden circles from the display case. "And no gentleman of refinement would dine without this." From the display came a tiny wooden tube. The shopkeeper opened the tube and extracted a three-inch sliver of ivory tipped in Leadville's most beloved ore, silver. "This is the very finest instrument for the cleaning of one's teeth."

Scotty thought that toothpick was about the fanciest thing he'd ever seen. "Add it to my bill," he said sticking the pick into his new jacket pocket.

The boy soon returned, and more whiskey bottles were passed around the barber shop, the haberdashery, and the bench out front. Toasts were made to the dashing good looks of each man as he came out of the shops. It was shaping up to be a magnificent afternoon.

But the haberdasher's wife was a high-strung woman who had little patience for the men's spiritedness. She insisted they not touch the bright white collars or finger the velvets. She completely lost her temper when a whiskey bottle tipped over and the contents ran over a bolt of fine yellow satin.

"Out, out, out!" she shouted, waving arms that bristled with pin cushions.

Just as she was shooing the men onto the boardwalk a young deputy arrived. Putting his hands on his hips, he announced in his most authoritative voice, "Public drunkenness and loitering will not be tolerated during daylight hours. I'm placing you all under arrest."

It was difficult work to get thirty drunks pointed in the same direction. A few of Scotty's recently acquired chums used the confusion to casually saunter off with their new duds and clean shaves. After several minutes of wrangling, the deputy escorted about two dozen no-accounts back to the pokey.

The sheriff pointedly looked at his pocket watch as Scotty and his friends reentered the jailhouse. "Two hours," was his only comment.

"Aw Sheriff, I believe the deputy is bit too fond of me," Scotty said with a lop-sided grin.

The shopkeeper arrived shortly carrying Scotty's valuable satchel. The haberdasher explained that he had taken out money owed him for the damaged merchandise.

"Tally up the fines for drunk and disorderly Sheriff and we'll be on our way. We still have loads to do," Scotty told the lawman.

A man of few words, the sheriff blew out a resigned sigh and presented Scotty with the sum required to spring him and his friends, who were now charged as repeat offenders.

The sun was sliding beneath the peaks as the gang stepped back onto the streets of Leadville. Scotty heard Young Henry's stomach grumbling and remembered how much growing boys can eat.

"I'm so hungry I could eat a horse. Would anyone like to get some dinner?" Scotty asked, looking at the kid with encouragement.

The youngster twisted his mouth with longing but shook his head. "I'm flat busted."

"No worries, I'm buying." Scotty ruffled the youngster's new haircut with a grin.

With that they headed to the fanciest restaurant in all of Leadville. Two large tables were set up and the staff was instructed to never let their champagne glasses get empty.

When Henry couldn't decide what to order, Scotty told the waiter, "Bring him and me one of everything on the menu." The table soon overflowed with food and drink. Everyone cheered when young Henry slurped down his first raw oyster, followed by a shot of whiskey and a gulp of beer.

Scotty was about to raise a toast to boys becoming men when the oysters, the whiskey, the beer, and half of a pork chop that Henry had greedily gobbled down

AN EPIC JOURNEY OF RESILIENCE, HONOR, AND THE RELENTLESS PURSUIT OF JUSTICE.

As the trusted lieutenant of the infamous Geronimo, Chato's days are painted in the hues of raid and revolt until personal tragedy strikes when his family are taken into slavery in Mexico. Hoping to secure their release, Chato strikes a deal to aid the U.S. Army in maintaining peace with his people. But when Geronimo denounces him as a traitor and departs, all hope for Chato's family flees with him. Forsaken by his former brothers-in-arms, Chato vows to hunt down the renegades himself, becoming a beacon of the Chiricahua peace faction clinging to reservation life in the process.

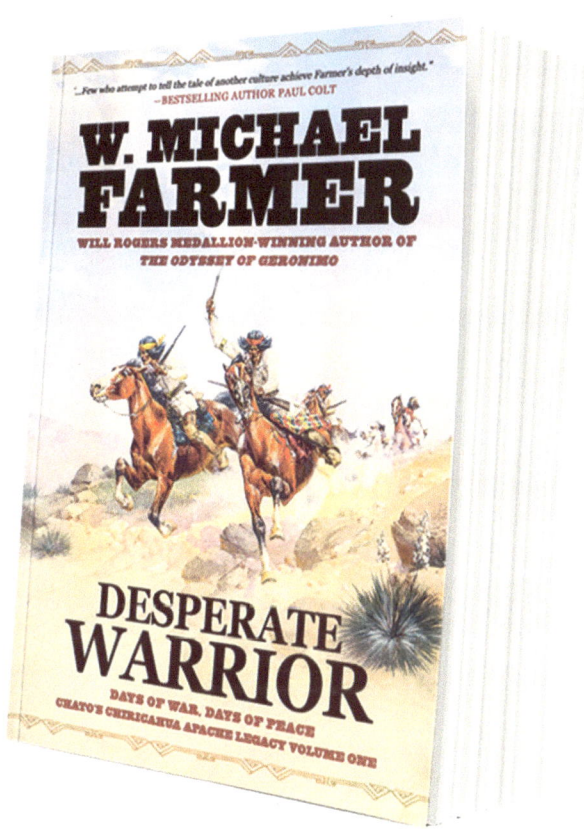

"... Few who attempt to tell the tale of another culture achieve Farmer's depth of insight."

—Bestselling Western author Paul Colt

came violently back up. The men sitting near Henry leapt back in disgust, lifting plates and glasses out of the gore and knocking over an ice bucket and champagne bottle in the rush.

The men at the adjoining table roared with laughter. The fella next to Henry, overcome by the stench and too much alcohol and rich food, began to gag. He too, lost his dinner.

"My new shirt," cried a man splattered with bile and wine.

took some sorting to separate the regular diners from Scotty's bunch. A few men used the cover of darkness to slip away.

About twenty drunken brawlers were escorted back to the hoosegow. This time, in addition to drunkenness, they were charged with fighting. Scotty was required to pay for food, drink, and damages as well as the cost to replace the missing silverware.

"If I didn't know better, I might suspect you were using our celebrations as a money making scheme,

When the wild bunch at the next table slapped their knees, pointing and laughing, it was too much. The muck-covered man picked up a chicken quarter by the leg and flung it across the room at his tormentors. They responded with a bowl of fresh peas and one of mashed potatoes. In a flash, the dignified air of Leadville's finest restaurant was filled with curses, flying plates, smashing glasses, and roasted vegetables. Quietly amid the chaos, one man began stuffing the silverware into his pockets.

It wasn't long before Sheriff Tucker and his deputies arrived. Nearly everyone was covered in food, so it

Sheriff," Scotty said as he and his dwindling parade of misfits friends were marched back to the jail.

Sheriff Tucker elected not to respond to that. He added up the cost of Scotty's crew's latest misadventure, and the sum was extracted from the thinning leather satchel.

Big John hesitated as the group, now numbering only about a dozen hardy souls, headed back out into the Leadville night.

"Won't you join us, friend?" Scotty asked. "We are off to enjoy all of the temptations that Leadville has to offer."

"Well, I don't know, Scotty," Big John said. He rubbed the back of his neck. His face contorted with hard thought. "Seems like we keep ending up back here." He hitched a thumb over his shoulder toward the jailhouse. "I don't want to spend another night in there."

"That's right." Scotty snapped his fingers. "Your wish was for a big ol' bed. Come on. Let's go get us rooms at the Clarendon Hotel."

The hotel, adjacent to the splendid Tabor Opera

of gaming tables rumored to take in more money every day than the Carbonate Bank.

After buying a round of drinks for the house, Scotty was invited to the second floor high rollers' tables where there were no limits and the whiskey glasses were never empty.

"Come sit over here by me," called a beautiful girl from a faro table. Her name was Dolly, and she proved herself to be a most charming companion, hovering near his shoulder and blowing sweet kisses in his ear.

Book 5 of the Award-Winning Abercrombie Trail Series

COMING 2024

Widow Solveig from Abercrombie Trail returns in

Award Winning Author Candace Simar

House, was the town's finest. Scotty arranged for everyone to spend the night sleeping in luxury after they hit the town. But Big John took one look at the lofty feather mattress and clean sheets and told the fellas, "I don't want to get drunk and not remember this night's sleep. I'm staying right here."

So the others bid Big John good night and went on their way to check off the next item on Scotty's list of things the newly rich should do—have a drink in all one hundred of Leadville's saloons.

They made it as far as the Texas House at 216 Harrison Avenue. It was a grand building with two floors

Scotty won several hands. The pile of chips before him grew so high Scotty thought he'd need a ladder to ante. That was about the time that Dolly declared her undying love for Scotty.

Indeed it was his lucky day.

But shortly after midnight his luck changed, and Scotty began to lose. The pile of chips before him shrunk to the size of an abandoned anthill.

"Time to change tables," said a stunning redhead in a short dress. "Dolly's rancid breath is blowing bad luck on those cards. Come play keno over here with me."

"Stay away from my mark," hissed Dolly.

STORIES FROM THE PAST STILL HAVE LESSONS TO TEACH US TODAY....

"A good introduction to Native American legends for young children."
—Children's Literature Review

2024 WILL ROGERS MEDALLION FINALIST
WESTERN YOUNG READER/FICTION/ILLUSTRATED CATEGORY

"Now girls, there's enough of me to go around," Scotty said.

He tried to explain he would gladly be both ladies' special friend. But the two women would hear none of it. They began to scratch and slap. The dealers from the faro and keno tables joined in. Tables were overturned, chips scattered, curses and fists rained down. Amid the ruckus, one man silently stuffed chips and banknotes into his pockets.

--- ◆◆◆ ---

Scotty slowly opened his eyes. The empty leather satchel, now thin and stained with food, drink, and God knows what lay lifeless beneath his pounding head. He looked like he was on the downhill side of a good time. His new jacket was filthy and split at the elbow. His shirt collar hung open, sweat-stained and limp. He gently felt his nose. It was swollen and tender. It must have gotten busted again in the whiskey-fueled mayhem of a day and night in Leadville. Perhaps his nose would look better when it healed.

He looked around the jail. Hovering in the far, dark corner of cell #8, the resident ghost stared at Scotty and sadly shook his head. The handful of men sleeping on the narrow bunks or huddled on the floor didn't appear to notice the apparition.

Scotty didn't recognize any of the morning's inmates. Gone was Old Ben and his fine suit, Stinky Pete and his freshly washed and cut hair, hungry Young Henry, the stranger who had put the silverware in his pocket, the fast-fingered gambler with the easy smile, and even beautiful Dolly, who had proclaimed her love for him. He reached into his pocket. Only the ivory toothpick remained from yesterday's bacchanal.

The sheriff and his deputy brought in breakfast, nodding a morning greeting to those awake.

"I suppose the carousel ride is over," Scotty said as he accepted the tin plate of grub through the bars.

The old lawman sighed but didn't say the words "I told you so" out loud.

Scotty shoveled the cold eggs onto the toast and remembered his dinner the night before. "Sheriff," he called. "What would you do if you suddenly struck it rich?"

The sheriff slowly turned to Scotty. His eyes squinted with the weariness of a man who has seen nearly every kind of foolishness. "I'd get a dog." ⍵

THE AUTHOR

Kimberly Burns *grew up in Colorado hearing stories about the colorful characters of the Old West. When she moved to the East Coast, few people knew these fascinating tales. Following her father's first rule of storytelling (never let the facts get in the way of a good story), Kimberly began writing novels based on the true stories of the wild women of the Old West. Her debut novel,* The Mrs. Tabor, *is based on the scandalous life of America's original gold digger. The book won numerous awards including the Western Fictioneers Peacemaker Award for Best New Novel, a gold medal for Best Regional Fiction from the Independent Publisher Book Awards, a National Indie Excellence Award, and a silver medal from the Colorado Independent Publishers Association EVVY Awards. Her most recent novel,* The Redemption of Mattie Silks, *tells of Denver's most successful madam and her feud with notorious con man Soapy Smith. It is already on the CIBA Laramie Award shortlist. Kimberly is a member of Women Writing the West and the Historical Novel Society as well as an associate member of Western Writers of America.*

BOB GIEL

AUTHOR OF SAVING THE TELL

STOLEN RIVER

NOW AVAILABLE AT ALL YOUR FAVORITE BOOKSELLERS

ALEX SLUSAR

THE DECEIVERS

A SHORT STORY

Jim Clayton and Arthur Durant said little as the train from Denver rocked and lurched through the night, winding up a dark line of steel and timber. They smoked and gazed out the window where black Colorado forest thinned out until the twinkling lights of Leadville emerged among the shadowy peaks. The train pulled in, squealing steel and exhaling billowing white vapour. They gathered their luggage, collected their horses from the stable car, and rode into town.

Clayton scanned the streets from atop his bay. Nine years since he'd ridden or walked them, he thought. The hoof-tampered dirt he remembered was framed now by ochre brick buildings with swooping white arches. Flickering iron gas lamps lined the street like sentries.

Durant sniffed the air. With his round spectacles and fair slender features he resembled a bird, perched up on his grey mare. His equipment jostled aside his saddle — a leather briefcase with compounds for mineral testing, a surveying tripod, and a case containing a theodolite.

"Just like you left it?" Durant said.

"No," Clayton said. "Silver's changed everything."

"Must be nice to be back, though."

"I ain't here to reminisce. You remember what we're here for."

The Grand Pacific Hotel was off Leadville's main drag. They put their names and professions in the ledger—Clayton, property agent; Durant, assayer/surveyor/geologist. Clayton appreciated using his real name. They received a shared room with two beds where Clayton set his luggage down, drew his blued steel Colt Single Action Army, checked the six .45 chambered rounds and the thirty which studded his belt. Durant unloaded his equipment and drew his nickel-plated Remington Frontier Army .44 revolver. He twirled it, cutting the air with flashing silver sweeps and circles.

"Don't," Clayton said.

Durant sighed and twirled the Remington into its oiled holster. He removed his spectacles and wiped them with a handkerchief. "Orders?"

"We oughta get a drink."

"Now you're talking."

Clayton remembered the place called the Board of Trade, on the main street. The regal Tabor Opera House sat across from it now, and the saloon had caught some of its opulence. Narrow walls of dark wood drew patrons toward the prominent mahogany bar and the archway to the gaming tables beyond. Electric lamps cast a waxy amber sheen. A lively piano sonata backed a boisterous, chattering crowd. The saloon smelled of whisky, juniper, horse musk and French lavender.

They went to the bar and ordered beer. The bartender sliced creamy foam off the heads with a silver scraper and passed them over.

"Think our boy's here tonight?" Durant said.

"What if he is?"

"Get to business."

"We'll find him. Just be attentive. Enjoy your beer."

"Sure," Durant said.

Clayton eyed the crowd. He found no familiar faces in it. It seemed the Leadville silver rush brought a new citizenry — younger, lean and sinewy from working in mountain air, with cosmopolitan tastes. He found his reflection in the silvery glass behind the bar. Nine years since it had been there. A different man stared back now — bearded, creased, his reddish-brown hair streaked with grey, his blue eyes sallow and deep-set. A man nobody from the old days would recognize as one of their diligent deputies.

He barely recognized it himself.

"Hold on," Durant said.

"What?"

"By the stairs. That must be the father. Lee Pilger."

Clayton looked. Near a carpeted staircase by the archway stood a stocky sun-browned man in a black coat and a bowler hat. His grey mustache drooped over a pluming cigar. He grinned sharklike at the whispers of a young, snow-pale golden-haired woman in turquoise hanging off his arm.

"You're right," Clayton said.

Lee Pilger followed the girl up the stairs.

Durant wiped froth from his lip. "What you think?"

"Could stay here, listen to chatter," Clayton muttered. "Or spend time with the people who know everything 'round here." He nodded toward the far corner of the room, where three young women in pleasant satin gowns stood coolly eyeing the crowd and batting their lashes.

"You're serious?"

"Works sometimes, if a man ain't pushy and pays well."

"This some test?"

"No."

Durant stroked his chin. "All right. If I must."

"Who said it'd be you?"

Durant's mouth opened slightly. He looked at the women, at Clayton.

"Go on," Clayton said. "Call it your next lesson."

Durant smirked and finished his beer. He sauntered away from the bar and approached a dusky sloe-eyed girl draped in purple.

Clayton left his drink. He slipped through the crowd and went outside. He walked along the gaslit street, seeking memory. Leadville was foreign terrain now, populated by tall structures and creatures that scurried to plunder the riches below and spend

them above. The earth held the same scent, though —dry, rich loam tinged with pine and something like the metallic tang of blood.

They breakfasted in the hotel salon. Clayton sipped coffee while Durant wolfed down bacon, eggs and biscuits.

"What'd you learn?" Clayton asked.

Durant mopped up runny yellow egg with biscuit. His eyes flashed behind the round spectacles. "That this work has its moments."

"Come on, now."

Durant shrugged. "I said Matthew recommended the place. Maisie—that's her name—asked if I meant Lee, since he's a regular. I said Matthew Pilger, we'd met in Chicago."

"And?"

"Said Matthew hasn't visited since he came home a couple months ago. Not in town much. Spends most of his time at his father's mine."

"Like we reckoned."

Durant nodded. "This could be easy."

Clayton finished his coffee. "Don't assume. But it's a good lead."

"So we'll go there?"

"Claims office, first. Then look at the mines, like a surveyor-geologist would."

Durant picked his teeth. "All this playacting."

"You don't like it, there's other jobs."

"It's just not direct."

"It's how it's done."

"You say so."

They finished their breakfast and got up from their table.

"Jim Clayton," a man said. "I'll be damned."

Clayton turned. Lee Pilger stood inside the salon entrance, grinning.

"Why, Lee Pilger. Been a spell."

"I knew it," Pilger said. "Even with that beard. Saw you last night at the Board of Trade, thought there was something familiar. How the hell are you?"

"Fine enough. You look well."

Pilger's coal-black eyes glinted. "I'm blessed, Clayton. Left wrangling for a silver concern nearby, the Prospero. Five years now, she's turned out steady."

"The way the papers talk, I thought Tabor held all the silver."

Pilger scoffed. "Tabor's busy failing in politics. A

DUSTY RICHARDS
THE NATURAL

EIGHT SECONDS CAN BE A LIFETIME

man with a claim can still succeed in Leadville. But you know that, or you wouldn't be here."

"I'm not in silver."

Pilger pointed at Clayton's chest. "But you ain't in tin, either."

"Left the badge here."

"What since?"

"Property, mostly."

Pilger nodded quizzically. He turned to Durant. "Who's your companion?"

"Lee Pilger, Arthur Durant. Arthur's a surveyor and geologist from Chicago."

Durant frowned, then smiled. "Pleased to meet you, Mr. Pilger."

Pilger's eyebrow raised. "A surveyor-geologist, and a property man. Interesting. You knew Clayton was law here once, Mr. Durant?"

"Indeed."

"Was maybe your age then. Eager, too."

"Lee knows firsthand," Clayton said. "When he wasn't wrangling for the Gas Creek outfit, he ran around with scum."

Pilger glared. He chuckled. "Time ain't softened your view, Jim?"

Clayton said nothing.

"You know about the dispute, Mr. Durant?"

Durant shook his head.

"In '74, a local rancher got killed by this ganged-up bandit Gibbs. But Gibbs walked. So we formed a safety committee to protect ranchers in these parts. Committee kept things in line."

"It was a gang itself," Clayton said. "Threatened people, killed people. Terrorized the county."

Pilger snorted. "I remember different. Judge Dyer thought like Clayton, though—posted warrants for committee members nobody wanted to enforce. But Deputy Clayton brought 'em all to court. That was a sight. I don't recall any going to prison, though."

"Because your committee threatened anyone who'd testify."

"Some had hot blood about it. But no evidence is no evidence." Pilger shrugged. "Anyway, it's in the past. Bygones."

Clayton scoffed. "Bygones? Even what happened after? Nothing bygone about that."

Pilger ran his tongue over his teeth. "Tragic, sure. But nobody knows who went into the judge's chamber and shot him, Jim. It's on his stone, 'shot by persons unknown.'"

"Somebody knows."

"Not I." Pilger glanced around the salon. "Nine years is like ninety in Leadville. Silver's brought success, progress. Taken us into the future. Few years, we'll be bigger'n Denver. Any old problems been forgotten."

Clayton's eyes narrowed. "Not by me."

Pilger smiled. "Glad you're back, Jim. Maybe see you at the Board of Trade again."

"Maybe."

Pilger tipped his hat and passed them, seeking a table. Clayton left the salon. Durant followed.

"What the hell, Clayton?" Durant said through clenched teeth.

"Shut up," Clayton said. "Get your things."

Durant went upstairs for the surveying equipment. He carried it down and outside, where Clayton smoked on the front porch, watching the street. Together they walked toward the stables.

"You going to explain?" Durant said.

"Explain what?"

"You—" Durant scoffed. "You didn't say you knew Pilger."

"I used to know everyone and everything in Leadville. That's why I'm here."

"Really? Or did you take this job because of that dispute? Settle old business?"

Clayton grunted. "Past ain't important. This job is."

"Put that in a wire to Chicago."

"Nobody's wiring anyone."

"The boss ought to know."

"There's little he don't," Clayton said, and pushed open the stable door.

The Leadville claims office held a list of top-producing silver mines. That Horace Tabor owned the best was no surprise. Lee Pilger's Prospero mine ranked forty-first overall and tenth-best among independent owners. Clayton and Durant rode to four other independents—the Maybell, the Eagle, the Black Ace and the Little Gail—and surveyed them. Clayton talked with workers willing to talk and asked about output. Durant fiddled with the theodolite and sniffed rocks.

By mid-afternoon they were up on a grassy ridge swathed in tall pines. Durant stood behind the theodolite and tripod. Clayton leaned against a tree, smoking a cheroot. Below them the Prospero lay in a narrow basin where boulders had collected like irregular marbles in a bowl. Three figures ambled among the sparse log structures—a bunkhouse, outhouse, shed, and a cabin—and ducked in and out of a ragged hole carved in the basin's northeast rise. They dumped rock chunks into a trough full of brown water.

Durant rotated the theodolite. "Don't know what the hell."

"Just look like you do."

Durant peered through a spyglass mounted beside the block of knobs and pips. "Don't see Lee nor Matthew. Two men there look weathered. Third has an old scalping wound."

"Must be Pete Grant. Had some trouble in Dakota territory, years back. I'd haul him in drunk every other week." Clayton nibbled the cheroot. "Nice of Pilger to give him work, I guess."

Durant hummed. "Pilger killed that judge?"

"Not directly."

"What?"

"I was down the street after the committee's acquittal," Clayton said. "Seven men, guilty as sin, walked. There was a small crowd of supporters, including Pilger. Three to five of them ran into Judge Dyer's chamber, I never learned who. But I know who ginned them up."

"Talked them into it?"

"Yeah. He went off about what was real justice if the court couldn't be trusted. Those committee boys were hopping, and he riled 'em. When the smoke cleared, he claimed he wasn't even in town at the time."

Durant frowned. "You were close with the judge?"

Clayton shrugged. "He wanted to do the right thing. They killed him for it. I gave up my badge after."

"Before they came for you."

"Like to think I wasn't scared they would."

Durant squinted through the spyglass. "There's smoke from the cabin down there, but nobody's gone in or out," he said. "I wager someone's inside."

Clayton extinguished the cheroot. "Let's go see."

They packed up the gear and rode down the basin slope. They rode the battered path to the mine, cantered up to the bunkhouse and cabin and approached the men at the trough. Two of them were slender, dark, balding, and slaked with dirt. The third was big and hairy, wearing a mud-caked union suit and suspenders. The scalping scar across his head looked like stained leather.

ANTHONY
WOOD

WILL ROGERS MEDALLION-WINNING AUTHOR OF *WHITE & BLACK*

STORM
of TERROR

A TALE OF TWO COLORS · VOLUME VI

"That's far enough," one of the slender men said.

"You the foreman?" Clayton said.

The man shook his head. "George Garrick. My brother Tom, and Pete Grant."

Clayton nodded. "Mr. Grant. Maybe you remember me, Jim Clayton. Deputy, years back."

Grant grunted. "I remember."

"Mr. Pilger around?"

"He's in town," George Garrick said.

"Who's in charge when he's in town?"

"We just work it," Tom Garrick said.

"Any questions, talk to Pilger," George said.

"You see him, tell him we were here," Clayton said.

Clayton and Durant tipped their hats and turned their horses around to leave. As they rode away, the door to the cabin opened. A man of around twenty, wearing unsullied work clothes, stood in the doorway. He was stocky, with wild curly black hair.

Clayton tipped his hat. Durant followed suit. The man closed the cabin door.

"That's Matthew, all right," Durant muttered.

"Like us to meet him soon," Clayton said.

It was approaching dark when they returned to Leadville. They took supper at the hotel. Durant went to see Ticket-of-Leave Man at the Tabor Opera House—burnishing his credentials, Clayton thought. Clayton went to the Board of Trade. It was as busy as the previous night. He nursed a beer at the bar. Lee Pilger sidled up beside him and ordered whisky.

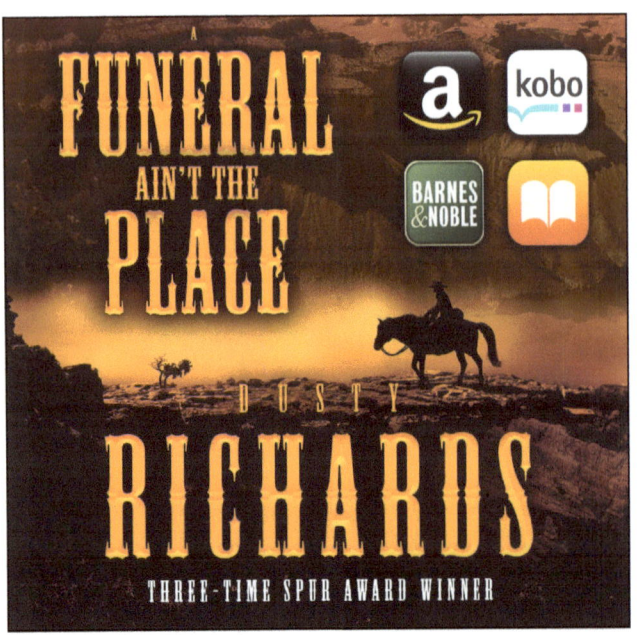

"Feeling more sociable tonight, are we, Clayton?" Pilger said.

"You're still standing."

Pilger chuckled as the bartender passed him a jiggling glass of amber. "That's good. Because you ain't fooling me."

"What?"

"Said you weren't in silver. But you fellows visited claims today. Including mine."

"Durant's a surveyor. Follows the land."

"He's from Chicago."

"That's right."

"You too?"

Clayton nodded.

"Thought so. You were honest when you were law, Clayton. Suppose things change."

"What you think I'm up to?"

Pilger drank. He jabbed the bar top. "The only reason to come to Leadville—silver. You know this area, and you're back after a near decade with someone from Chicago that knows terrain. If you were in it for yourself, you'd have come back with the rush, so I figure you got sent here. You're workin' for someone. Chicago's full of millionaires. Which one is it?"

"For an old wrangler and crook, you're pretty smart, Lee."

"Is it Field? McCormick? Pullman? I won't tell nobody. But I know I'm right."

Clayton leaned in. "All right. It's Pullman."

Pilger grinned. "Well, now."

"You know how much silver goes into gilding his rail cars? Tabor supplies Pullman, but Pullman's sick of his money going to Tabor's politics and his highfalutin new wife. He wants a reliable supplier of Colorado silver, for a premium, if it's a good source. He hired me to help Durant find the best."

Pilger stroked his moustache. "You're looking to supply Pullman cars?"

"I'm only telling you this because Durant said your claim is the one he'll recommend to Pullman."

Pilger's eyes flashed wide. "The Prospero?"

Clayton nodded. "Has to do with the land. Durant's a genius, can figure where the silver is and how much, based on how the land is and the ore quality."

"Pre... premium?"

"If it's good enough. We'll need to make sure."

"How?"

"Bring Durant to your mine. He'll read the ground, and any samples."

Pilger rubbed his chin and nodded. "Tomorrow?"

"Sure. Say around noon."

"Alright."

"It's just you owns it, right?"

Pilger nodded. "Matthew looks after it for me."

"Your boy? He was just a sprout."

"You've been gone long, Clayton. He's filled out. Strong kid. After Constance died, he spent some time out east sowin' his oats, but found his way home a few months ago." Pilger grinned. "The Prospero is a family concern."

"Have him there, then. He ought to know."

"Noon, then." Pilger turned from the bar, then stopped and turned back. "I...I know we didn't always agree, Clayton, but I'm glad of your return. Seems Providence has brought us together for some benefit."

"To cross our palms with silver?"

Pilger chuckled. "I suppose."

"You said it yourself. A man can do well here. Provided he's the right man to deal with."

Pilger winked. "Tell Pullman he'll find none better. I promise that." He started back into the crowd.

Clayton finished his beer. He drummed his fingers on the bar. He hoped Durant would be ready. He reckoned they'd both have to be.

The Prospero cabin was cramped and drafty. Clayton leaned against the wall beside a marbled glass window through which he saw their horses hitched and Grant and the Garricks sorting rock in the trough under the noonday sun. He turned toward the table in the center of the cabin. Durant sat on one side. Lee and Matthew Pilger sat across. Three pebbly chestnut-sized silver nuggets and a lit candle stub lay between them. Durant examined the nuggets with a loupe.

"Yes," Durant said. "Oh, my, yes."

"Oh yer yes, what?" Matthew said.

Durant held silver against the flickering light. He brought it closer. "I've only seen this weight and pattern in high-yield deposits."

"High-yield?"

"Meaning, a lot."

Matthew scratched his neck. "How you so sure?"

"My family's worked in silver for seven generations. We used to buy it for the King of France." Durant set the nugget down. "It's all that I know."

"You just look at it, and know there's more?"

"Much more. See how...uniform the color is?"

"Uh, sure," Matthew said.

"No flaking or crumbling. Better than any I've seen in Flanders, Portugal or Spain."

"No kiddin'?"

"It'll please Mr. Pullman?" Pilger asked.

"I can't speak for him," Durant said. "But this is what he's looking for. How much does your assayer pay? In line with average?"

"Dollar-five an ounce, say."

Durant tsk-tsked. "This quality is worth more. At least a dollar-twenty, which Mr. Pullman won't mind paying. Over perhaps ten years."

Pilger sat back in his chair and exhaled. "Incredible. I was worried the Prospero would play out."

"Your mine is the forty-first in the county. With four men, it would be. But with Pullman's support, you'll hire more, tap into bigger and deeper veins. Could run Tabor out of the county in a year."

The shark-grin they'd seen in the saloon broke across Pilger's face. "When do we start?" he said.

"There are formalities. Clayton and I will leave for Chicago tonight. We'll return with a contract offer within, when would you expect, Clayton?"

Clayton shrugged. "Two weeks."

"Incredible," Pilger said again. He slapped Matthew on the back. "This calls for a drink. A toast. And then, a night on the town." He got up and went to a cabinet in the corner of the cabin.

Matthew stared at the nuggets. He looked up and eyed Durant. "If you know all this, how come you don't work for Tabor?" he said.

"He can't afford me," Durant said.

Matthew picked at a nugget. "This some of the best you've seen?"

"Pretty well. Although the best silver I ever saw was some earrings."

"Earrings?"

"Worn by a girl in Chicago. Catherine Stanton."

Matthew looked up from the nuggets. His smile fell away. The colour drained from his cheeks. "What?"

"Catherine Stanton," Durant said. "Beautiful girl. Or she used to be."

Matthew swallowed. Pilger brought a bottle of whisky out of the cabinet. Tin clattered as he rummaged for cups. Clayton left the window and stood between Pilger and Matthew. He hovered behind Matthew with his eyes on Pilger and his hand near his gun.

"I know, I've got something," Durant reached into his vest pocket and brought something out in a closed fist. "Something to compare to your silver."

"W-what?" Matthew said.

Durant opened his palm and flicked something onto the table. It flashed silver in the candlelight. The badge came up emblazoned with an unblinking eye which stared up at Matthew Pilger over the words *PINKERTON NATIONAL DETECTIVE AGENCY*.

Matthew started out of his seat.

Clayton drew his Colt and cracked the butt over Matthew's head. Matthew dropped like a sack of wet meal and hit the table. The nuggets scattered.

Pilger whirled around at the noise. He stared open-mouthed down the barrel of Clayton's revolver.

"Hold it," Clayton said.

Durant got up. He dragged Matthew over the table and threw him to the floor. Matthew landed on his face and howled. Durant crouched over him, pulled a knife from the small of Matthew's back and threw it against the far wall where it embedded point-first in a log. He heaved Matthew up by his shirt collar and slugged him hard across the mouth. Clayton heard something snap.

"No," Pilger said.

"Catherine Stanton," Durant landed another blow on Matthew's face. Matthew reached up feebly. Durant swatted his arm away and hit him again.

"Stop him, Clayton!" Pilger exclaimed.

"No," Clayton said.

Pilger stammered. The whisky bottle dropped and shattered on the floor.

Matthew gurgled, spat molars and blood. Durant dropped him, picked up the badge on the floor, drew his Remington and cocked it. He flung his spectacles off. They cracked against the wall. He wiped his mouth and trained his .44 on the mewling, bloodied man at his feet. "Enough playacting," he said.

Pilger trembled. Clayton opened his coat. Another Pinkerton badge was pinned on the inner lining.

"We came for your boy, Lee," Clayton said. "Three months ago, in Chicago, he took his hands to a girl wouldn't do what he wanted. Beat her near blind. Ruined her."

"No," Pilger said.

"Her family hired us. We put it together and tracked him back home." Clayton stepped forward with the Colt trained on Pilger. "Were you surprised when he came back? Or maybe you knew what he'd done, and wanted to keep him safe here."

"I... I...." Pilger trailed off. "You mean you're a goddamned Pinkerton?"

"Left one badge. Took another."

Pilger turned to Durant. "And you...you ain't..."

"Name's Sam Durant, not Arthur," Durant said. "I just started with Pinkerton. I rode for Wells Fargo, and I can lie pretty good."

"What... what you said about Pullman, the silver?"

"Made it all up. We're gettin' real with your boy now, though."

Pilger shivered. "Let him go."

"We're taking him back to Chicago for trial," Clayton said.

"Or I finish him here," Durant said.

"Sam."

"I Didn't," Matthew moaned. "I didn't."

"Yeah, boy, you did," Durant said. He rolled Matthew over, pulled a rawhide loop from his pocket and cinched Matthew's wrists behind his back.

"He ain't goin' nowhere," Pilger said.

"Reach for your gun or try and stop us, I'll send you through that cabinet," Clayton said.

"You won't make it to your horses. The boys outside are loyal, won't let you leave the mine."

Clayton stepped forward. Pilger flinched. Clayton removed the pistol from Pilger's holster—a blued Remington like Durant's but pitted and weathered — and clipped Pilger with it. The trigger guard and butt raked across his face. He went down with a yowl.

"Nine years you've had that coming," Clayton said, tucking the pistol at his front waist.

Pilger rolled, clutching his nose. "Help!"

Durant brought Matthew up. He looked out the window. "Those boys are coming," he said.

"Armed?"

"Yeah."

Clayton stepped over Pilger and looked out. The three miners were closing in on the cabin. Grant carried a shotgun. The Garricks held revolvers.

Clayton threw the cabin door open with his Colt raised. "Stop now or be shot," he said.

The miners flinched. They stopped. They eyed him. The Garricks held their pistols low. Grant's shotgun stock was tucked against his shoulder with the barrel cantered down.

Clayton flashed his badge. "We're bringin' Matthew Pilger out," he said. "He's wanted in Chicago."

"Bullshit," Tom Garrick said.

"It's the truth. Sam, bring him out."

Durant pushed Matthew before him, jamming the Remington in his neck. "We're detectives, takin' in a wanted man. You don't want any of this."

The miners eyed each other. Slowly, Clayton and Durant led Matthew away from the cabin, toward their horses. Durant pushed Matthew ahead with the Remington. Matthew wept silently through blood. Clayton held his Colt on the miners.

"Easy," Clayton said.

"Clayton!"

Pilger stood in the cabin doorway. His mouth was a matted, bleeding slash.

"Back inside, Lee," Clayton said.

"Let him go!"

"Get back."

"Stop 'em, George!" Pilger said. "I paid you extra to watch my boy, for God's sake."

"I... I don't..." George Garrick stammered.

"Grant," Pilger said. "Grant, shoot them now."

Pete Grant's eyes darted. "I don't know," he said.

"Grant," Clayton said. "I was always fair to you. Drop that scattergun."

"They're kidnapping my boy, Pete," Pilger said. "They ain't law, they're killers. Assassins. They'll take Matthew and kill him."

"That ain't true," Clayton said.

"Remember who pays you, Grant," Pilger said. "Who gave you this job, gave you silver."

Grant twitched. The shotgun came up.

Clayton fired. His round caught Grant dead center and exploded in Grant's chest as the big man's shotgun belched flame. Clayton felt a gale-force wind of white-hot bee stings down his left side. He spun, toppled, heard himself scream. He met the earth face-first. It was dry, sun-warm, and hard.

Someone shouted for him. He heard gunshots—heavy .44 blasts in quick succession, two cries of pain, a smaller pop. Something jabbed his stomach—Pilger's Remington, jammed in his belt. He reached his right hand out, seeking his Colt. His whole left side was wet, sticky, burning. Immobile.

He rolled over. The pines at the top of the basin swam and swayed. He came up on his right elbow. He hissed and spat. The Colt lay before him. He picked it up, came to his knees and looked.

The Garricks lay splayed out on their backs near Grant. They were stone dead and perforated. Durant had thrown Matthew down. The barrel of his Remington smoked faintly.

Pilger stared at the scene, frozen in place.

Clayton looked down. His left arm and part of his chest were shredded and swathed in blood. It dripped freely down his shattered arm and into the yellow basin grass.

"C-Clayton," Pilger said.

Clayton cocked the Colt and shot Pilger in the left leg. Pilger screeched and dropped to his right knee. Blood soaked his trouser leg as he clutched the wound.

"Look what you did," Clayton said.

He fell back. He felt something catch him. Durant held him, propped him up off his wounded side.

"Jim. You're hurt bad."

"Yeah," Clayton said. He coughed. His arm stung and hung limp.

"I'll get you to the doctor. We'll stow Matthew with the local law."

"Can't trust law in a silver town," Clayton spat. "They ain't likely to...appreciate us. Get him...to the train. Chicago. I'll get help."

"Not on your own, you won't."

"Got enough on your hands right now. Don't worry about me."

Durant looked at Clayton's wounds. He shook his head. "Go on. Something I gotta do, anyway."

Durant gazed over to where Pilger snarled on the ground, gripping his leg.

"Thought old business didn't matter."

Clayton wheezed. "Guess I lied."

"Damn, Jim," Durant said. "Now what the hell do I tell Pinkerton?"

"Whatever you like. I'll come by later," He coughed. "Fill in the details."

Durant swallowed. He got his arm under Clayton's good one and hauled him to his feet. Clayton grunted in pain, then stood up rigidly.

"Be seein' you, Sam."

Durant nodded. He turned, went over to Matthew, and hauled him up. He marched Matthew to their horses, heaved him up into his saddle, then mounted his own mare.

He rode off down the path leading Matthew captive beside.

Clayton's dead arm burned cold. Blood dripped steadily to the ground. He holstered his Colt, pulled

the Remington from his belt and tossed it. It landed beside Pilger.

"Just us now." Clayton limped over. "Nobody else you can rile up or do your bidding. Pick it up."

Pilger hissed. "You bastard, Clayton. You'll answer for this."

"You'll answer... for the judge."

"Christ's sake."

"Mine. I'll hear you confess."

"To what?" Pilger's face reddened and his eyes got very large.

"You talked the committee into killing Dyer."

Pilger spat. "They'd have done it anyway. There wasn't reason to stop 'em."

"Pick it up."

"Look at you. You're dead anyway."

"You want me to answer, Lee? You've done well in silver. Let's see how you do in lead."

Pilger bellowed. He reached for his Remington. Grasped it. Raised it.

Clayton drew his Colt. It thundered in his hand. The bullet caught Lee Pilger directly between the eyes and the force snapped his head back. He stared forward, almost confused.

Clayton emptied the Colt into him, sending Pilger backwards into the grassy dirt of the basin.

Pilger shuddered once and lay still.

With a sigh, Clayton holstered the pistol. He turned and limped down the path toward his horse. He got as far as a lone pine at the foot of the basin ridge. Short of breath, he leaned against the tree and winced, then slid down to the base of the trunk. *It's comfortable enough,* he thought.

He felt cold, but the air was fresh with pine, and the earth underneath him was warm and full of silver. He could sleep here for a bit, he figured—gather strength, head back down the mountain.

He wheezed. *Pinkertons,* he thought—the one thing he wasn't supposed to do was sleep. Yet the job was done. The business of years ago was concluded. If he wanted to sleep, nobody else was around to know. It was just him and the silver-rich earth, the turquoise sky, the soft rustle of mountain wind. *This time will be alright,* he thought as his breath grew shallow and he looked up beyond the ridge at the white Colorado peaks.

This one time would be fine. ♘

THE AUTHOR

Alex Slusar *was born and raised in Saskatchewan, Canada. His writing explores crime, horror, living with nature, and life in the West (in both historic and modern contexts). After obtaining his Master's degree in political science, Alex worked in a suite of capacities as a political consultant, operative and organizer, and also enlisted with the Royal Canadian Navy. He continues to work in both national political affairs and military defense matters. In 2022 Alex was selected as an apprentice for the Saskatchewan Writer's Guild Mentorship Program, which assists developing writers in refining their craft, and is developing a collection of neo-Western short stories. Alex divides his time between the provinces of Saskatchewan, Ontario and Quebec, and can often be found traveling, kayaking on the St. Lawrence River, trekking deep in the wilderness of northern Canada or hiking the Sonoran Desert. He tweets intermittently @axslusar and celebrates adventure through photography on* **Instagram @alex.slusar**

A WORD (OR TWO) ON WORD

*If you're a fan of Westerns and you don't know
who Rob Word is, stop reading this.*

STORY BY

GEORGE "CLAY" MITCHELL

Rob Word has spent a lifetime as a fan of movies, especially Westerns. They captivated his attention as a child, and he still maintains that wide-eye excitement when talking about Westerns and bringing the stories behind the iconic films and television shows to life.

That passion also led Word to be part of a project of an unproduced script by a legendary Western screenwriter and director.

NOT YOUR AVERAGE FAN

Word devoured publications that featured his big and small screen heroes. He began collecting magazines like *Favorite Westerns of Filmland.* One of the covers featured John Wayne beating up the bad guys. Word has the original painting of that cover that was done by Jack Davis, who made a career and name for himself as one of the key artists for *MAD Magazine.*

He also collected (and still has) comic books featuring Western movies and television shows like *The Rifleman* and *The Grey Ghost.* Word poured through and kept the Marvel Westerns featuring the *Two-Gun Kid, Rawhide Kid, Kid Colt,* and *The Apache Kid.* He kept magazines and articles featuring B-movie icons like Al Adamson and Ed Wood. Word even collected *Leave It To Beaver* comics.

"I still have all those old magazines," Word laughs. "I'm not your average fan. My wife asked me what would happen to all the stuff when I'm gone. Luckily, my son grew up surrounded by all that stuff. He appreciates and values it. I do have instructions for him, though."

"I just love all that stuff."

EARLY BEGINNINGS

Word's family went to the movies once a week. He remembers that his first movie was a Western, but it was either *High Noon* or *Shane.* His dad picked the film.

Dad was a Navy pilot in Clearwater, Fla., when the only things there were the airbase, the beach,

> ## MY DAD AND THE NEXT-DOOR NEIGHBOR HOOKED UP THE TV. IT WAS ALL FUZZY. BUT IT DIDN'T MATTER. IT WAS A MAGIC BOX.
>
> ### —ROB WORD

and about 1,400 people. His dad was a flight instructor for the Navy and an essential component of the war effort in the 1940s.

"I remember my dad and the next-door neighbor hooked up the TV," Word said. "It was all fuzzy, but it didn't matter. It was a magic box." Television programming was different back then. Local stations started at 3 or 4 p.m. and were often live variety shows. When the FCC began allocating licenses in 1953, stations were desperate for programs. This became a boon for the small Western feature producers.

"Gene Autry had the right idea. If you can get kids hooked on Westerns, you'll have them forever," said Word, and he was hooked from watching them on TV or going to the noon movies at the mall or shopping center. "The stores gave away free tickets so the moms would dump the kids to watch the serials from nine to noon."

Word said it was a cool time to watch television, especially if you were a fan of the genre. "There was just an explosion of Westerns on TV. There were just three networks, and two, maybe all three, had Westerns going at the same time."

He and his friends would play cowboys with their toy metal guns. Word learned the fast draw in front of a mirror. "It was all a major influence," Word said.

Family trips were in a 1949 Ford with no AC, pulling an Airstream trailer with no bathroom. "We would just go out west. I saw my first snow on one of those trips." Their travels west only cemented Word's love and passion for the West and the stories being told.

OUT FROM BEHIND THE CAMERA

Word graduated college from Stetson University in Florida and got a job as a cinematographer/editor at an ABC station in Central Florida.

He continued his work at a station in Orlando

Rob as a child in 1952, on summer vacation in front of his parents' '49 Ford and Airstream trailer.
Photo Courtesy of the Rob Word

where the owner was a fellow movie buff. Word talked him into giving him an audition to host movies. Soon, Word was hosting movies six nights a week. "Our ratings were high," said Word. "You couldn't get movies anywhere else on TV at that time, and we were beating Dick Cavett and Johnny Carson."

Word couldn't afford cue cards, so he had to memorize all the movie facts he wanted to share. They would shoot six episodes at a time. He would do the intro. There was a bit where he talked about the movie about two-thirds of the way into the feature and the outro. He wore a clip-on bow tie that became his signature look.

"People wanted to see the movie, and I wanted to talk about the movie," he added. In 1972, Orlando changed when Disney World opened. Disney soon called him to ask if he wanted to interview any of the stars who might be coming to

Rob doing the intro for an episode of *A Word on Westerns* on *The Lone Ranger*.
Photo Courtesy of Rob Word and A Word on Westerns

Portrait of Rob out on the trail during a recent trip to Arizona.
Photo Courtesy of Rob Word

Orlando to visit the park. He chatted with Frankie Laine, Mel Tormc, Judy Garland, Ron Howard, Don Knotts, and many others. He transcribed what he talked about with the stars and the movies into a weekly column for the *New York Times*. Local radio stations wanted him to cut five minutes of interviews he did for broadcasting.

After a while, he decided he needed to move on. "I felt like a big fish in a small pond in Orlando. No one else was doing this sort of thing then," said Word. "I needed bigger toys. With no real connections, he packed up his Betamax and B-movies and came to California to do a series called *Focus On Film*. That later evolved into another series called *Stardom*. He would record short 2.5-minute interviews that would be played on local stations across the country. He would record five shows at once. He saved some of those interviews and is trying to restore most of them so they can be seen again

on the internet. "The quality isn't that great, and it feels like I'll be watching home movies when I see them again."

THE SHOW FINDS A NEW HOME

Rob's previous show began as a hobby for 25 years and ended with the final Golden Boot Award in 2007. With some prompting from Bo Hopkins and others, Word started his show again at a restaurant at the Saddle Ranch Chop House. It featured guests like Ernest Borgnine, Robert Culp, and Ted Post, who directed *Hang 'Em High* and episodes of *Rawhide*.

He would later bring the show to a cafe at the Gene Autry Museum. Mike Clark ran two cameras, and they conducted interviews at 1 p.m. when the cafe opened. Folks lined up at 10 a.m. to get a seat for the 20-minute show. Eventually, the museum asked if he would like to host his show in the Wells

Rob at the Autry Museum of the American West with Bruce Boxleitner, Robert Carradine, and Robert Woods
Photo Courtesy of the Rob Word

Fargo Theater on the site. Now, they have two hours to do a live show.

"When we first came to the museum, we had to create a 12-month schedule. It was a bit different because sometimes we didn't know who we would talk to at the restaurant. Sometimes we would pull someone from the audience who worked behind the scenes and are still fans of the Westerns," Word said. "So we put together a list that included folks who were part of the production of *Lonesome Dove* and *How the West Was Won*. Producers, production assistants, actors, we got as many as possible."

Word's little show, which began as a hobby, was now being filmed with four cameras, and more fans continued to fill the theater seats.

"I was lucky to have interviewed Julie Adams, Johnny Crawford, Robert Forester, and others who are gone now, but I have recorded all these wonderful conversations," Word said. "I hope these shows will still be out there when I'm long gone."

Sometimes, the scheduled guest couldn't make their designated time to appear on the show. However, in the studio audience there would be actors, directors, producers, or other folks who worked behind the scenes. Word would bring them onto the stage, and they would talk about their passion for making Westerns.

Word has released over 500 shows that are now on YouTube, and a new one is released every Sunday.

"THE LADIES FROM LONESOME"

One of his favorite moments was doing a live reading back in April of an unproduced script written by Burt Kennedy, who directed such classics as *Return of the Seven, The War Wagon,* and *Support Your Local Sheriff!*

Kirk Ellis, whose past credits include *Into the West, John Adams,* and *Ben Franklin,* mentioned that while Kennedy mentored him, Kennedy had penned a script called *The Ladies from Lonesome* about how the prostitutes became cattle drovers. Word said that people knew he was working on it, but no one knew it was done.

Word on Westerns decided to do a script reading with actors for the show. Actors Bruce Davidson, Stephanie Powers, Bobby Carradine, Bruce Boxleit-

Rob, his wife, Laura, and their son, R.J., posing with Sidney Poitier after Rob was awarded the Golden Boot Award in 2007.
Photo by Jennie Knudsen

Rob poses with the cast of *The Ladies From Lonesome* after a live script reading at the Wells Fargo Theater at the Autry Museum. *Courtesy of the Rob Word & A Word on Westerns.*

ner, Delanna Studi, and 14 others came together for a recorded live reading at the theater.

"We read it once at home and had such a good time. But that was the only rehearsal we had," Word said. "It had wonderful lines and was so distinct that you knew what each character was about. It was a lot of work. We had a blast doing it, and the audience had a great time. It was a tribute to one of the all-time greats."

RELAX THE GUEST

Word's interviewing technique is simple: Relax the guest. However, he can only do that because he prepares for each interview, like cramming for a test.

"What I do is amazing," he said. "I have conversations. We're just sitting around and talking. If I can trigger a memory, that usually gets them started. That memory awakens something in their memory. That's the nicest thing I can do for my guests. This is my hobby that got out of hand. I love Westerns and movies and want my guests to have fun. Several months later, the guest will return and sit in the audience to watch my other interviews, which makes it all worthwhile."

Not every guest was cooperative, though. For instance, Word said all he could get from Don Knotts was a single sentence. So, during the in-

terview, Word spent most of his time discussing Knotts' past credits and history.

"I had people come up to me and say how they learned so much about Don Knotts," Word said. "It was because I did my homework and all the talking. Years later, I got to interview Tim Mattheson, who worked with Don Knotts while filming *The Apple Dumpling Gang Rides Again*. Tim was a fabulous guest. He told some very funny stories about Tim [Conway] and Don. Tim was a fan of those guys, and the audience can see that. I'm happy with every guest... mostly."

Word added that a good interviewer will listen to their guest. "Find exceptional hosts at what they do," Word said. "Right now, no one does it better than Jimmy Kimmel. "He listens to his guests, does his homework, and gets stories from them. Most importantly, have a good time."

If you're a Western fan and would like to tune in to *A Word on Westerns,* you can find it on YouTube at **www.youtube.com/@AWordonWesterns.**

George "Clay" Mitchell *is an award-winning reporter and photographer, a founding partner of* Saddlebag Dispatches, *and Executive Vice President and Publisher of its partner company, Roan & Weatherford Publishing Associates. He lives in Lavaca, Arkansas, with his wife and two daughters.*

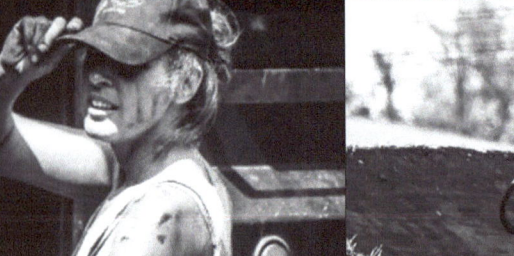

JAMES A. TWEEDIE

LEAVE HER BE

A SHORT STORY

"Sir!" I said in as quiet and firm a voice as I could control. "Let go, stand back, and leave her be!"

It was mid-July, 1878, and I was riding the Denver Pacific night train to Cheyenne. There must have been eight or ten other passengers in the car, but when the man in the seat behind me started choking the woman next to him, I was the only one who stood up and said or did anything.

The man looked to be in his mid-twenties, perhaps fifteen years younger than I was.

His fingernails were worn short, with traces of dirt underneath what were left of the nails, and his fingers were attached to two rough and calloused hands which, as he turned to face me, were tightly clenched.

A dark beard framed a face that was red with anger—a meanness that had quickly torn itself away from the sobbing woman and redirected itself at me.

"I don't know who you are, and I don't rightly care to know!" he growled. "But you'd best be mindin' your own business and be leavin' me to deal with my wife as I see fit!"

When I didn't immediately respond, he continued his rant, "Do you understand? Or do I have to pound it into your head like you was a woman?"

I didn't want to engage in a fight, especially with a rough-hewn miner who looked strong enough to level me with one blow. Even so, for the sake of the woman, I refused to back off.

"This is not the time or place to be disciplining your wife," I answered. "I suggest that you step between the cars for a time and cool off."

He responded by trying to sucker-punch me with a looping right hook.

I was quick enough and experienced enough to deflect the blow but a straight left hand caught me full on the forehead above my right eye.

If my head had been a bell, it would have rung loud enough to be heard all the way to San Francisco.

I went down in a heap and looked up at my adversary standing over me in the aisle.

I caught a glimpse of a metal flask poking out of his front trouser pocket, then watched as the expression on his face turned from anger, to disgust, and then to distain.

"Leave me and my wife alone," he said as he shoved my leg with his foot.

He then bent over and lowered his face to less than six inches above my own.

"Or I'll kill you," he whispered.

The car fell completely silent, including the woman who—although I couldn't see her from where I was lying on the floor—appeared to have brought her sobbing to a full stop.

"What's this?" called out the Conductor as he stepped into the car and took in the scene.

"It's nothin'," said the man who had just brought me low. "We had a difference. He pushed me, and I pushed him back."

He turned his head from the Conductor and locked his eyes on mine.

"Ain't that right, Mister?" he said to me. "It's the truth, ain't it? Tell the man that it's the truth."

I slowly pulled myself into a sitting position.

"It's close enough to the truth for me not to argue against it," I said as I crawled back onto my seat with my head pounding in pain.

As soon as the Conductor left the car, the man behind me opened his fists long enough light up a cigar. He then spent the next thirty minutes blowing the smoke onto my head until I could neither see nor breathe. When the smoke became intolerable, I took my own advice and stepped into the space between the cars in order to breathe and in order to keep myself from doing something that I would immediately regret.

Let it go, I told myself. The man is right. It's none of my business.

But, even so, I feared for the safety of the poor woman and wondered how many times her husband had threatened to kill her the same as he had threatened me.

At Cheyenne, I would be transferring to the Union Pacific, heading west on my way to Sacramento to meet with the major shareholders in the Central Pacific Railroad.

If the man and his wife made the same transfer, I promised myself that I would do what I could to keep the woman safe but otherwise I would wash my hands of it.

As for myself, I was traveling as an agent for Jay Gould, one of the wealthiest and most powerful men in the country—a man associated with Boss Tweed and Tammany Hall as well as being the man whose attempt to corner the gold market led to the Black Friday gold panic in 1869.

Gould had a keen interest in acquiring control of railroad lines, an interest that dated as far back as 1857. After acquiring a controlling interest in the Union Pacific in 1873, his next project, and the reason for my trip, was to find a way to gain controlling interest in other western railroads, including the Kansas Pacific, Denver Pacific, and Central Pacific. The Central Pacific was a long shot since Stanford, Huntington, Hopkins, and Crocker still held full control of every inch of track from Promontory, Utah, to Sacramento.

But if Gould could acquire enough shares and negotiate a merger with the Kansas and Denver Pacific railroads, he would wield political and economic control of virtually everything in the United States

between the Mississippi River and the Great Basin of the Intermountain West.

My assignment was to meet with the owners and major investors of the railroads, make various "enquiries," see which way the wind was blowing, and then report back to Gould.

The newspapers said that Gould was "corrupt" and a "robber baron" and, in support of that opinion, the cartoonist, Thomas Nast, had lampooned him more than once in *Harper's Weekly*—most recently for Gould's loss of control of the Erie Railroad the previous March—part of a corruption scandal that put Tweed in jail for life the following year.

Gould had somehow avoided prosecution, though, and as far as I was concerned, as long as what I was doing was on the up and up, I'd work for anyone willing to pay the sort of money that Gould had offered for my services. As for my private life, I'd say I was a little more of a Mama's Boy than a Ladies' Man.

My father was a mean drunk who beat my mother until he unexpectedly died one night in his sleep. Even as a child I had always taken my mother's side

in their arguments and I took some beatings for it. But when Pa died the town gossip was that Ma had poisoned him and maybe she did, but no one could prove it so I grew up with Ma.

The scuffle on the train triggered memories I would have preferred to have left forgotten. But I've never thought it right for a man to take advantage of someone unable to defend themself whether it be an old man, a woman, or a child. I consider such men to be cowards—no better than mad dogs foaming at the mouth and needing to be put down.

And as far as I'm concerned, God didn't create marriage for a man to lord it over his wife with a whip any more that he intended for the whip to be in the hands of the wife. It seems to me that if a marriage isn't a safe and peaceful place for both man and wife then it's a lie to call it a marriage at all.

But then again, it's none of my business what other folks do so long as what they do doesn't cause me any harm. So, I try to love my neighbor without being my "brother's keeper," even though it's sometimes hard to tell the one from the other.

When the train stopped at Greely to exchange

Mockingbird,
Make Up Your Mind!

Written & Illustrated by
Victoria Marble

passengers, I went back to my seat and found the seat behind mine empty.

I figured they'd gotten off at the stop, but they must have just changed cars, because when I stepped off the train in Cheyenne they were standing on the platform, waiting for their bags.

Later, when I went to step on the west-bound train, the husband came up from behind and elbowed me to the side so he and his wife could board first.

People have shot each other for less than this, I thought to myself as I tried with some difficulty to control my rising anger.

Instead of shadowing them onto the train I walked to the following car and found a seat facing another young couple who turned out to be a brother and sister returning from a family visit to New York. They were most engaging and the boy regaled me with stories about the dungarees he was helping his uncle Levi make back in San Francisco. He gave me his card and told me to stop by and see him if I got as far as San Francisco. Their names were Jacob and Caroline Stern and their uncle's family name was Strauss.

I never did get to San Francisco, but I kept the card as a memento of my cross-country trip.

It was a trip that almost ended nine hours later when we made a dinner stop in Rawlins.

The train's meal of water and coal was predictable, but so also was the tasteless mix of carrots, potatoes, gravy and flecks of meat—rumored by some to be prairie dog—that was slopped on a plate for any passenger willing to trade a dollar for it—which was a day's wage for some of the passengers.

The railroad only allowed thirty minutes for meals so when the train whistle started blowing folks left the tables in a hurry whether they'd finished eating or not.

"Don't you go tellin' me what to do!" an angry voice echoed through the emptying dining area.

It was the husband and wife at it again and this time the man stood up and gave his wife a vicious slap across the face with the back of his hand.

To her credit—even with a touch of blood showing at the corner of her mouth—she stood her ground and pointed at the table where the flask I had seen earlier was now lying empty on its side.

"You're too drunk to know what you're doin', Todd," she yelled. "And you're too drunk to get back on the train without my help, but I'm done helpin'

you and I'm done puttin' up with your excuses for bein' so mean to me...."

She paused long enough to catch her breath.

" ... so why don't you just crawl into the privy out back and throw up with your face buried in the shithole...."

Todd was breathing hard like a bull about to charge, but he was unsteady on his feet and leaning on the table to keep his balance.

"... and when you wake up in the morning, you'll have a hangover but you won't have me because I'll be long gone!"

With that, she spit in his face, but before she could turn to leave, he stumbled forward more quickly than she expected, wrapped his arms around her shoulders and dragged her face down onto the floor.

Like a street-brawler, he knelt on her back, grabbed her hair and started to beat her face against the floor.

He never got the chance to do it twice because I raced over, grabbed the back of his shirt and pulled him off. In a moment he was back on his feet in a fighter's crouch, facing me with a knife large enough to take down a bear in a fair fight.

I had nothing to defend myself since I carried neither gun nor blade, unless you counted my penknife as a weapon.

Todd charged and I grabbed a nearby chair to fend him off, but before he got close enough to take me down there was a flash and a bang followed by a puff of black smoke rising from the floor where Todd's wife was now balanced on one knee.

Her derringer only had one bullet but she'd made good use of it, seeing as it left its mark dead center in the back of Todd's head.

His eyes went from raging-red to dead-blank in an instant, and his forward momentum carried him, still stumbling, ten feet past me before he fell face down and lifeless to the floor.

When the town marshal was called in, he ordered the train to stay put until he'd gotten statements from everyone who had seen what had happened.

I was the last passenger to be interviewed.

"Can't have women shooting their husbands," the marshal said as he nodded his permission for me to board the train. "Maybe in Denver or one of those big places like 'Frisco or Omaha, but not here, not in Rawlins."

He turned and gave a name to the woman who

JOHN T. BIGGS

THE
OWL OF
DEATH ROW

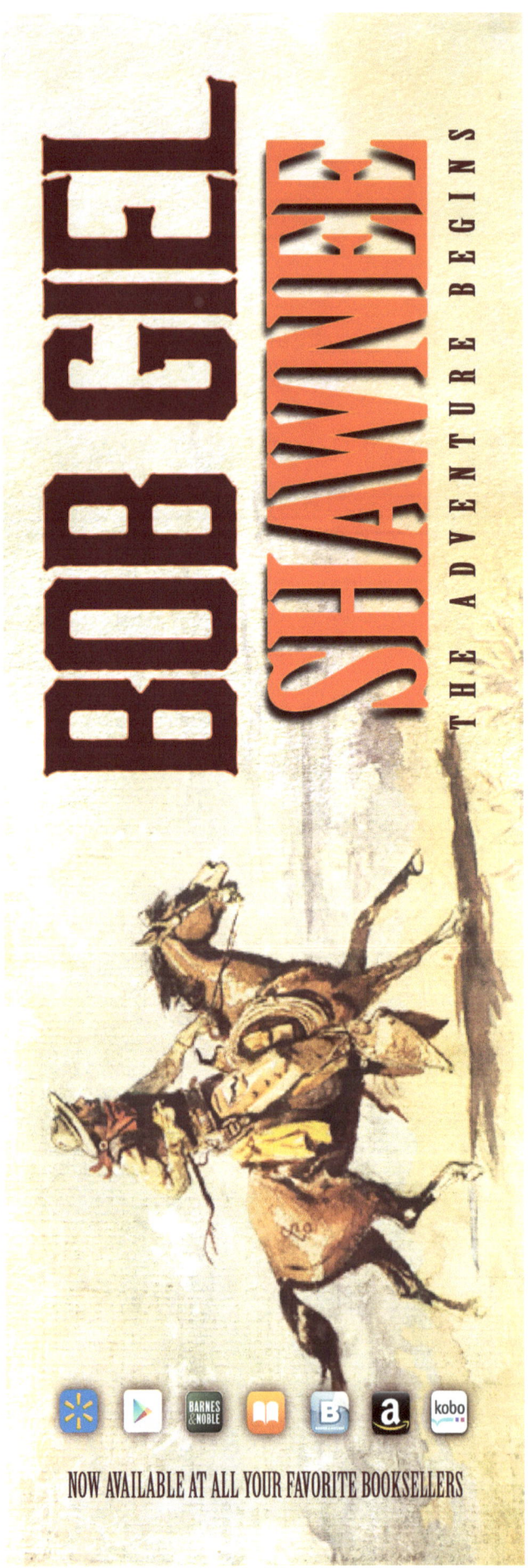
had stood up to her bully husband and shot him dead to save my life.

"Rebecca Parsons," he declared, "I'm arresting you for the murder of your husband, Todd Parsons."

"You can't do that," I interrupted. "She saved my life. It was self-defense...."

He didn't let me finish the sentence.

"I thought I told you to get on that train and go," he said with a scowl. "I didn't say she was guilty or not. I just said what I was arresting her for. It will be up to a jury to decide whether she hangs or goes free."

He abruptly turned to his deputy.

"Did you get their luggage off the train?"

The deputy nodded and the marshal turned his attention back to me.

"I thought I told you to git," he said.

"Not until I'm allowed to have a word with Rebecca... Mrs. Parsons... if that's all right with you?"

"Seein' how everyone here says she saved your life, and seein' that you'll prob'ly never see her again, then I guess I'll grant you a minute with her. But mind you, the train's tired of waiting, so make it quick."

She'd been sitting in a chair unshackled and untied now for nearly two hours, with her eyes alternating between watching the marshal do his interviews and staring at her hands as if she was still finding it impossible to believe what those hands had just done.

As the folks around her stepped back to give me room, I pulled up a chair and sat facing her.

For the first time I had the opportunity to see her full in the face as a real person.

She looked younger than I had originally imagined, perhaps no more than seventeen or eighteen. Her brown hair was braided into a tight bun, and while her face was soft and unblemished it was also plain and expressionless—except for her blue eyes, which burned like two fuses about to set off a pile of explosives.

"Rebecca," I began. "I'm sorry things turned out the way they did. I'm sorry I couldn't do...."

Usually I'm a good talker, which is one of the reasons Gould hired me as his agent. But sitting and staring at the tearless grief in this young woman's face left me speechless.

"I want to thank you for saving my life. You didn't have to do that, but you did, and I hope they don't hold it against you, because it wasn't your fault. It was Todd... and... there must be a whole lot of other things that I don't know about, but I just wanted to say thank you and let you know that if there's a trial I'll do what I can to help you get free.

"I guess that's all I have to say. They tell me I've got to go. I won't forget you. I owe you my life."

Her expression never changed but her eyes followed mine as I stood, and I have no doubt that those burning blue eyes followed me all the way out of the room.

The train whistle welcomed me back on board, and as it headed west, it left Rawlins and Rebecca Parsons behind to face an uncertain future.

Five weeks later, on my return trip, the train made another dinner stop in Rawlins.

The only thing I wanted to know was what happened to Rebecca.

It didn't take long to find out because Rawlins was a small town and the murder trial had practically shut down the place for two days.

The first man I ran into told me that the jury deliberated for only fifteen minutes before returning a unanimous verdict of "not guilty."

"What happened to Rebecca?" I asked

The man smiled and traced the toe of his boot in the town's Main Street dirt before giving an answer.

"Well," he drawled, "the women in town were mighty pleased with the verdict and celebrated by taking up a collection and offering to buy her a train ticket to anywhere she wanted to go."

"And where did she decide to go?" I asked.

"She decided to go back to Denver—back to the cabin she'd been living in up in Leadville."

"And that's it?" I asked.

His grin grew wider. "Except for one thing."

"And what's that?" I asked.

"I heard that when she got back to Cheyenne, she walked up to the Denver Pacific ticket agent and demanded a refund for her used ticket and a free ride back to Denver."

"And...?" I asked as I encouraged him to finish the story.

"Well I'll be darned if the Agent not only refunded her full fare from Denver, but gave her back the full fare for her husband's ticket along with it!"

I laughed and smiled back at the man.

"I like the Denver Pacific's style," I said as I slapped him on the back "And the next time you see me, I might just own a piece of it." ♞

THE AUTHOR

James A. Tweedie *has lived in California, Utah, Scotland, Australia, Hawaii, and presently in Long Beach, Washington. He has published six novels, four collections of poetry, and one collection of short stories with Dunecrest Press. His award-winning stories and poetry have appeared in regional, national, and international print and online anthologies. He has twice been honored with a Silver Certificate award from Writers of the Future and was awarded First Prize in the inaugural Edinburgh Festival Flash Fiction Contest. He is a regular contributor to* Frontier Tales *and* Saddlebag Dispatches.

He recalls moving from San Francisco to Logan, Utah, in 1979 and being both baffled and amused when he was asked, "What made you decide to move out West from California?"

In that moment, he learned that "the West" was not just a direction, but a cultural space infused with traditions and tales embracing a heritage of mountain men, pioneers, Native Peoples, cowboys, homesteaders, prospectors, ranchers, railroads, and a host of conflicts that stretched and expanded the United States into the country it is today.

His favorite corner of the West is the Sierra Nevada, where he has hiked and fly fished since he was old enough to walk.

LAW & MERCY IN EARLY LEADVILLE

Law Enforcement and Medical Services:
two separate pieces of Leadville's early history that were a
contributing factor to the city's survival and growth.

STORY BY

DORIS McCRAW

Leadville, that city sitting high in the Rocky Mountains of Colorado, is just over 10,000' feet above sea level. With tree line averaging 11,500 feet and the mountains, Mount Elbert, being the tallest in Colorado is just about twelve miles to the southwest. In addition, Mt. Massive and Mt. Harvard in the area complete the top three highest in the state.

Into the area thousands came to either make their fortune from the ore in the ground or from the people who were digging for that ore. As with any quick growing town there were elements of lawlessness. In addition, many who made their way to Leadville didn't make that big strike and found themselves either working the mines for others or perhaps tried other trades.

With the rapid growth there was also a need for medical personnel and hospitals to tend those who fell ill. These two opposites, especially in the early

days, can be illustrated by looking at Marshal Martin Duggan and the Sisters of Charity. Both were active around the same time, 1879, and help illustrate the growing pains of this booming 'city'.

Beginning with the law part of this story, we will look at the journey Leadville took from the beginning with the election of Horace Tabor as mayor and the appointment of T. H. Harrison as city marshal to the two terms as marshal of Martin (Mart) Duggan.

As with all booming mining towns, Leadville was no exception to the pangs of rapid growth. In the book Deadly Dozen the author, Robert K. DeArment, says this about Leadville and the criminal element: "from its earliest days Leadville seemed to attract more than its quota of violent ruffians and gunmen". This criminal element ran T. H. Harrison out of town only two days after Horace Tabor had appointed him.

The next appointed city marshal managed to last almost a month before he was shot and killed

A buckboard makes it's way down Leadville's bustling Harrison Avenue circa 1881.

by his own deputy after a disagreement about the deputy spending too much time in the saloons and dance halls.

According to the news report in a Leadville paper, Marshall George O'Connor, on April 25, 1878, went to Billy Nye's saloon with his deputy James Bloodsworth. As an argument the two were having escalated, Bloodsworth pulled his pistol and fired five shots into O'Connor, then fled the scene never to be seen or heard from again.

It was from this situation that Mayor Tabor called on Martin Duggan to 'pin on the badge.' One wonders if he could have fast forwarded to the future would he have accepted?

At the time Martin Duggan proved to be what Leadville needed. This square faced man was exactly the person the situation called for. The Rocky Mountain News, a Denver newspaper, had this to say, "his courage and nerve were supplemented by a fine physique. He was of medium height, but of compact, massive build. His hair and complexion were light and his eyes blue. He was a man that you would look at twice as you first met him."

This was a far cry from the young Irish immigrant boy who arrived in New York prior to the draft riots that had killed many of his countrymen.

There are some differing stories of Duggan's early years. One source says he started out alone from New York while another source, supposedly a friend who knew him well, said he came to Colorado with his family in 1861. This same friend's account has him working for his brother tending bar in Georgetown, being a prospector, and keeping a saloon in Ouray.

The local newspaper in Leadville stated that when he arrived, he brought with him the reputation of a fighting man, equally dangerous with guns or fist, although there was no official document of the truth of those statements.

One thing that is certain, according to news reports from his time in Leadville, Duggan was no one to mess with. It seemed he feared no man or group of men.

As one report in the local paper illustrated the truth of this statement. Shortly after being appointed he confronted a group intent on hurrahing a local restaurant. Duggan stepped up to the leader in the restaurant and ordered him outside. The recorded

1880 view looking down Harrison Avenue from the West, showing the many stores, offices, and saloons in operation.

following conversation went something like this after Duggan had issued his order.

"What if I don't go?" The leader sneered.

"Then say a 'Hail Mary 'because you're dead where you stand."

The story continues with the confronted man, after looking Duggan in the eye, blink and head out the door.

For a brief space of time Leadville experienced a period of "peace." However, Martin Duggan declined the badge after his term ended. That term was what remained of the initial time of the two city marshals prior to him. In April of 1879 he stated he and his wife Sophia wanted to travel to Michigan to visit her family.

He was followed by P. A. Kelley, whom the papers say was not up to the standards of Duggan. It said the criminal element was again threatening to take over the town. By November of 1879 the city

Council wired and asked Duggan to reconsider. Duggan returned and again served the city as marshal from December 1879 to April 1880.

During his tenure Duggan executed his duties as he saw fit. No one was truly exempt. He once arrested mining magnet August Rische, one of the wealthy mine owners, and who Tabor had grubstaked, for drunk and disorderly conduct. When Rische resisted arrest Duggan hit him over the head with the nightstick and took him to jail. Horace Tabor, still the mayor, let Duggan know that Rische, because of his position, should have special consideration. Duggan informed Tabor, if he continued in that vein, he would join his friend in lockup for obstructing justice.

However, he had his detractors. One of Duggan's flaws included becoming violent when drinking. When in this inebriated state no one was immune. Yet, his abilities to control the criminal element gave him a pass with many of the residents in Leadville.

While Duggan and the rest of law enforcement were engaging in their battles for the control of Leadville, the rest of the growing town was working to create a vibrant city.

In 1879 Postmaster Smith moved the post office from cramped quarters to a larger space which he was able to rent for $2000 a year. It was reported the postal employees were handling 1500 pounds of

Looking East down Harrison Avenue toward Fryer Hill.

The Lake County Courthouse on Harrison Avenue, circa 1881.

incoming mail and about 1000 pounds of outgoing mail on a daily basis. This included sorting 7000 incoming letters and 6000 outgoing letters. Within four days, according to one report, they issued 895 money orders worth $9354 and paid out 58 money orders worth $1820.

There were, as of June 1879, according to *The Chronicle* newspaper, three daily newspapers, four banks, four theaters, five gun shops, seven drugstores, twelve real estate offices, thirteen assay offices, thirteen livery stables, sixteen corrals, fifteen blacksmith shops, thirty-one restaurants, thirty-five houses of prostitution, forty-four hotels and lodging houses, and one hundred twenty saloons.

There were also five ministers, four churches, two fire companies, and four brass bands. It was estimated that the city cemetery contained 303 burials. Yet, even with fifty doctors, there was no hospital listed.

Leadville was on its way, in the minds of the res-

idents, and leading the way were the women. Despite having little to say in business they were busy working to improve the conditions of those living in the city. During the summer the women of the Catholic Church held a festival in the unfinished Tabor Opera House. They collected, according to one report, over $5000.

Shortly after this fair the 'Ladies Relief Society', an organization set up to aid the ill who could not afford medical care, met to discuss the feasibility of having their own fair. Although this fair never happened, they sent the following letter to the editor of one of the local newspapers. It said in part:

"It is the desire of the friends of the ladies relief hospital that your enterprising paper should place the needs of this institution before the citizens in such a way as to bring to its aid their support and sympathy for want of which it is almost powerless to do the

Fryer Hill was a major mining district in the 1880s, as well as the location of Horace Tabor's famed Matchless Mine.

work daily brought to its doors. There was a meeting recently held at the house of us in Wells for the purpose of electing officers and the transaction of business looking into the enlargement of facilities and plans of operation. It is proposed, by the consent of the donors, to sell the present property... And secure a location beyond the reach of confusion and the smoke of the smelters at little or no expense. It is thought that the money realized from the sale will do much in the erection of a building such as the cause demands.

"The society is now taking shape to be able to meet the wants of all who may need its care, and with the hope and energy now manifested among the ladies, it is believe the people will give such aid as will provide care and nursing for the increasing numbers of sick and suffering in our midst."

However, it appears not all was as most believed. A later article seemed to point to a reorganization of the society. The article read in part:

"The ladies relief hospital... Has been a successful one to date. Many an unfortunate stranger has here found kind treatment, but alas, alas. A misunderstanding has arisen, or perhaps more properly speaking, this mischief maker cunningly crept into the peaceful fold. To strike the nail square on the head and tell the whole story in a single sentence, "Doctor" Bowker in some way or other sanctum modified his way into the female fold that settled it. Everything is discord, and the good work so successfully commenced by the noble ladies of the original society, is liable to come to naught."

However, it was said even with all the disruption, the hospital continued to function, influenced in large part by the efficient work of Mrs. Kelly and Dr. Mary Barker Bates. At the time Dr. Bates was the only female doctor in Leadville.

While the Ladies Relief Society was working to get their hospital built there were others working for the same goal—a hospital.

During Catholic fair mentioned in the Ladies Relief Society article, two Sisters of Charity from Leavenworth also visited the fair. The two, Sisters Francis Xavier Davy and Apollonia Rohr, stationed in Denver, were visiting the mining camps to raise funds to aid in paying the incurred debt from the building of the St. Joseph's Hospital in Denver.

They came to Leadville from Fairplay over Weston pass. Once there, Father Robinson encouraged them to attend the fair. With the help of Miss Anastasia McCormick, the sisters received a large sum of money to aid their mission. It was during this time the residents of Leadville requested the Sisters of Charity think about building a hospital in their town. Father Robinson sent their request to the Mother Superior in Leavenworth. In the fall of that year, he received word the Mother Superior had granted the request. The Sisters would be building a hospital in Leadville although the sisters did not have to try raise funds to build the hospital. It was named St. Vincent's Hospital, and they had secured the funds prior to building. However, news reports at the time indicated there was concern about their making ends meet after the building was complete. One of two things that would help them stay afloat was the city and county paying for the indigent patients they treated and the fact that all the work was done by the Sisters.

Before the hospital was even finished, for there was a scarcity of lumber and shortage of carpenters in the area in addition to all the other structures being erected in the town at the time, an unidentified man came into the unfinished building and placed an unconscious man that he was carrying in his arms on a pile of wood shavings. Sister Mary Pendergast pointed out that they still didn't have any doors or windows installed and that patients could not be cared for because the hospital was far from complete. The story in the paper said the man shrugged his shoulders and turned to leave saying "I'll leave him anyway. He might as well die here as on the street."

The Sisters decided that despite the fact the hospital was unfinished they would do what they could for the suffering man. With cooperation from various workmen, window openings were boarded up, a stove was set up, and in addition to a few doors being hung a mattress and blankets were obtained. Thus Thomas Krating was the hospital's first patient.

The next day the workmen created rooms in the unfinished hospital by putting up canvas and calico partitions. Unfortunately, the severely frostbitten Krating died three days later. However, the Sisters had several patients prior to the official opening of the hospital.

The papers also reported that during the summer at one time the sisters of St. Vincent's Hospital treated close to 100 patients. The city's doctor, Ernest Meire stated he had sent 38 patients to the hospital. According to the doctor all 38 had been diagnosed with pneumonia yet only three had died.

It was obvious that Leadville was growing, and St. Vincent's was part of that growth. An example of the mindset of those coming to Leadville is found in the following excerpt from an article about the hospital:

"Would you please tell me the number of patients?" Ventured the reporter, hardly knowing where to commence or why he came.

"I shall have to get my book if you require statistics," and taking down a large register from the shelf, she [the sister in charge of the hospital] found that on the 13th day of March last the hospital was opened with one patient from that date till last evening, June 2, there had been 181 patients admitted of whom 14 died, there being 50 now in the hospital. In speaking of the 14 who had died, the Sister remarked that it seemed like a good many to lose, but as the physicians would testify, they were scarcely alive when they came. Here, in this anxious, busy, exciting mining country, men are loath to lay down as long as there is a breath of life left in their bodies.

"Now sister—should I call you Sister?"

"Oh, yes, everybody calls us Sister."

"Well, what I wish to learn is this: I am near 3000 miles from home and friends. Now suppose I should fall into a well or take the pneumonia, what would become of me?"

"Why, you could come here, and we would try and take care of you."

"But I am not a member of the Catholic Church."

"That makes no difference. We never inquire about a patient's religion. So long as there is room, we take all who come, whatever may be their color, creed or nationality. Otherwise, it would not be a charity."

"But you Sisters are all members of the Catholic Church."

"Yes, that is true, but that does not prevent us from trying to do good for others."

"You receive no reward for your labors?"

"Not in this world. We look to our reward in the next."

The article continues...

...although every room in the building is overcrowded, each is scrupulously neat and tidy. The convalescent patients are provided with bedding and obliged to sleep in the halls.

One small room visited by the reporter had three beds. There was a man in each. On entering, two turned their heads toward the door. The third did not stir. He was dead. The undertaker had been notified in the morning, but had not yet arrived, and as there was no vacant room in the building, the corpse must necessarily be left in the same room with the living.

St. Vincent's again appeared in the news when after reports of the Denver and Rio Grande officials buying ground just north of the hospital. Suddenly the hospital was on very valuable real estate. One news report said 'lot jumpers' had sent letters to the sisters of Charity, ordering them to move the hospital to some other location or the lots on which it stood would be taken by force. Sister Mary Bridget told Fathers Robinson and Walsh of the threats. These two went to the church parishioners and with their help about one hundred men took turns guarding the hospital. The note the 'lot jumpers', as they were called, was a threat to set fire to the hospital unless the fence which was enclosing it and the adjoining lots they owned was torn down. Later that night two men snuck up onto the grounds and began to tear down the fence. One of the guards that shouted for them to stop but the men paid no attention. A pistol was fired and the two ran

off. A number of the men guarding the hospital ran after them and another pistol shot sounded out and one of the men fell. Although his accomplice tried to lift him to his feet they were soon surrounded by the guards. A police officer by the name of Roger Sweeney grabbed the uninjured man and took him to jail the other was taken into the hospital where his leg wound was treated before he too was taken to jail.

As Leadville continued to grow and thrive so did St. Vincent's. The same could not be said for Martin Duggan. After leaving law enforcement, Duggan at one point shot and killed a man in self-defense. He turned himself in after the incident and was cleared of the charges. However, the victim's widow swore to wear mourning until Duggan was dead then she would give her widow weeds to Duggan's wife. When he was later shot and killed, the story is told the widow was seen dancing where Duggan's blood had spilled on the walk and later a shadowy figure was seen throwing something on the porch of Duggan's house.

Today, Leadville has St. Vincent's Health, the descendant of that original hospital. As for Marshal Duggan, his story has only recently come to light, yet these two separate pieces of Leadville's early history were a contributing factor to the city's growth.

Doris McCraw *is an Author, speaker, and historian specializing in Colorado and Women's History. She is a member of National League of American Pen Women, Western Writers of America, Women Writing the West, Western Fictioneers and the Pikes Peak Posse of the Westerners. She also writes fiction under the pen name, Angela Raines.*

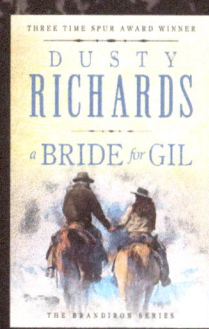 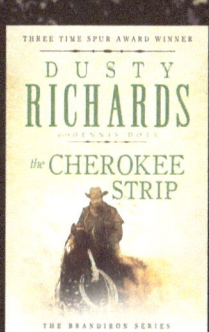 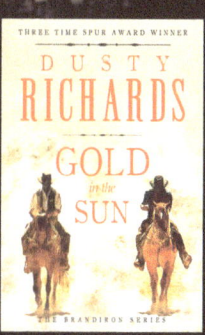 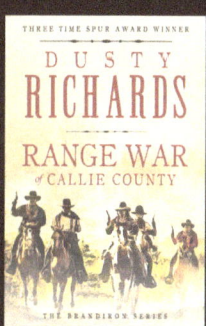 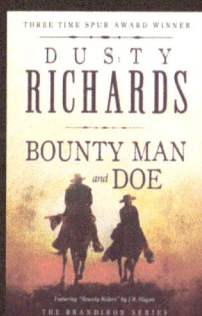 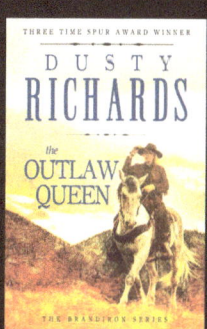

BESTSELLING AUTHOR OF *FRIENDS CALL ME BAT*

PAUL COLT
LUNGER

THE DOC HOLLIDAY STORY

PAUL COLT

DOC VISITS LEADVILLE

AN EXCERPT FROM THE WILL ROGERS MEDALLION AWARD-WINNING NOVEL *LUNGER: THE DOC HOLLIDAY STORY*

BOARD OF TRADE SALOON
LEADVILLE, COLORADO
JULY, 1882

After righting the matter of Johnny Ringo, Ah followed Lady Luck to Leadville. Upon ma arrival in Leadville, Ah determined to become a model citizen of upright demeanor and proper decorum starting with the Leadville ordinance prohibiting the carrying of firearms in town. Going about unheeled, Ah scrupulously avoided troublesome situations and so doing lived peaceably, despite disease tightening its relentless grip on ma lungs.

The town boomed out of a silver strike in the '70s. Silver production petered out by the onset of the '80s, but boom town gaming and vice remained strong. Ah took to the tables in various of the more than one hundred gaming establishments along Harrison Avenue, among them John Morgan's Board of Trade saloon. Ah took residence in Mannie Hyman's saloon, occasionally dealing faro there.

Cugh, cugh, cugh… cugh.

Ah poured another drink in hopes whiskey would quench the fire in ma chest or at least render me dull to its effects.

"Doc, that stuff ain't helpin' none."

John Morgan, ever solicitous of ma health. "Consumption no, consumption some, ma friend." Ah poured another drink.

"Been to the doctor lately?"

"To what good?"

"Maybe he could prescribe something to ease the cough. Whiskey sure ain't helpin'."

Laudanum Ah thought to ma self-diagnosis. Perhaps, couldn't hurt to give it a try. "Thank you, John, I shall take you up on your advice."

Ah can't say the laudanum helped. It certainly did not hurt, though when mixed with whiskey, which Ah continued to consume, one had to strike a balance to remain competitive at the tables. Ah survived the fog of disease, managing to stay ahead of the horseman for the next two years.

HYMAN'S SALOON
JULY, 1884

Ma conditioned worsened in spite of the opium elixir better serving ma tolerance to discomfort. Better, though dull comfort did little to slack my thirst. It served to fortify ma drinking. As things progressed John may have come to regret his medicinal advice. Ah accepted as inevitable the rider's pursuit.

To ma condition, Lady Luck added insult to infirmity. She deserted ma game. She is a fickle wench, though some speculate medications may have played a part in the deleterious decline of ma acumen at the tables. Ah placed no store by such notions. The faithless whore to fortune was not to be trusted. Perhaps such thinking further offended her, for she tripped me with yet another pair of tricks when two disreputable characters from ma Tombstone past found their way into town.

Johnny Tyler, with whom Ah had contentious relations during ma time at the Oriental dealing in Wyatt's concession along with former Ike Clanton Cowboy, Billy Allen. Tyler came into Hyman's saloon one evening backed by rowdy cronies he sought to impress with bravado directed to ma person. I sat at ma usual corner table, medicating ma dissipation with whiskey.

"There he sits boys, Doc Holliday, the Cowboy killer himself. Killed any Cowboys lately, Doc? No, I suppose not. No Earp to hide behind here."

"Ah, Johnny Tyler. No, no Earp here, for if there were, you'd surely tuck your scallywag tail between your bowed legs and slink out of town."

"Big talk for a scrawny lunger a stiff breeze might blow away. Now, if you was to back up your palaver, you'd pull so I could return the favor of your killin' my friends."

Ah laid ma hands on the table. "Not armed, Johnny. You must know there's an ordinance against carrying firearms in Leadville."

"Listen to him, boys. Doc Holliday's become a law-abiding citizen. Goes right nice with the yellow streak down his back, don't yah think?"

With that, Ah stood and turned to the stairs to go to ma room.

"Look there, boys, he turns tail and runs, yellow streak and all."

"Ah should bide ma tongue if Ah were you, Johnny. One never knows when one might have to eat it."

"That a threat, Doc? If it is, get yourself heeled and back it up."

Ah climbed the stairs.

"Yellow son-of-a-bitch."

Ah found the incident an embarrassing insult to ma honor. Time was, Ah might have killed the impudent rascal for half as much. Time was. Time passes. Time passes. Honor does not, though the passion one feels for it may waste away. Ah felt ma-self past killing for it.

AUGUST, 1884

Ah should have known better when it came to Billy Allen. Ma judgement was surely fogged by medication, though Ah cannot now recollect if it was whiskey or the opium elixir on that occasion. No matter. Ah found ma-self impecunious and in need of a small loan. Five dollars seemed a trivial amount, and Billy Allen, for all our past troubles, was more than willing to oblige for a promise of re-payment within the week. The week passed. Regrettably, Lady Luck turned her back on me once again. Ah found Billy tending bar in the Monarch Saloon.

"Come to pay up, Doc?" He said polishing a glass.

"Regrettably no, Billy. Misfortune besets me. Ah shall need a little more time."

"What the hell you think I am, a bank? Listen here, you stinking drunk, pay me by noon Tuesday or I'm comin' for you and all them dead pards you an' Earp killt."

Ah took ma leave without further incident. When Tuesday arrived, Ah received word Allen was armed and asking around for me. Ah took the precaution of having ma Colt hidden behind the bar in Hyman's. Unable to repay a five-dollar-loan, the fine for a firearm violation posed prospect of financial ruin. On ma way down to the saloon, Ah explained ma plight to Mannie Hyman and asked him to notify the police Billy Allen was about courting trouble. Ah hoped police protection might avert trouble. Once in the saloon, Ah took a place at the end of the bar within reach of ma weapon.

Billy Allen entered Hyman's with his hand in his pocket in the fashion of concealing a gun. He scanned the room. His gaze came to rest on me. Ah pulled ma pistol and shot him a wounding graze to the arm. Ma second shot narrowly missed killing him as he slumped to the floor. At this, the bartender disarmed me, sparing the miscreant's life.

Ah was promptly arrested and charged with attempted murder. Bail was set at five thousand dollars. It might as well have been five hundred thousand for ma impecunious circumstances. John Morgan, owner of the Board of Trade Saloon, made bail. Consider the irony. Had Ah borrowed five dollars from John to repay Alan's loan, the whole ugly matter might well have been avoided. Pride precluded me from seeking such aid.

Pride. Honor. The code of a southern gentleman. Such things prove a heavy burden amid the vagaries of real life.

LEADVILLE MUNICIPAL COURTHOUSE
AUGUST 25, 1884

The bailiff strode to the bench. "All rise. Court is now in session, Justice of the Peace William W. Old presiding."

"Be seated. We have before us the *People vs. John Henry Holliday* to be arraigned on a charge of attempted murder in the shooting of Billy Allen. Attorneys present."

"District Attorney William Kellogg for the prosecution, Your Honor."

"Your Honor, Charles F. Fishback representing the defendant, Judge Milton R. Rice, assisting."

"The bench calls Leadville Police Captain Edmund Bradbury to the stand."

"Do you swear to tell the truth, the whole truth, and nothing but the truth, so help you God?"

"I do."

"Be seated."

Captain Bradbury testified to ma request for police protection from the person of Billy Allen. Frank Lomeister tended bar that afternoon and testified to the same request for a police presence. He also allowed as how killing me would have boosted Allen's notoriety as a gunfighter. Allen's cronies denied he intended any harm to me in coming to Hyman's looking for me.

Ah got ma say over the loan and the threat, the threat having been confirmed by another witness who heard it. Ah told the court Ah saw him with the butt of a pistol in his pocket and shot him. He fell wounded. Ah fired again, for Ah could not have survived him physically on account of ma infirmed condition and the fact he had me bettered by fifty pounds.

Judge Rice offered closing on ma behalf, stressing the threat of violence to ma person, ma requests for police protection, and the physical risk posed by even a wounded Billy Allen. Kellogg, the prosecutor, gave a stem-winder closing in which he declared ma act of self-defense to be no less than murder, premeditated by the placement of a firearm within reach. The prosecutor's accusation in no way supported by the facts of the case or the testimony heard. Justice Old, being a justice of the peace and not a circuit judge, passed the buck. Ah was bound over for trial by jury when the next session of circuit court convened that November.

After twice being continued owing to congested court dockets, Ah finally came to trial the following March with District Judge George Goldthwaite presiding. Witness depositions were read to the jury followed by closing arguments for the prosecution and defense. The jury reached a verdict on the facts of the case, promptly finding me not guilty.

WINDSOR HOTEL
DENVER, COLORADO
MAY, 1885

Bucking the tiger at Missouri House, word reached me. Wyatt Earp was seen checking into the Windsor Hotel. Ah cashed out. Reaching the Windsor lobby, Ah inquired after the desk for Wyatt Earp. As the clerk scanned the register, someone approached ma elbow.

"Doc Holliday, as I live and breathe."

"Wyatt Earp." Cugh, cugh… cugh. "Wish Ah could say the same."

He apprised me with eyes saying more than words at the appearance of ma condition. Behind him, the statuesque and stunningly beautiful Josephine Marcus gathered all the light in the room around her natural glow. Her dark eyes, too, registered disbelief at ma emaciated frame, though she was too much the lady to say more.

"Ah heard you were in town."

"Just checked in. You remember Josephine."

"Ah do," Ah said with a slight bow. "Ah don't mean to intrude. Ah thought we might have a drink."

"Josephine has been talking about a bath since we had lunch on the train. Now might be the ideal time if you'll excuse two old friends a few moments time."

She smiled. "My pleasure." She kissed Wyatt on the cheek and set off for their room. We watched her go.

"Ah see Ah was right."

"Right?"

"About San Francisco."

"You did say something about that, didn't you?"

"Eighty-two, wasn't it?"

"It was. So, I did."

"Near certain you would."

"That obvious?"

"That obvious."

"Where's the bar?"

"This way."

"I knew you'd know."

"That obvious?"

He laughed.

Ah led. The Windsor Saloon was in tasteful company with the standard of elegance the hotel set for itself and its guests. Polished pegged wood lobby gave way to hushed atmosphere furnished in dark wood, with red velvet upholstery, draperies, and massive mirrored bar lighted by cut crystal chandelier. Ah took us to a corner table and signaled the waiter for a bottle. Wyatt declined as usual and ordered a beer.

"How long do you plan to be in town?"

"Just passing through. We leave for Cheyenne tomorrow, westbound for California."

"San Francisco?"

"Josephine likes it."

"And what Josephine likes, Josephine gets."

"I seem to recall Kate having some sway over you."

"Haven't seen her for some time."

"Likely you will again."

"Likely and seeing people again,"—cugh, cugh... cugh—"don't go together the way they once did."

"That bad?"

"That bad. Had to give up a good run at the tables in Leadville last year. Couldn't take the winter cold up there. Things are a little better down here. More to the air. As things stand, these lungs must breathe twice as hard to get half as much done."

"Sorry to hear that, Doc."

"Ah know, old friend. Nothing to be done for it."

He lifted his chin to the bottle. "Little less of that might help."

"Man's gonna die. Better dulled than not. Now let's not spend this time given to maudlin reflections on matters beyond our control. We have better things to reminisce about."

"We did have some interesting times together."

"And look at us. Here we are. Walked away from all of them."

"We did."

"Any... *regrets* over the way things ended in Tombstone?"

"Lost Morg. Virg is a cripple. Regret all of that. Righted the family honor. No regrets over that. Did it with the help of good friends like you, Doc."

"What friends are for."

"Doesn't always come with killin'."

"Does when its necessary. True friends in for a penny, are in for a pound."

"Spoke like a damned phil-os-ofer."

"Damned is probably the right of it."

"Well, some of that goes with the territory for men like us."

"Some. So, what are you and Josephine planning to do?"

He shrugged. "Take it a day at a time, I suppose. Find a way to make some money."

Ah laughed.

"What's funny about that?"

"For all the differences in our circumstances, our occupations are the same."

"There you go phil-os-ofyin' again. Hadn't thought of it that way."

"Man in ma condition has occasion to think. The only difference between us is the amount of occupation left to us."

"Well, hell's bells, Doc, none of us is more than a call away from the hereafter."

"Maybe so, but some of us hear those bells louder than others. Those who don't hear them miss out on all the anticipation. Gives a man purchase to think."

"Hadn't thought of it that way."

"Course not. No reason to."

Silence fell across the table. Ah knocked back ma drink and poured another, sensing unsaid words for farewell.

"Doc, it's been good to see you, but I suspect Josephine is waiting."

"Ah'm sure she is. Fine looking woman, Wyatt. Ah wish you both the best."

"And the same for you."

He rose to take ma hand. We shook holding on to the moment before he turned to go. I watched him. Hell of a man. Hell of a friend. He was gone. Ah sat back down, brushing something wet at the corner of one eye. Picked up ma bottle and poured.

Kate....

Hadn't thought much about her for some time. Seeing Wyatt and Josephine together brought her to mind. Wonder if she still has that boardinghouse in Globe. Probably so. Made her a respectable living to hear her tell it. Couldn't picture ma-self in a settled down life such as that. Settled down and life. Too much of the first let the demons catch up with the last of the second.

HYMAN'S SALOON
LEADVILLE, COLORADO
FEBRUARY, 1887

The cold like to collapsed ma lungs... cugh, cugh, cugh... ah. The potbelly stove in the corner fought a losing battle. Words hung misty in kerosene fog. Ah poured another drink.

"Don't sound good, Doc," Manny said.

"Don't feel good, either."

"It's the mountains and the cold. Ain't good for you. I like havin' you around, but no doubt you'd do better someplace warmer."

"You're a good friend, Manny. Come spring I'll

do something. Can't bear the thought of traveling this time of year. Just have to take a seat closer to the fire."

Kate...

Ma thoughts drifted. Ah wrote.

Dearest Kate,

I hope this finds you well. Surely better than I. I write of plans to seek treatment at the hot springs in Glenwood come spring. You have recommended it to me on more than one occasion. I am now in full appreciation of the wisdom of your advice. I write in hope you will consider joining me. We have enjoyed so many good times. I should like to see if we might find a few more as time permits. Join me if you will. If you do not, I shall understand. I have not been the best of companions to you. For that I am truly sorry. For your part you have been a rock to me when I found myself most in need. I hope you can forgive the times I behaved badly. It was not in any way your doing. It is the curse I carry in my chest where love should be. I hope we have time to make amends.

In all affection,
Doc

THE AUTHOR

Paul Colt's *critically-acclaimed historical fiction crackles with authenticity. His analytical insight, investigative research, and genuine horse sense bring history to life in dramatizations that entertain and inform.* Lunger: The Doc Holliday Story *is a finalist for the 2024 Will Rogers Medallion Award for Traditional Western Fiction. Paul's Great Western Detective League series does action-adventure western style.* Grasshoppers in Summer *and* Friends Call Me Bat *are Western Writers of America Spur Award honorees.* Grasshoppers in Summer *received Will Rogers Medallion Award recognition.* Boots and Saddles: A Call to Glory *received the Marilyn Brown Novel Award, presented by Utah Valley University. Reviewers recognize Paul's lively, fast-paced style, complex plots, and touches of humor. Readers say, "Pick up a Paul Colt book, you can't put it down."*

Paul lives in Wisconsin with his wife and high school sweetheart, Trish. To learn more, visit Facebook @ **paulcoltauthor**

POETRY BY
JOHN McPHERSON
SADDLEBAG DISPATCHES POETRY EDITOR

POKER ALICE

POKER ALICE SMOKED CIGARS AND WORE THE LATEST FASHIONS,
BUT PLAYING POKER WITH THE GUYS BECAME HER CARDINAL PASSION.

SHE GOT HER START IN LEADVILLE IN ITS EARLY ROUGHSHOD DAYS,
WATCHING WHILE HER HUSBAND PLAYED IN A GIN MILL'S SMOKY HAZE.

SHE DIDN'T SMILE OR ROLL HER EYES AS TROLLOPS SOMETIMES DO;
HER POKER FACE BECAME HER ACE AS HER REPUTATION GREW.

AN EXPLOSION TOOK HER HUSBAND SO SHE HAD TO MAKE IT ON HER OWN.
SHE HAD THE FLAIR SO A DEALER'S CHAIR BECAME HER EARTHLY THRONE.

WHEN THE MINING FRAYED SHE PLIED HER TRADE IN CREEDE AND OTHER PLACES,
WHERE SHE MET BOB FORD AMONG THE HOARD OF FAMOUS WESTERN FACES.

THEN DEADWOOD CALLED AND OFF SHE HAULED TO THE LAND OF THE LAKOTA
TO SETTLE DOWN IN THE FRONTIER TOWN OF STURGIS, SOUTH DAKOTA.

HER CLAIM TO FAME MIGHT BE THE NAME SHE MADE IN SILVER CITY—
WHEN SHE WON 6K IN A SINGLE DAY AND LEFT THERE SITTING PRETTY.

SHE HELD HER OWN IN A GAME THAT'S KNOWN TO BE A MAN'S AFFAIR,
AND OUTLIVED THREE THAT CAME TO BE ONE-HALF A WEDDED PAIR.

AT SEVENTY-NINE IT CAME HER TIME TO FOLD HER CARDS AND PASS,
BUT SHE LEFT BEHIND A LIFE DEFINED BY GRIT, AND NERVE, AND BRASS.

Terry Alexander
ENTERTAINMENT EDITOR

Two Colorado Originals

Spring Byington and Kelo Henderson

SPRING BYINGTON

Spring Dell Byington was born on October 17, 1886, in Colorado Springs, Colorado. Her father, Edwin, was a college professor and superintendent of schools who died in 1891. Her mother, Helene, placed her sister, also named Helene, with their grandmother in Port Hope, Ontario. Spring stayed with relatives in Denver. Her mother went to Boston where she studied to be a doctor. Spring developed an early interest in theater. As a high school teenager, she put an acting company together and toured the mining camps in the area. After high school, she joined a stock company and toured on the circuit in the U.S. and Canada.

At the onset of World War I, she joined the Belasco De Mille company of New York enroute to Bueno Aires, Argentina. She married Roy Corey Chandler, the company's manager. The couple had two daughters, Phyllis and Lois. Spring learned fluent Spanish during her time in South America. The marriage ended in divorce four years later, and Spring and her daughters returned to New York. She never remarried.

In 1924, she made her first Broadway appearance at age thirty-one in the comedy satire *A Beggar on Horseback*. She worked exclusively in theater for the next nine years, building a reputation as a dedicated performer. She made her film debut as Marmee Marsh in 1933, in Louisa May Alcott's *Little Women*. She shared the screen with Katherine Hepburn, Joan Bennett, Jean Parker, and Francis Dee. She was nominated for an academy award for Best Supporting Actress, losing to Mary Astor for *The World Changes*, and never returned to Broadway. She appeared in the horror film *Werewolf of London* with Herbert Hull and co-starred with Olivia De Havilland and Errol Flynn in *The Charge of the Light Brigade*.

Spring was a lifelong science fiction fan, and once said that she read the genre daily.

Spring was nominated for an Oscar for Best Supporting Actress for her role as Penny Sycamore in *You Can't Take It with You* in 1938. Fay Bainter won the Oscar for her role in *Jezebel*. Ironically, Spring was also in this movie.

Spring Byington was a native Coloradan who made a name for herself on stage, radio, and the silver screen. In the Western genre, she is best known for playing Daisy Cooper on the television show *Laramie.*

She acted steadily in movies for years. In 1950, she co-starred in *Devil's Doorway*, directed by Anthony Mann. The movie starred Robert Taylor, Louis Calhern, and Edgar Buchanan. The movie told the story of an Indian who fought in the Civil War for the Union. When he returned home after the war ended, he found hatred and bigotry from the whites and the Indians. She received a Golden Globe nomination for Best Actress in a Comedy or Musical for the 1951 movie *Louisa,* losing to Judy Holiday for the film *Born Yesterday.* She won a Golden Laurel for her role in the film. She appeared in over eighty movies, including eighteen of the Jones Family films. She appeared in two films that won Best Picture Oscars, *Mutiny on the Bounty* in 1935 and *You Can't Take It with You* in 1938.

When her career began to wane in the fifties, she moved on to radio, then to TV. She starred in the comedy *December Bride* on the radio in 1950. In 1954, Desilu brought the comedy to the small screen; her co-stars were Vera Fulton and Harry Morgan. The show ran for five years. Spring was nominated for Best Actress in a Television comedy in 1958 and 1959, losing to Jane Wyatt for her role in *Father Knows Best*. In 1960, she appeared in her last movie role in the comedy *Please Don't Eat the Daisies,* playing Doris Day's mother. She received a nomination for a Golden Laurel for her role.

She played Daisy Cooper in the western television show *Laramie*. The show starred John Smith and Robert Fuller as two cowboys running a stage relay station, including cowboys working on the

Kelo Henderson hailed from Pueblo, Colorado and starred in a number of Westerns on both the big and small screen, including *The Brand, Tales of Wells Fargo, The Last Stagecoach West, 26 Men,* and *Saddle the Wind*. He passed away in 2019.

ranch. They changed out the teams for the stagecoach, repaired fences, did the cooking, and washed dishes on occasion. Spring played a grandmotherly figure to young Dennis Holmes, who also joined the show with her. Spring continued to work in TV. She was in an episode of *Mister Ed* in 1963 and appeared as heiress J. Pauline Spaghetti in a 1966 episode of *Batman* starring Adam West and Burt Ward. She even played Larry Hagman's mother in a 1967 episode of *I Dream of Jeanie,* which starred Barbara Eden. Her final television role was in a 1968 episode of *The Flying Nun,* starring Sally Field.

She has two stars on the Hollywood Walk of Fame. Spring and Marjorie Main were alleged to be close companions, and Main said after her death that "She didn't have much use for men."

Spring died on September 7, 1971, at her home in Los Angeles, California from cancer. She was survived by her daughters, three grandchildren and two great grandchildren. She donated her body for medical research.

KELO HENDERSON

Paul Lars 'Kelo' Henderson was born on August 8, 1923, in Pueblo, Colorado. He appeared in a handful of western roles from 1957 to 1965. He first appeared in an episode of Cheyenne in 1957. He played Doc Pardee in the episode *The Brand*. The series starred Clint Walker in the title role. Ed Brynes guest starred as a young outlaw. He played an uncredited henchman in the movie *Last*

THREE-TIME SPUR AWARD WINNER

DUSTY
RICHARDS

the PRIDE
of TEXAS

THE
BRANDIRON
SERIES

AVAILABLE EVERYWHERE SEPTEMBER 2024

Kelo Henderson on horseback during the fiming of 26 Men, in which he played Arizona Ranger Clint Travis.

Stagecoach West. The coming of the railroad to Cedar Center meant the end of the stagecoach mail contract. The movie starred Jim Davis, Mary Castle, and Victor Jory.

He played Ike Clanton in a 1957 episode of *Tales of Wells Fargo.* The series starred Dale Robertson as troubleshooter Jim Hardy. In the episode "The Target," a pony express rider was found dead on the Wells Fargo Stagecoach route and Jim had to find his killer. He returned to the big screen in late 1957 to play a police dispatcher in the science fiction/horror film *The Monolith Monsters.*

He played a guard in the 1958 film *Return to Warlow.* After he spent eleven years on a chain gang, Clay Hollister escaped from prison and returned to his hometown where his brother hid the money from a robbery years before.

He also appeared in an episode of *Sergeant Preston of the Yukon* that year. In the episode "Escape to the North," two criminals blackmailed an ex-con into helping them escape from the law. The series was written by Don Beattle, Robet C. Bennett and Fran Striker, the man that wrote the early adventures of *The Lone Ranger* and *The Green Hornet.* The series starred Dick Simmons, George Eldridge, and Yukon King.

Saddle the Wind, a 1958 release, saw former gunman Steve Sinclair's efforts to settle into life as a peaceful rancher go terribly wrong when his wild younger brother arrived with a fast gun and a fiancée in tow. The writer for this film was *Twilight Zone* creator Rod Serling, along with Thomas Thompson and Daniel Fuchs. It starred Robert Taylor, Julie London, John Cassavetes, Donald Crisp, Royal Dano, and Ray Teal.

He appeared in seventy-three episodes of the western series *26 Men* as Ranger Clint Travis. The series told the true stories and tall tales of the Arizona Rangers and their adventures during the late 1800s and the turn of the century.

His last film appearances were *Treasure of the Aztecs* and its sequel, *Pyramid of the Sun God,* directed by Robert Siodmak based on the novel by Karl May. The full story takes place during the American Civil War and starred Lex Barker as Dr. Karl Sternov. It also starred Jeff Corey. Dr. Sternov was hired by the Mexican Government to find lost Aztec treasure and return it to the Leaders in Mexico. Kelo played Frank Wilson in this epic, which was initially filmed as one movie. After the film was completed, the investors decided to split the film into two halves for a better chance to recoup their expenses on the film and show a profit.

Kelo was awarded a Golden Boot award for his work in the western genre in 2003. He died in Ridgecrest, California, following a surgical procedure on December 10, 2019.

Terry Alexander *and his wife, Phyllis, live on a small farm near Porum, Oklahoma. They have three children, thirteen grandchildren, and four great grandchildren. If you see him at a conference, though, don't let him convince you to take part in one of his trivia games—he'll stump you every time.*

TRIBAL PASSAGES

Regina McLemore
FEATURES WRITER

Dangerous Ground

Kit Carson, Chief Ouray, and the Ute of Colorado

"The Ute Must Go!" Despite having camped in and hunted the lands of Colorado for thousands of years, the Ute had little choice when Frederick W. Pitkin won the Colorado Governor's race in 1879 with this campaign slogan. After years of battling with government officials, they came to agree with Chief Ouray's words, "The agreement an Indian makes to a United States treaty is like the agreement a buffalo makes with his hunters when pierced with arrows. All he can do is lie down and give in."

Ouray, whose father was half Jicarilla Apache, was born around 1833 in the Taos area and grew up speaking Spanish and English. When he was eighteen, he moved to Colorado where his father, Guera Murdah, lived as the chief of the Tabegauche band of the Ute. When his father died in 1860, Ouray became the chief of the Tabegauche. His patience and diplomacy would earn him the name "the White man's friend."

According to the May 23, 2023, edition of *The Leadville Herald Democrat,* the Ute have always lived in their homeland and have no migration story. They roamed from what would become Oregon to New Mexico and through all surrounding areas until they met the Spanish in the late 1500s or early 1600s. They were referred to as "Yuta" in Spanish documents, which is likely the first derivative of their name. The Spanish also introduced them to horses and changed their lifestyle forever. Having horses enabled them to cover more ground at a much faster pace.

The source of the Arkansas River lies near Leadville, and it was a regular stop in the Tabegauche band's annual migration. This was not a problem until gold was discovered in the area in around 1860. The prospectors soon learned many of the Ute they encountered were friendly, but author Virginia Simmons in *The Ute Indians of Utah, Colorado, and New Mexico,* relates when some gold hunters tried to follow an old Ute trail, they were killed. Usually, all Indians were considered to be ordinary "pests," confining themselves to asking for food or stealing loose articles like axes or clothing. With the passing of the 1862 Homestead Act, Congress encouraged farmers and ranchers to join the miners in settling Colorado and all of the West. What was once Indian land now became public land.

Ouray was chief of the Tabeguache (Uncompahgre) band of the Ute tribe, then located in western Colorado.

Christopher "Kit" Carson was one of the greatest explorers of the American West. In 1854, he was appointed Indian Agent for the Ute, Jicarilla Apache, and Taos Pueblo tribes.

There had always been instances of resistance, which were lumped together as "the Ute Wars" and involved the states of Utah, Arizona, New Mexico, and Colorado. These wars were considered to begin in 1849 and end in 1923. Perhaps the earliest major Ute conflict in Colorado occurred on Christmas Day 1854 when a group of Ute and Jicarilla attacked El Pueblo, Colorado, killed 15 men, captured two women, and ran off the stock. Later they attacked a settlement near Alamosa, Colorado. After several scrimmages, the resistance was broken when Dragoons, led by Colonel Thomas Fauntleroy, killed forty Ute and burned all the lodges, food, and supplies of a large village. The Ute sued for peace the following July.

Ouray came into prominence in 1863 when he helped complete a treaty in Conejos in the San Luis Valley. In this treaty, the Ute relinquished all land east of the Continental Divide as well as part of Middle Park. Essentially, it was a formal relinquishment of land already claimed by white homesteaders and miners.

As Ouray found his place in Colorado history, he encountered one of its most famous citizens, Christopher (Kit) Carson, well-known frontiersman and one of the greatest explorers of the West. In his capacity of Indian agent, Carson developed a friendship with Ouray as he worked with the Ute and Jicarilla Apache. This friendship was strengthened when Ouray helped stop an outbreak of violence by Ute Chief Kaniache in 1866, waged in retaliation for the death of his son by Mexican herders.

When one of the herders escaped to Fort Union, the fort authorities refused to turn the man over to the Ute for their brand of justice. Kaniache swore vengeance and attempted to enlist Ouray in a series of raids. Instead, Ouray went to Fort Garland to inform Carson of Kaniache's plans. Carson wrote to his superiors, "An outbreak might occur at any moment and the loss of life and property in the Settlements would be enormous."

Carson sent Captain A.J. Alexander and a company of the 3rd U.S. Cavalry to talk to Kaniache. Kaniache admitted he had stolen corn and cattle from nearby farms but said, "The land belongs to us and when our children are hungry we will take food for them." Alexander told Kaniache that they would resume their talks the next day.

Kaniache didn't show-up for the talks, and an infuriated Alexander learned that Kaniache had left on another raid. When Alexander found Kaniache, he ordered a charge, resulting in thirteen dead Utes and two wounded cavalrymen. The surviving Ute fled. Alexander sent a message to Carson, saying Kaniache had killed several men along the Huerfano River and had taken an American lady and her four children captive. He was currently trailing Kaniache.

After explaining his desire to "avoid a general war with the Utes," Carson sent word to Ouray to come immediately to Fort Garland for urgent peace talks. Ouray assured Carson, "I will do my best to restrain the young men." Carson sent a protective force to accompany Ouray and his men.

Ouray convinced Kaniache to release the captives, but he refused to come back with Ouray. When Ouray returned to the fort with the captives and over one hundred peaceful Utes, Carson rejoiced. He wrote in his report, "Yesterday all the hostile Indians came in under the guidance of Uray [sic] and I made peace with them. No more of the outrages that makes humanity shudder have been perpetuated here."

In 1868, with the assistance of Chief Ouray, Kit Carson helped to create The Treaty of 1868, which is sometimes referred to as the "Kit Carson Treaty." The signers of this treaty included Ouray and Guero representing the Tabegauche, Kaniache and Ankatosh from the Mauche, and Nicaagat (also known as Captain Jack) for the Yampa. In all, seven bands. The Ute agreed to give up a large portion of their lands, and Colorado's Consolidated Ute Reservation was created, which took in most of the Western Slope, amounting to approximately twenty million acres.

The delegates were given a silver peace medal and a promise that each family would receive a cow, five sheep, and farm implements. In addition, the tribe would receive sixty thousand dollars in annuities over the next thirty years. Schools, sawmills, and other useful structures would be built, and unauthorized non-Indians would not be allowed on the reservation. To continue receiving annuities, all Ute children would be required to attend a white school, and those Ute suspected of wrongdoing would be turned over to United States authorities for trial. In addition, Ouray was named as the Chief of the Ute. This title and the treaty itself made Ouray a target of re-

sentment among his fellow Ute.

The 1868 treaty was the last official business in which Kit Carson was involved. He died at age fifty-eight on May 23, 1868, of an abdominal aneurism in Fort Lyon, Colorado.

History has recorded Carson's mostly successful record as an Indian agent to be somewhat muddled. One of the chief complaints was that he called on his friends among the Ute to help him forcefully subdue other tribes such as the Navajo, the Comanche, and the Kiowa.

No doubt Ouray missed his friend Kit Carson when the 1868 treaty was broken a few years later as the miners began encroaching on the Ute reservation. They discovered gold and silver in the San Juan Mountains. At first the government ordered them to leave, but when the miners refused, state and federal officials began working on a plan to annex the mountains to Colorado.

Initially, Ouray said, "We did not want to sell a foot of our land, that is the opinion of our people. The whites can go in and take the land and come out again."

Things changed when Felix R. Brudinot, chairman of the Indian commissioners, learned Ouray's son had been abducted by an enemy tribe years earlier. Brudinot persuaded Ouray to agree to sell the land if Brudinot found and returned his son. Brudinot searched but was not successful. Even so, Ouray, being impressed by his sincerity, agreed to sell the land in exchange for hunting rights in the mountains and twenty-five thousand dollars a year, plus other deliverables. The arrangement, the Brudinot Agreement, was signed in

1873 and included a one thousand dollar annual payment to Ouray.

A new Indian agent, Nathan Meeker, was appointed to the White River Agency in 1879 and brought more trouble to Ouray and the Ute. Meeker, who had had no experience with Native Americans, tried to force the Ute into farming and Christianity. When he plowed under a field the Ute had designated for horse racing, they decided he had gone too far. After a tense confrontation with a Ute chief, Meeker was injured and driven from his home.

Meeker wired the military for assistance, and the Ute took his action as a declaration of war. Soon, his would-be rescuers, Major Thomas T. Thornburgh and his troops, were ambushed near Milk Creek. The Ute attacked the White River Agency on September 29, 1879, killing Meeker and several others. The Ute also took some women and children hostage, including Meeker's wife and daughter. Additionally, the Ute Chief Colorow killed Major Thornburgh and most of the officers.

The surviving soldiers dug in behind the wagons and animal bodies for defense after one man got away to ride for reinforcements. Many settlers living in the area fled to Leadville for safety. After several days, reinforcements came to rescue the soldiers. Among them were thirty-five Buffalo Soldiers from the 9th Cavalry, led by Lieutenant Francis Dodge and Sergeant Henry Johnson. Both men later received the Medal of Honor for their heroic actions

Ouray and his wife Chipeta negotiated for the return of the hostages. After three weeks they were released, and Ouray took them back

Lieutenant Francis Dodge and Sergeant Henry Johnson of the 9th U.S. Cavalry Regiment were both awarded the Medal of Honor for their heroism when their unit helped break the Ute tribe's siege of the White River Agency in 1879.

to their ranch. Ouray would not reveal the names of the Ute who were involved with the murders, but he was forced to turn twelve men over to be tried in Washington, D.C. These men were selected because they were named by the witnesses as suspects for the murders.

According to author Simmons, the ailing Ouray, Chipeta, Agent W.H. Berry, and eight other Ute traveled to Washington to attend the trials. They were met by angry mobs who threatened to lynch them, and several hundred jeering people pelted them with rocks, lumps of coal, and sticks. They couldn't leave the train they were on because they encountered aggressive mobs at every stop. When they reached Washington, they were hungry, dirty, and bedraggled. After several days of an intense trial, the Ute were all acquitted.

The incident in which Meeker and his men were killed became known as the Meeker Massacre. It greatly increased bad feelings toward the Ute and led to Ouray and other Ute leaders being coerced into signing an agreement to move to a reservation in Utah, which would be named the Ouray Reservation. Many Ute refused to go, and Ouray, who was in bad health, spent his last days traveling in an attempt to collect more signatures for the agreement. He died of Bright's Disease at age forty-seven on August 24, 1880, far from home.

Many of the Ute who agreed to move to the reservation didn't feel bound to remain there. There were numerous incidents of the Ute camping and hunting for long periods of time outside of their assigned reservation.

Earlier that same year, on May 15, 1880, the *Leadville Weekly Herald* proclaimed, "Prospectors are leaving Leadville for the borders of the Ute reservation. They are not liable to remain outside the line if they see a good thing inside."

Leadville locals Doctor William Bell, and Thomas Blake, led bands of approximately 125 armed men, composed of miners and investors, from Leadville for the, as they stated, "unalterable purpose of exploring and developing the country known as the Ute Reservation."

In response to these actions, the government sent military troops to keep the peace. The white men stayed in the area for several days and collected assay samples which only showed low grade ores. Realizing there would be no mining boom on the reservation, they returned to Leadville and to other known boom towns.

By 1880, Leadville had become one of the world's richest and largest silver camps with a population of over fifteen thousand. As Leadville and many other Colorado cities prospered, the fate of Colorado's original inhabitants was not as happy. The Ute endured several years of upheaval and deportation until Congress abruptly changed their minds in 1894. They stated Colorado's Utes should not be moved to Utah or anywhere else, and those who were already in Utah were to return for allotment enrollment. Some of the Utes complied and eventually accepted individual allotments. Others continued to live as they had always lived, moving when and where they wanted as they hunted and lived off the land.

Regina McLemore *is a Will Rogers Medallion Award-winning author and retired educator of Cherokee heritage. Her great, great grandmother, Susie Christie Clay, survived the Trail of Tears in 1839. Regina's Young Adult Trilogy, Cherokee Passages, is a fictional retelling of her family's history from the Trail of Tears down through the modern day.*

CATATONIC LEADVILLE

During its mining boom days, Leadville was well known nationally for its high altitude, which at the time was believed to have a lethal impact on cats.

STORY BY

PRESTON LEWIS

Virtually all mining booms in the Old West were followed by corresponding cat booms as mining towns spawned rodents by the thousands, and enterprising entrepreneurs recognized the need and imported felines that they sold for exorbitant prices.

Cats delivered to Leadville, however, had a higher mortality rate than in the typical mining town. Observers at the time blamed it on the high altitude. Here's how some newspapers of the time reported on the inexplicable feline fatalities:

ALTITUDE SICKNESS

One of the queerest of the many queer things about Leadville is that in all the length and breadth thereof there lives not a single cat. Cats have been imported here by the hundreds and in all varieties of color, breeding and size; but not one has ever survived the second week of residence. No one seems to understand why it is that the cats all die, but they do. The healthiest, sleekest cat in St. Louis, if brought to Leadville would lose all interest in life the moment it reached here, and after moping around in a sickly and disconsolate way for a few days would resignedly have a fit and give up the ghost.

A saloonkeeper on State Street brought a big strong Maltese from Denver a few days ago, hoping the animal would survive the fits long enough to become acclimated; but it was no use. The cat had a fit the first day, two or three the second, and then the number of attacks increased in a geometrical progression until, as the saloon-man said, "There were more fits than cat, and the cat had to give in."—*St. Louis Globe-Democrat*

Fort Worth (Texas) *Daily Gazette*
Saturday, August 30, 1884, p3

THIN AIR

In Leadville, Colorado, the atmosphere is too thin for cats, or their common prey, rats and mice, to live. What a blessing some persons in other places would consider it if they could have that atmosphere for a

A NOVEL OF WORLD WAR II

SHORT GRASS

JOHN J. DWYER

WINNER OF THE WILL ROGERS MEDALLION AWARD
GOLD MEDAL FOR INSPIRATIONAL FICTION

while, when the cats are on their back sheds at night, making enough noise to raise an Egyptian mummy.

Colleyville (Kansas) *Weekly Journal*
Saturday, September 6, 1884, p3

NO CATS

There is not a single cat within the limits of the town of Leadville, Colorado. Cats have been imported there by the hundreds, and in all varieties of color and size, but not one has ever survived the second week of residence. However, as there are no rats and mice in Leadville, there is no real need of cats, and it makes little difference whether they live or die. The thin atmosphere at that altitude (10,200) is as fatal to the vermin as to their foe, and the inhabitants are thus mercifully spared the inflictions of both.—*Chicago Inter-Ocean*

Wyandotte Gazette, Kansas City, Kansas
Friday, November 7, 1884, p1

THAT LECTURE

Prof. Hoenschel's lecture at the M.E. church on Saturday night last was highly enjoyed by an appreciative audience. Pike's Peak was his subject and he interspersed anecdotes with solid facts in such a way as to hold the attention of his audience. ... Cats can't live at Leadville, but the man who made the most money on his investment in '59—the first year of the Pike's Peak excitement—was the man who took out a load of cats. They cost him nothing, but sold for good round prices to the miners—to stand over their flour, which at $25 per sack, was too dear to be turned over to the army of wood-rats that preceded the gold seekers and the mice that went along for company. ... The lecture was good, and as the cats were excluded, we can say without fear of contradiction that the talk was enjoyed by the entire audience.

The Alma (Kansas) *Signal*
Saturday, April 18, 1896, p1

Preston Lewis *is the award-winning author of more than 50 novels and nonfiction works, including* Cat Tales of the Old West *and* More Cat Tales of the Old West, *from which this article was adapted.*